SAVING QUINN

A WINDSOR FALLS NOVEL

Kimberley O'Malley

WHERE ROMANCE IS TRUE BLUE & RED HOT!

Published by Carolina Blue Publishing, LLC

Copyright 2018, Carolina Blue Publishing, LLC

ISBN: 978-1-946682-06-2

To first responders everywhere. These brave men and women, whether police, firefighters, or EMTs, willingly lay their lives on the line for strangers on a daily basis. Where would we be without them?

Praise for
Kimberley O'Malley

Coming Home

"There was so much emotion in the story that you will definitely need to keep a box of tissues close by. I felt the heartache, joy, and love that the characters were feeling throughout the story. The author writes a beautiful story that kept me hooked until the end."

–Alpha Book Club

"Kimberley O'Malley really manages to captivate the reader with her words and descriptions. I felt their heartache and joy and loved the ups and downs."

–Texas Book Nook Blog

Taking Chances

"A wonderful witty sarcastic banter love story that shows you that patience and understanding are rewarded and taking risks is worth it in the end when it comes to love."

-Books Are Love

"Ms. O'Malley has a fan for life. Older characters, plots that actually make sense, smexy times, family, characters that you fall in love with, realistic dialogue, perfect pacing, interesting jobs, but above all...LOVE, LAUGHTER, and LIFE. You'll regret it if you don't pick it up."

-Harlie's Book Blog

Second Chances

"This was a good read. Not easy, because it has lots of emotional topics, but it grabs the reader into it. I have truly enjoyed the writing style of Ms. O'Malley and I really look forward to read more from her."

-More Books Than Livros Blog

"Second chances should all be so sweet...I love this series and the characters that inhabit it! Drama and turmoil stirs up this small town and gives these relatable characters an extra snap to their step."

-Nerdy, Dirty, & Flirty Book Blog

Chapter One

Quinn Adams sat down to breakfast in the station kitchen. The aroma of a freshly cooked egg sandwich teased his nose. His mouth watered as he picked it up to take the first bite. Then alarms echoed throughout the building. He shook his head and took one large bite before jumping up from the table. *Why did it always have to be when he sat down to eat?* Quinn listened to the dispatch while he pulled on his turnout gear and grabbed his helmet. They were headed to a multiple vehicle accident with possible entrapment.

All around him, other members of Station Fifteen rushed to respond to the call. The huge bay doors rolled open. His best friend, Andrew Jefferson, or A.J. as he was known, slid into the driver's seat of the rescue truck, even as Quinn pulled open the passenger door. They grinned at each other. Although theirs was a serious business, nothing started the day like a "good trauma".

A.J. drove the engine out of the station. Quinn glanced ahead at the thick, cloud-leadened sky. The storm was worse than when he arrived this morning. A curtain of rain beat on their windshield. Even with the wipers on high, visibility dropped off past the front of the truck. The dry spring was over. This storm had been raging on and off throughout the night, making sleep spotty at best for Quinn. Lightning split the sky in front of him. The otherwise dark, dreary morning was blindingly bright for a moment.

"Might be a bad one with this weather," A.J. muttered. His friend was normally chatty but maneuvering the engine in the storm required his complete attention.

"Yeah," Quinn agreed. Another bolt of lightning split the gloom. A frisson of uneasiness slithered down his spine. People didn't drive well in rain. They tended to either go too fast or too slow. Either one could spell disaster in these conditions.

A few minutes later, they rounded a bend in the road, and Quinn could see their call. Three cars, in various degrees of ruin, spread out before him. People milled about, but he couldn't tell yet if they were victims or bystanders wanting to help. He hoped for the latter. The street was blocked. Several police cars had pulled over at odd angles, and officers were directing traffic.

"Guess this is as close as we get."

A.J grunted under his breath and pulled the engine over to the curb.

Jumping down from the truck, he approached Captain Wells, who sent him ahead to survey the scene. He approached the vehicles, taking care to look for downed wires or leaking gasoline. A small, four-door sedan was the worst of them. The bright blue car was wedged up against a light pole on the driver's door. The person behind the wheel, who didn't appear to be conscious, slumped against the door. With other fire and rescue personnel dispatched to the other two cars, he made his way cautiously to this one. He eyed downed wires warily as he approached.

Shaking his head, he knew they would need more assistance and radioed to his captain. "We're going to need the power killed in this area if it's not already. Send the medics to the small, blue car." The older firefighter replied that his message was received. Quinn continued to the car, checking for other hazards as he went. Thankfully, the wires were not on top of the car. There didn't appear to be any gas or other fluids leaking from it either.

Quinn approached the vehicle. The closer he got, the worse the damage looked. The passenger side had sustained extensive damage. However, the damage was to the rear door, leaving the front one accessible. *Thank goodness for small favors.* The heavy rain continued to pour down, but he paid it no heed. The too still body of the driver captured his attention. He didn't know if they were unconscious or dead. He pulled open the door and slid into the front passenger seat, brushing glass fragments onto the floor as he went. He pulled off his helmet to give himself more wiggle room. From his vantage point, he saw a curtain of long blonde hair and a slender form covered by a rain coat and seat belt. The last may have saved her life.

Away from the noise of the storm, he heard a faint moaning. "Miss, my name is Quinn, and I'm with the fire department. Stay still, okay?" He wasn't sure if the young woman could hear him, but it didn't stop him from trying. A calm but firm voice would help her if she regained consciousness.

He ducked his head back out into the storm to call for a cervical collar, long board, and some bandages. Given the amount of damage done to her car, there was no way to predict the types of physical injuries she might have sustained. He had to protect her neck and spine. Once another of the crew handed him a collar and bandages, Quinn maneuvered back into the car.

He kneeled on the center console, not an easy task folding his 6'2" frame into the space and brushed back hair from her face. Most of it was sticky with her blood and clinging to her skin. Too much blood. The driver appeared to be several years younger than his thirty-five. She was slim and dressed casually. So far, the only damage he could see was the left side of her face and head which had apparently impacted the door. But Quinn knew from experience looks could be deceiving. There was no telling what type of internal damage she may have suffered.

Her eyes fluttered open. They were a bright blue but shadowed by pain and confusion. She lifted a slim hand to her bloodied face. "Where am I? What happened?" Her voice was faint and unsteady. She seemed to notice her hand was covered in her own blood. She made a small, pitiful noise in her throat. Her eyes drifted shut once again. Tears rolled down her face.

"Hey! You're okay," Quinn murmured. "Welcome back. My name's Quinn, and I'm with the fire department. I'm here to help you. Right now, I need you to hold your head still." Quinn placed the cervical collar around her neck, explaining as he went. He tightened it accordingly, taking care to ensure her hair was not stuck in it.

"Miss, you were in a car accident. Right now, we're working on getting you out of here. I put a collar around your neck to hold it still. I know it's not comfortable, but it will protect you from further injury. I'm need you to listen to me and follow some directions." Quinn placed a reassuring hand on her shoulder. "Let's start with not moving your head or neck. When I ask you a question, don't nod your head. Just talk to me." Not waiting for consent, he continued. "So, you know who I am, but I have no idea who you are. What's your name, Miss?"

Her eyes opened again. "I can't see very well. What's wrong?"

Quinn cringed at the pitiful tone of her voice. He couldn't imagine how terrifying it was to awaken in her situation. "You were in a car accident, Miss. There's some blood running down your face and into your eyes. Keep them shut for now, and I'll try to clean it up for you." Quinn squeezed one of her hands. "I know you're scared. I'm right here with you. Can you tell me your name?"

"Paige."

Quinn leaned in to hear her over the rain pummeling the roof. "Okay, Paige, nice to meet you. You have a bump on your head and a nice gash there as well, which is where all the blood is coming from. You must have hit the window. I know it seems like a lot of blood. Head wounds are funny that way. Right now, I need you to sit tight. I'm with you, and I'm not going to leave you. You'll be out of here before you know it." He didn't tell her car was totaled. No use making her more upset at this point.

"I'm so sleepy," she muttered. "I need a quick nap." Her voice drifted at the end.

Quinn rubbed her arm. "Come on now, am I boring you?" Her lethargy scared him. "You need to stay awake."

She nodded and winced. "Why does my head hurt so much? What's your name again?"

Where were the damn paramedics? "It's okay, Paige. My name's Quinn, and you've been in an accident. The ambulance should be here any minute, and then we'll be getting you out of here. Until then, I need you to stay with me, okay?" He squeezed her hand, dwarfing her tiny one. She returned the squeeze.

Although she wasn't saying much, Quinn was relieved to see she was at least still awake. "Does anything else hurt?"

"Chest hurts. I can't breathe."

"That's not uncommon with seat belt injuries. It tightens up on impact. You're probably going to end up with a bruise there."

"Quinn, I'm so tired." Her thin, unsteady voice gave out at the end.

He grabbed both of her hands with his gloved ones. "Come on now, Paige, you can't expect me to hold up the conversation on my own. You have to talk to me."

He leaned closer to her as she tried to say something. He thought he heard her mutter the name Finn. Of course, he had no idea who Finn was. She was alone in the car.

He turned towards the door. "Where is the damn ambulance? She needs to go now!" He filled the remaining time talking quietly to her and bandaging her bloodied head.

She floated up to the surface again. "I'm scared. My head is killing me, and I can't remember anything. I need to be somewhere, but I have no idea where." She fumbled for the door handle with her left hand.

"Shhh," he murmured. "It's all right. I need to you to sit still. Help's coming." He removed his work gloves. Pulling a pair of rubber gloves from the pocket of his jacket, he put those on. He needed to keep her as still and calm as possible.

He took both of her hands in his. The human contact seemed to calm her. "Paige, listen to me. Help will be here any moment. All I need you to do is stay still. I'm right here, and I'm not going anywhere. Listen to my voice." He was pleased to see she had stopped thrashing and settled back into her seat. He could feel her pulse bounding rapidly in her wrist, probably due to fear and blood loss.

After what seemed an eternity, he felt a tap on his shoulder. "Hey man, we've got this." As the words were spoken a small, female medic slid into the tiny backseat and placed her hands on either side of Paige's head, taking control of her cervical spine. He looked up to see his friend, Mac, standing behind him with a long board and stretcher. The cavalry was here. Still, he felt oddly reluctant to leave Paige's side. Something about her, in her vulnerable state, brought out the protectiveness in him. Maybe it was because she reminded him of his younger sister, Lauren.

Quinn and Mac traded places as he gave a brief run-down of what he had encountered. He stepped back to give the medic room and dragged the stretcher up closer, locking the wheels and bracing it with his legs. He called for a few more guys to come help.

After Mac performed a brief assessment, Paige was out of the car and secured to the backboard. He walked alongside the stretcher as she was wheeled to the ambulance, holding her hand the whole time. Her skin was the color of paper. She didn't notice when he was forced to let go of her hand as she was loaded into the waiting ambulance. She had drifted off once again. He waited until Mac got settled in the back with Paige before closing the doors and motioning for the driver to take off. He stood for a moment, watching until the flashing lights of the truck vanished in the storm.

He didn't have time to think about Paige. He moved on to where he was needed. There were still two other cars and more victims to deal with. The rest of his crew was already occupied. He jogged over to the next vehicle to lend a hand.

Over two hours later, they arrived back at the station. The accident had looked far worse than it was, which was not always the case. Only one other driver had been taken to the hospital. He had been driving behind Paige's car and had not been able to stop in time. His injuries appeared minor, at least compared to Paige's. The driver who had started the whole thing, the one who had hit Paige's car, was a seventeen-year-old on his way to school. Inexperience mixed with a bad storm made for a bad combination. Although shaken, he was not injured and had been released to worried parents at the scene.

Quinn cleaned and stored the equipment as he always did after a call. They never knew when the next one would come. Windsor Falls might be a small town, but they still had their fair share of excitement. One of the aspects he most loved about being a firefighter was the uncertain nature of the job.

A.J. approached as he was hanging up his protective gear. "What was the deal with the victim? She looked pretty bloody when they rolled her by."

"Her name is Paige, and she's going to be fine. You know how head wounds can be. They look worse than they are."

"Paige, huh? Since when do you remember a name? Or even get one? Was she pretty?"

Quinn shoved his hands in his pockets and scowled. "I felt bad for her. She was scared and in pain." Seeing how upset Paige had been made him glad he didn't know her. This job was so much worse when the victims weren't strangers. A.J. was still looking at him funny, so he added: "Besides, she reminded me a bit of Lauren."

A.J. smiled. "Ah, now it makes sense. Maybe Paige is also someone's little sister. They'd be happy to know you were looking out for her." A.J. walked into the kitchen, whistling as he went.

He was relieved when his friend let him off the hook. He couldn't say why she had affected him so much. Everything he had told A.J. was the truth. His sister and she probably were about the same age. And he did feel badly about her injuries. But there was something more. He could see how scared she had been; how vulnerable. He had wanted to take away the fear and the pain, make things better for her. That didn't happen.

He also wondered who Finn was and if he had been told of her accident. He shook his head to clear those thoughts. There was no use in wondering about a woman he would never see again. Remaining professional, and distant, allowed him to do his job.

*****

Several miles away, Paige was back amongst the conscious and not sure if this was a good thing. Her head ached, and the noise in the busy emergency department wasn't helping. She picked at a fingernail, wondering why someone hadn't told her what was going on with her head.

There was a soft rap on the glass divider. Her friend Charlie Avery walked in, concern written across her beautiful face. "Hey, Paige, nice to see you back with us. Please don't scare me like that again, arriving here bloodied and unconscious. We need you for book club." She stepped forward and placed her hand on Paige's shoulder. "I'm so sorry this happened to you. Tell me what hurts."

Paige struggled to sit up a bit higher in the bed. Even the slightest movement hurt, so she gave up. "I'm okay, I guess. Lucky really, when you consider what could have happened." She smiled slightly but stopped when it hurt her head. She raised a hand to it only to find a bandage had been applied.

"You may not believe this, but you already look better. There's more color in your face. But you're going to be sore, so don't move around too much. And you're right. It could have been so much worse for you. I understand your car didn't fare as well." Charlie grimaced. "Sorry. Sometimes I don't think before I speak. I only meant the medics always report any damage to the vehicle, so we can get a complete picture of the impact." She shook her blonde head ruefully. "There I go again."

Paige squeezed her hand. "I'd rather you tell me the truth, Charlie."

"Okay, let's talk about your head. You have a minor laceration right at the hairline. I'll have our plastics guy come down to suture. There shouldn't be much of a scar. The bigger issue, however, is the bump you got. The goose egg on your forehead along with your loss of consciousness says moderate concussion. The CT scan didn't show any bleed. So far. These things can develop over time. We'd like to keep you at least overnight."

She opened her mouth to protest, but Charlie cut her off. "I know, I know. No one wants to hear that. You need to take this seriously. The impact was pretty severe, and combined with your earlier symptoms, I would feel better if I knew we were keeping an eye on you."

Tears welled in her eyes. *Really? After everything today, she was going to cry now?* "I know you're right." All she wanted was to go home and sleep in her own bed. She sighed deeply. "I'll stay."

"Good. It's a little after noon now. I'm waiting on a bed assignment for you, and then we'll get you up to a room." She leaned down to hug her friend. "You'll be much more comfortable. Now, I need to see other patients. Ring the call bell if you need anything else. I'll come running."

"Noon?" Paige tried to sit up but the pain racing through her head stopped her. *No more sudden movements.* "I have to call the school. They're going to think I blew off work today. My poor students will wonder where I am. Do you have a phone I can use?"

Charlie handed her a phone with a long cord, plugged into the wall. "No one who knows you will think that, Paige. And I'm sure they've made arrangements by now."

"You don't know Principal Morton. She thinks I'm undependable. This won't help." She took teaching six-year-olds very seriously. Too bad her boss didn't think so. This was another in a long line of 'infractions'.

"Dial nine to get out. Try to keep it to a minimum though. You need rest." After hugging Paige one last time, she left the room.

She closed her eyes to the situation and lowered her head back to the pillow. This was really a mess. She clutched the phone in her hands. How was she going to tell Amy without worrying her? Then she remembered Finn. Who was going to take care of her new puppy tonight? Although she knew these things were minor, they seemed insurmountable. Her pounding head made thinking nearly impossible. She would rest for a moment before calling the school. What was another few minutes after all this time?

But rest was impossible in the chaotic ER. Many voices fought for her attention. The shrill cry of an unhappy toddler split the air. Paige gave up on resting and dialed the school's main number. After a few rings, Madge, one of the office secretaries, answered. Hearing the older woman's voice was almost enough to unravel Paige completely.

"Hey Madge, this is Paige Harrington. I need to let you know I was in a car accident on my way in this morning. I'm so sorry it took me so long to call you."

"Oh, my goodness, Paige! I knew something must have happened. We were so worried! Are you okay? Do you need help?"

Paige winced. The shrillness of the other woman's voice cut through the phone to her already tender head like a hot knife. "I'm at Memorial in the emergency department. My head hurts and I have a small cut, but I'm fine." She crossed her fingers against the small white lie. Paige still hadn't taken a deep breath since the accident.

"Oh, I'm so glad it's not worse, honey."

"Me too, Madge. Could you let Principal Norton know please? Of course, I won't be in for a few days. How's Amy doing with my class?"

"Well, when we didn't hear from you, dear, we called in a substitute. Luckily, someone was able to come in by 9:30, so Amy has only her own students again."

"Please let her know I'm okay. Ask her to call me when she gets a second. I don't have my cell phone, and I don't know which room I'll be going to, but she can call the main number of the hospital and ask for me."

"Of course, dear."

Paige assured her once again she would be fine and ended the conversation. The effort of making one call exhausted her. Maybe staying overnight wasn't the worst idea after all.

She drifted off again, remembering the firefighter with the deep, calm voice. Quinn, she thought his name was. Whether it was his first or last name, she couldn't be sure. All she could remember is how comforting his voice had been. Paige had been terrified by the accident, especially considering her history. Her last car accident had ended mush worse than this one. She was grateful for his presence at the scene. Someday, she should find him and thank him.

*****

Quinn awoke at the sound of movement in the hallway. Glancing at his phone, he realized the night had passed without interruption. His twenty-four-hour shift was over, and he could go home. He grinned as he sat up and stretched his arms over his head, working kinks out of his back. He could see sunshine outside. Yesterday's stormy weather was gone.

He dressed in khaki shorts and a fire department T-shirt, gathering his few personal items and stowing them in his locker. He was looking forward to a few days off in a row. He loved his job, but sometimes his time on duty could be very intense. He was always glad for a break.

Running down the stairs, he stopped when he heard his name being called. Turning and walking into the bay, he spotted Donna waving him over.

"Hey, what's going on?"

Donna, one of their two female firefighters, grinned up at him. She was small and slender, barely breaking 5'3", but Donna was strong and brave. He had no problem with women being in the service. If they could pull their weight and be depended upon, he didn't care about gender. Unfortunately, not everyone shared his opinion. Female crew members sometimes had a tough time with some of the guys. So, he went out of his way for them in a show of support.

"My Aunt Carol needs some painting done. Do you have time to go look and give her an estimate?"

Quinn, like many firefighters, had a second job. Unfortunately, firefighters didn't make a lot of money, especially when you looked at the danger of their jobs. But they all knew it going in. He didn't have a family to support like some of his co-workers. For him, it was more about keeping busy in his days off. And he loved working with his hands. He had a side painting business. Some of his firefighter buddies helped when they wanted to pick up some extra cash. Having days off between shifts came in handy.

"Of course, Donna. I'll even give her a good deal. You know how much I enjoy her baking." Donna's aunt made killer brownies. A lovely older woman who wholeheartedly supported what her niece was doing, she also appreciated most of the guys at the station accepting Donna without reservation. She repaid them for their kindness in home-made baked goods.

"Great! She'll be thrilled. I'll text her number to you." She resumed placing items in a plastic bag.

"Hey, can I help you?"

Donna shook her head. "Don't worry I'm almost done. These are the things I grabbed from the smaller car in the wreck yesterday. I heard the driver is still in the hospital, so I thought I'd take these by on my way home this morning. I can't imagine being without my purse and phone." She looked at her watch. "In fact, I'd better get going. I like to catch the kids before they leave for school if I can."

He tensed. She was talking about Paige. The young woman had been the last thing he thought about before going to sleep last night. Surely it wouldn't hurt to swing by and drop her belongings off to her. Then he could get an update on her condition.

"Hey, I'll do it for you. I'd like to see how she is. Besides, it's on my way home, and no one's waiting for me." He reached down to pick up the bag, ending any need for discussion.

She smiled at him. "If you really don't mind, thanks. It's actually a bit out of my way."

Quinn fished his car keys from his pocket and left the station before anyone could figure out what he was doing. He didn't even know what he was doing. He didn't get involved with the people he assisted during accidents or fires. No emotional entanglements. They stayed anonymous. As much as one could in a small town. Other than general comments on a patient's condition offered up by one of the paramedics, he usually didn't know learn anything further about them.

As he slid behind the wheel of his pickup, Quinn wondered if what he was doing was smart. He had never gone to the hospital to drop off a patient's belongings. Why this patient? It was too late to wonder now.

Chapter Two

Paige grimaced as she viewed the damage in the tiny bathroom mirror. After a restless night, during which she was awoken frequently to 'make sure she was still with them', Paige had given up trying to sleep and gotten up to go to the bathroom. She didn't think the stern nurse would appreciate her going alone, but she was beyond caring. It was less than fifteen feet from her bed. *What could happen?*

Hadn't her grandmother always warned her about putting ideas out into the universe? The thoughts were still floating in the air when she was hit by a wave of dizziness and nausea. Grabbing the sink for support, she acknowledged the nurse might have known what she was talking about after all. She closed her eyes and took a steadying breath. She felt a bit better after a few moments.

Raising her head and opening her eyes, she stared at her reflection. There was a small, neat row of black sutures along her hairline giving her somewhat of a Frankenstein look. The bruising on her forehead now a deep black and blue with purple at the edges. Still, all in all, not too bad. Considering what could have happened, she'd take it.

She thought back to Amy's stricken face when her friend had burst into Paige's hospital room late yesterday afternoon. Her best friend had been beside herself, imagining the worst possible scenarios. Their friend, Tom Gibbons, a gym teacher at the adjoining middle school, had come with her. Tom was a rock next to Amy's hysteria.

The two had come to visit, or as Amy had put it, to ensure Paige was still alive. She had to laugh when she thought of her dramatic friend. But with their shared history, she could understand why Amy was so protective.

She had been able to convince her best friend, despite her horrific appearance, she was fine, or at least she would be in a few days. Amy relaxed, and she and Tom stayed only long enough to get instructions for Finn's care. Amy had gladly agreed to take the puppy home with her until Paige was feeling better and able to care for him herself.

A soft knock at the outer door brought her out of her reverie. Unfortunately, she turned her head too swiftly. The room swirled around her as pain shot through her head. She cried out as the floor rushed up to greet her. Strong arms caught her just in time. She looked up into a somewhat familiar face. She should know him, but for the life of her, she couldn't place the face.

"Hey there! Are you sure you should be up so soon by yourself? Let's get you back to bed, shall we?" He guided her out of the bathroom and back into her hospital bed. His large hands were rough with calluses in spots. The sensation was far from unpleasant. A tingle travelled all the way up her arms. She spoke to break the moment.

"Aren't you the firefighter from yesterday? What are you doing here?" Paige hoped it hadn't come out wrong. She didn't want him to think she was ungrateful. But his presence flustered her. She hadn't noticed yesterday how handsome he was.

He smiled and laughed. The sound curled her toes. "I guess I should explain. Sorry. I'm Quinn Adams, and we did meet yesterday at your accident I didn't think you'd remember me." He held out his hand towards her.

"Oh, I remember you. At least I remember your voice." She stopped as she felt a warm blush travel up her face. "What I mean is I remember talking with you in the car. You were very kind to me."

"No worries. That takes care of who I am. As for why I'm here." He paused and reached over to the chair, picking up a plastic bag. "I brought these to you. They were in the car. I'm guessing you might need them."

Paige was happy to see the bag contained her purse and briefcase. Her identification was in there, not to mention her phone and hopefully her keys. She was relieved to know she wouldn't need to replace all her identification. And her briefcase held her student's grades and homework.

Paige smiled at him until her head hurt again. She eased her head back, resting on the soft pillow. "Ugh! I keep forgetting how much my head still hurts. Thanks so much for bringing those to me. To be honest, I hadn't even thought of them. I've been lying here trying to not feel as though my head contains a marching band."

"Well, I saw the other guy, so to speak, so I can imagine how you're feeling. But seriously, how are you?" His warm, brown eyes shone with concern.

"Considering everything, I'm great. I know how fortunate I was. It could have been so much worse." She smiled as much as her headache would allow. Reaching out to touch his arm, she gazed into his eyes. "I know I have you to thank. I'm just not sure how one thanks another for saving their life."

He squirmed in his seat. "There's no need to thank me. I was doing my job. Besides, you were never in any danger of dying."

"Well, you may not have literally saved my life, but you made a terrible situation bearable. I was really scared. You have no idea." Paige thought back to the other time in her life she had been in a similar situation. There hadn't been a Quinn back then to keep her calm. She could have used one. She still had the occasional nightmare… "You may have been doing your job, but it meant a lot to me. I want you to know."

"You're more than welcome. My sister Lauren is about your age. I would want someone to be there for her."

Paige found herself frowning at being compared to his sister. Unfortunately, her head hurt from the movement. She raised a hand to soothe it.

He leaned forward in the chair he had pulled up to her bedside. "Are you okay? Should I call a nurse?"

She could have groaned at her ridiculousness. She was lying in a hospital bed, wearing a so-not-sexy cotton gown, not to mention the line of sutures in her forehead. What did it matter if he was comparing her to his sister? She was someone he had rescued. *Get over yourself, Paige.*

"No, please don't. I'm fine. I need to be careful. No sudden movements. As I keep telling myself, this could have been *so* much worse."

"I admire your attitude, Paige. Others might not see it the same way. How long do you have to be here, anyway?"

"I'm not sure. The emergency room doctor said 'at least' overnight. I haven't seen anyone yet this morning, so I guess I wait. Thanks also for saving me from my own stupidity in there. I wasn't supposed to be in the bathroom alone, but I really had to…" She blushed furiously now and cleared her throat. "Uh, you know. I didn't feel like waiting and thought I'd be fine. I guess I overestimated my strength."

"No big deal. We all need help sometimes. Even big, tough firefighters." He smiled, and the dimples bracketing his mouth captivated her.

"Well, good to know. That you're not Superman I mean. Could be intimidating." She laughed. She liked Quinn. He was funny, and he had come out of his way to help her.

He arched a brow. "Superman, huh? Not even close. Sorry to tell you I have feet of clay like everyone else."

"Well feet of clay or not, you're still special in my book. Being there in the car with me meant the world. How can I ever repay you?"

He stuck his hands in the pockets of his shorts and dropped his gaze to his shoes. He seemed embarrassed by her praise. He raised his eyes and stared directly into her hers. "You don't owe me anything, Paige. I was doing my job."

She felt the intensity of his gaze to her very bones. The room suddenly felt smaller and warmer. Hot even. "So, tell me, how bad off is Betsy? She's dead, right?" At his stricken look, she clarified. "Betsy is my car; or was my car. The one I was driving when we met yesterday. I figured she's probably a goner. And how are the other people? Wow, I forgot to ask about them. Was anyone else hurt?"

"You named your car? Betsy?"

His expression told her what he thought of her mental health. *Great.* "Well of course I named my car. Don't you? We do spend a lot of time together." She was only making this worse. "In case you're wondering, I only have a moderate concussion. I'm not brain damaged per se. And I named my car long before the head injury." If it wouldn't hurt so badly, she might be tempted to smack herself in the head. She had just confirmed his suspicions.

Quinn laughed, a rich sound she felt to her toes. "I can't say I know anyone who names their car." He smiled. "Now I do."

She felt her face heating again. "Anyway, tell me what you can about the other drivers. I was worried about them. To be honest, I don't remember a whole lot about the accident."

He settled back in his chair. "I can't really divulge information on them, but you had the most severe injuries."

"I'm glad."

"Nice of you to say, especially since the accident wasn't your fault. You know your car, or Betsy, is totaled, but you don't seem to upset about it."

Paige reached out and touched his hand. "I may have named it, but it's only a car. There'll be another Betsy. Or maybe a Gunther this time."

"Gunther? You'd name a car Gunther?" He had a look on his face that said he might think she was crazy after all.

"Well, of course, but only if it's German made."

He burst out laughing. She tried to join in but was immediately reminded of the bruising on her sternum. Holding a hand to her chest, she stifled the laugh threatening to bubble up. "Oh, I must remember no laughing anytime soon." She grabbed a pillow and held it against her chest as a nurse had shown her last evening.

Quinn leaned in, a look of concern over his handsome face. "The seat belt got you, I see." He pointed to her chest. "Painful for sure but better than hitting the steering wheel. Can I do anything?"

"Stop making me laugh!" She looked at him then, really looked, and saw how cute he was. He wasn't model handsome, but his features added up to something more than ordinary. He had thick, dark blond hair, worn short, and warm, chocolate brown eyes. His lashes, which any woman would envy, were incredibly long and curled slightly. His nose was straight, and he had a firm chin. His skin was lightly tanned. Looking downward, she could see he was physically fit. The navy-blue fire department T-shirt he was wearing outlined rather than concealed the muscles in his arms and chest.

He smiled as if he noticed her checking him out. But she was sure he was used to it. After all, he was a ruggedly handsome firefighter. Women probably checked him out daily.

"So, let me get this straight. Your car is totaled, but your big concern is what you're going to name the new one?"

Paige leaned forward and smiled. "Yes. It was only a thing. Things can be replaced. People can't." She gestured to her forehead. "Other than some minor bumps and a few stitches, and of course a head injury, I got off lucky. It could have been much worse. Believe me, I know."

"Well, your attitude is amazing. Not many people would feel that way. I'm glad you're going to be fine." He stood and patted her hand. "I should let you get some rest. It was nice meeting you. I wish you all the best." With a wave, he left the hospital room.

Paige sat back, wondering what had happened. They seemed to be hitting it off, and then he bolted. Who knew? It was probably for the best. She was busy with her career and graduate school. She had a long way to go to prove herself. Even though the car accident wasn't her fault, she had a feeling Principal Milton might view it as another black mark against her.

She sank further into her pillows and sighed. She wouldn't worry about something she couldn't control. Besides, thinking about it would only make her head pound. It wasn't worth the effort. She closed her eyes and drifted to sleep.

Chapter Three

Quinn set down his paint brush and straightened, stretching out to his full height. He rolled his shoulders to lessen the knots forming there. He glanced around the living room he had finished in a soft, neutral color. This house was the third he had purchased in the past few years. The previous two he had "flipped" and made a tidy profit. It helped that he did most of the renovations himself.

The house was in an up and coming neighborhood with excellent schools, all things which had figured into his buying it. The house had gone into foreclosure and stood empty for over a year, making it the target of teens looking for a place to party. It needed work when he bought it. But that only drove down the asking price, allowing him to buy it at a fraction of its worth. If all went well, he would stand to make his biggest profit to date.

He was smart when it came to houses. It was women he had trouble with. He shook his head. If he was smarter with them, he wouldn't still be thinking about Paige. Several weeks had passed, and he still thought about her wavy, blonde hair and tinkling laugh.

She was exactly what he didn't need in his life. Quinn didn't date much. He liked women, and he certainly enjoyed sex, but he wasn't a long-term relationship kind of guy. He knew better. He didn't believe in 'happy ever after'. At least not for himself.

Shaking off these thoughts, he closed the paint cans and washed his brushes. Painting was tedious and at times back breaking work. But it didn't take a lot of thought. He had thrown himself into this project hoping it would take his mind off Paige. But he had been wrong.

Maybe, he mused, it was because he didn't have any distractions. A.J. and some of the other guys at the house had been teasing him ruthlessly about 'needing to get laid'. Maybe he did. But he dismissed the thought as soon as it formed. It wasn't what he needed. Not that he didn't have plenty of opportunity. There were women who would sleep with him because of his job. But it had grown old years ago.

When he was a rookie, barely out of the fire academy, he had learned about these women. He was a little ashamed to think about exactly how he had learned, but that was then, and this is now. Now he was older, and he hoped, smarter.

These days, when he did date, it was one woman at a time for as long as it lasted. Generally, he was the one to end it. He didn't have any interest in getting married and having kids. He was always honest and up front with any woman he dated. They didn't always believe him. He had hurt more than one woman, although it was unintentionally.

What he needed was a beer. He glanced at the clock, and seeing it was after eight, he knew he would find some of his friends at Smitty's. Taking long enough to change out of his paint splattered clothing and clean up, Quinn grabbed his keys and headed out the door. He hoped a few rounds and some darts with the gang would take his mind off Paige.

****

Across town, Paige was busy reviewing her lesson plans for the week. Sundays were generally spent catching up on schoolwork. She rolled her head on her neck, first to the right and then to the left. She grimaced slightly at the dull ache in her head. Although the worst of the headaches were gone, she still suffered some residual ones from her concussion.

She walked into the kitchen for a bottle of water. She glanced at the Keurig sitting unused on the counter. It seemed lonely and dejected to her. She pushed off such fanciful thoughts. She had been banned from drinking caffeine for the first two weeks of her recovery. It was the longest time she had abstained from coffee. She could drink it again but was reluctant to start. She could freely admit she had been addicted. Water was the better choice.

She grabbed a bottle from the fridge. The chilled water felt great sliding down her parched throat. Summer was rapidly approaching, and even late in the evening, the temperature was warm and muggy. That was North Carolina for you, but Paige wouldn't have it any other way,

With a sharp yip, Finn pounced on Paige's bare feet, reminding her he needed to go out to relieve himself. She was so proud of the little guy. Only twelve weeks old, and he hadn't had an accident in the house in a few weeks.

Paige opened the back door and turned on the flood lights. The little dog bounded out to the grass and squatted down. She praised him, causing him to run back to her and prance around her feet. The two stepped back inside, and Paige locked the back door and turned off the lights. The coffee debate made her think about the accident. Of course, she couldn't think about the accident without thinking about Quinn. The two were linked in her mind. She thought about the hunky firefighter a lot.

Amy had asked endless questions about him. What did he look like? Cute! Was he married? No ring... When would Paige see him again? She smiled. Very soon.

Paige had not heard from him. No surprise there. He had made it clear in his hasty retreat he was not interested. But how would she know for sure if she didn't give it the old college try? In her defense, she hadn't been at her best on the two occasions on which they met.

Since she had not stopped thinking about him and because she owed him a proper thank you, she had arranged a visit to the station for her class. She had personally spoken with Chief Henry Wells, Quinn's boss. She had ensured he would be on shift the date of the outing. Furthermore, she had asked his commander to not tell Quinn, citing the firefighter's modesty. She assured the chief her students had their hearts set on thanking the brave men who had saved their teacher.

Okay, so maybe it had been a stretch. But, they were excited about the visit as any six- year-old would be. They had also spent many hours constructing a banner and cards to thank the brave men and women of station Fifteen. If he was still not interested, then at least she could say she tried.

Paige felt the flutter of a thousand butterflies in her stomach. She was excited to see him again. But she was also nervous. She didn't want him thinking she was stalking him. She dismissed the thought. After all, she had two, legitimate reasons for visiting. She knew for a fact schools visited local fire departments all the time. Why would Station Fifteen be any different? And more importantly, she did want to show her appreciation.

*****

Tuesday dawned bright and beautiful, typical of late spring in North Carolina. He always thought of these as his happy-to-be-alive days. The trees were blooming. The sun shone brightly from the sky. He looked around his small town as they returned from a call. People waved as he drove past. He waved back. He was a part of this town. He mattered here.

The call had been a simple one. A quick-thinking employee had reacted quickly and called 9-1-1 for a small dryer fire in the laundry of a local nursing home. The fire itself was contained within minutes, and they had stayed to ensure everything was okay. He loved calls like this one. Everything was solved, and no one died. He couldn't ask for much more.

He was driving the rescue truck, and for once he had managed to go several hours without thinking about Paige. As much as he was attracted to her, as much as he wanted to get to know her better, it wasn't a good idea. He had gotten the sense she wasn't the type of woman meant for casual flings. So, he had done the only thing he could do and stayed away from her. No point in starting something he couldn't finish.

That didn't mean he didn't think about her. That didn't even mean he didn't know where she lived and worked. After all, the information had been provided on the accident report. He had gone so far as to drive by one night, slowing down as he saw her bright red car in the driveway. Since it wasn't a BMW or Volkswagen, he had wondered what she named it. He knew he was in trouble. He grunted.

A.J. looked up from his phone. "Did you grunt? What's gotten into you, man? You've been a bear to work with lately."

"Nothing. I'm fine. What is this, Dr. Phil?" Because Quinn was annoyed with himself for allowing his personal issues to spill over onto the job, he came off gruffer than he had intended. By way of apology, he offered to clean the truck when they got back, but all it got was raised eyebrows.

"OK, now I know something's off. Spill."

He drove around the corner and on to the apron outside of the station. Parked off to the side was a large, yellow school bus. Although his captain hadn't mentioned any planned trips, it looked like they were being invaded by ankle biters. Now it was A.J.'s turn to groan. This was far from their first school visit, and his friend was not a fan.

He hit the button for the bay doors. Turning to look at his friend, he grinned. "This is what you get for busting on me, A.J."

Quinn hopped from the truck and started into the station. His senses were on alert before he ever spotted Paige, standing inside the door. She was surrounded by small children and smiling at something his captain was saying. He watched in complete disbelief, and more than a little jealousy, as she placed her hand on his arm and laughed. Surely, he couldn't be jealous of a man who was thirty years his senior? What was she doing here?

As though she sensed his presence, Paige turned and looked straight at him. Smiling, she leaned down and said something to the gaggle of children seated at her feet. They jumped up and ran towards him, all screaming at once and swarming around him. He noticed A.J. was nowhere to be seen.

She approached him, calling for quiet from her students as she did. He was amazed when they all dropped back to the floor. He looked on expectantly as she signaled a little girl.

"Jasmine, are you ready?" The little nodded and stood up. She approached him, admiration shining from her eyes, instantly melting his heart. He squatted down to be on her eye level and waited.

"Firefighter Quinn, we all want to tell you how happy we are Miss Harrington didn't die. Thanks for saving her." The little girl then launched herself at him, wrapping her arms around his neck tightly. Blushing furiously, she turned around and ran back to her spot on the floor.

Paige stepped forward and placed her hand on his arm. She laughed before speaking. "Not quite how I would have said it, but true enough. There aren't enough words to thank you, Quinn." She hugged him before stepping back. This brought a loud round of oohs and ahs from the crowd. He was rewarded with her sweet blush.

Seeking to shift their attention, he asked in a loud voice, "Okay, who wants to sit in a fire truck?" He was mobbed by a sea of small bodies, leading them away like a modern day Pied Piper.

*****

Paige watched him go, placing a hand over her stomach to quiet the quivering there. In his work gear, he looked even better than she had remembered. She turned to catch her friend's eye. Amy had been speaking with Quinn's captain. She shook his hand and walked over to where Paige stood.

Amy grinned at her friend. "I see why you've been keeping him to yourself. He's gorgeous!"

Paige sputtered in return. "I haven't been keeping him to myself, as you well know. I haven't even seen him since the day in the hospital." The warmth she felt on her face was a dead giveaway.

Amy pounced. "Aha! I knew you liked him! All the talk about gratitude was a smoke screen. Well played, Paige, well played!" She was still laughing as she walked off to join the children.

"Well, you certainly look a lot different than the last time I saw you." The deep, masculine voice behind Paige drew her attention. She turned to see a very tall, muscular man standing there. He had to be over six five.

"Have we met?"

The man tipped his head in her direction. "Andrew Jefferson, ma'am. But you can call me A.J. I was on scene the day of your accident. You're so much prettier without blood running down your face."

Paige laughed out loud. "Well that's certainly a different compliment, but I'll take it. Nice to meet you, A.J. I'm sorry I don't remember you, but all I really remember is Quinn's voice."

"No worries, Paige. He's my best friend since my rookie days here."

Paige extended her hand which was swallowed up in his. "Well then, I'm pleased to meet you, A.J. Although my memory is a bit foggy, I know there are many people to thank. So, I guess I'll start with you." She leaned in and hugged the big man.

He walked around the side of a fire engine. He slapped A.J. on the back. "Paige, I see you've met A.J. Don't believe a single thing he says about me."

"If you're not too busy tomorrow night, why don't you stop by Smitty's after work? Wednesday night is Ladies' Night, and there's a live band. He and I, plus pretty much everyone else on our squad will be there. You should drop by."

Paige grinned up at A.J. "Smitty's, huh? Live music? Going out on a school night?" Amy rejoined her. "We were invited out to a bar tomorrow night, Amy. Sounds like fun. Doesn't it?"

Turning to the two firefighters, she smiled brightly. "Hi, I'm Amy Windsor. I teach with Paige and happen to be her best friend. And you are?"

A.J. stared at her, seemingly unable to put two words together. Quinn extended a hand towards her. "Nice to meet you, Amy. I'm Quinn Adams, and this unusually silent guy is my friend A.J. Say hello to the nice lady."

A.J. snapped out of his fog. "Sorry. My mind wandered for a second there. Hi, I'm A.J., as he said. It's Andrew Jefferson, but everyone calls me A.J. Pleased to meet you, ma'am."

Paige wasn't exactly stunned to see the huge, tough firefighter reduced to rubble by her friend. Amy *was* gorgeous! The kind of gorgeous that made men stupid. She was 5'11" and willowy with long, curly hair in hundreds of shades of blonde not from a bottle. It made men want to run their fingers through it. Her bright green eyes were captivating. In fact, sneaking a look at him, she was shocked he hadn't fallen under her friend's spell. Although Paige knew she herself was attractive, it was more in a girl-next-door way. She wasn't the type to make men speechless.

Amy turned to A.J. and placed her hand on his forearm. "I think I prefer Andrew. So, you were part of the crew that saved Paige, huh? Well, I thank you. Paige is very important to me, to my whole family. We are indebted to y'all." Her smile was sincere but blinding, and it seemed to keep A.J. off balance.

Paige swallowed a laugh at A.J.'s expense. She could already tell he was a goner. "A.J. was telling me about a bar called Smitty's. They have live music tomorrow night. What do you say?"

Whatever Amy might have said was lost in the din of the returning children. Chief Wells looked relieved to hand them back to their teachers. The children swarmed around Paige and Amy, each vying for attention. Within seconds, silence reigned. he looked at Paige, bewilderment clear on his face. She smiled in return. He obviously didn't work with small children regularly. All it took was she and Amy crossing their arms and wearing a certain look on their faces.

She continued to glance at the children, waiting until they were silent, and she was sure she had their attention. Smiling, she addressed the students. "Okay, then. Not bad. Under ten seconds! Now it's time to thank the kind firefighters for taking time out of their busy days to show us around. Then we're going to line up in pairs and walk out to the bus."

The children all said thank-you and filed out of the station in an orderly fashion, with Amy leading and Paige bringing up the rear. From the look on his face, he might believe she dabbled in witchcraft. She had learned very early on in her training she needed to always have control or else she would be lost. As much as she loved her students, she had to have the final say.

She turned to look back at him one last time. "See you tomorrow night." The students boarded the bus, and as Amy made sure they were settled in their seats, Paige did the mandatory headcount. Twice. It certainly wouldn't impress Principal Milton if she left behind one of her precious charges.

*****

Quinn and A.J. stood in the now empty and quiet bay. He realized he hadn't said goodbye to the women. He turned to A.J. "Well, that was something."

A.J. grinned back at his friend. "I think she liked me. Don't you?"

Quinn laughed and slapped him on the back. "Really? She said five words to you." He grinned at A.J. "And you couldn't even string five words together."

"Oh, she likes me. I could tell. Besides, we'll see them tomorrow night. I'll do better then."

"Tomorrow night? You really think they're going to show up at Smitty's? Honestly, A.J., I don't really think they're the type."

A.J. had a strange look on his face, part curiosity and part insult. "What does that mean? They're not the 'type'. What type are they?"

He spread his hands. "All I'm saying is they don't strike me as women who go after firefighters. I wouldn't have your heart set on seeing Amy again."

"What about you?"

"What about me? Not sure what you're asking." He tried to sound casual. The last thing he needed was A.J. catching onto his growing attraction for Paige.

"You can't fool me. I saw the way you were watching her." A.J. laughed at his friend's raised eyebrows. "I know you like her. Besides, it's been way too long since you've dated anyone. It's time to get back out there, my friend."

Quinn knew when he was defeated. He and A.J. had been friends way too long to get away with anything. He sighed. "Okay, yes, I like her. I think she's very cute. But I won't be asking her out."

A.J. shook his head. "Let me guess. You like her too much to get involved with her. You're not interested in anything permanent, and you don't want to hurt her. Am I close?"

He hit the bulls-eye. "I know you don't agree. I feel the way I do for a reason, A.J. It's not only the possibility of dying in the line of duty. It's also the worry every time I go to work, wondering if I'll make it home this time." He shook his head. "I won't be responsible for ruining someone's life."

This wasn't unfamiliar territory for them. Although A.J. didn't share his beliefs, he also hadn't grown up in a firefighter family. He wasn't in a position to judge.

"All I'm saying is you two seemed to hit it off. Why not give it a try? Ask her out. See where it leads."

"I do like her. Enough to back off. I'm not going to start something I can't, or won't, finish."

"At least tell me you'll come to Smitty's tomorrow night."

He smiled at his friend. "It would almost be worth it to see your face when they don't show, but no can do. I've got a date with a paint brush. I still have a long way to go with this house."

A.J. grinned. "Oh, they're going to show. You'll see."

Chapter Four

Paige graded her last quiz and slid the papers into her briefcase. She was so thankful to be done for the evening. She stretched and yawned. They all enjoyed the field trip, but it made for a long day. Even though she and Amy had managed to corral the kids back on the bus in an orderly fashion, they had remained giddy with excitement. Paige had to redirect their energy throughout the remainder of the school day.

She picked up Finn from his fluffy dog bed and curled up in the corner of the couch. The little puppy yawned and nuzzled his face under her chin. He was asleep again within moments.

Paige thought back to the day, a few weeks ago, when she first met him. She had gone to the shelter with Amy's mother, Susan. The older woman was looking to adopt a cat, having lost their ancient Siamese over the winter. Paige was along for moral support only. Then she spotted Finn.

The tiny puppy was barely eight weeks old and cowering on an old towel in the corner of his enclosure. Something clenched in her chest as she watched from outside the pen. Knowing she would later regret the move, she crouched down and whispered to the terrified pup. When he ignored her, she sat down on the cold, cement floor and waited him out. Eventually, he inched towards her, sniffing her outstretched fingers. His tiny body shook. She knew she had made a friend for life when he began to wag his little tail.

A shelter worker had come along and told Paige what little they knew about Finn. He was part spaniel and God only knew what else. He had been found abandoned in a box on their front step one morning, skin and bones and full of fleas at the time. They figured he was only a few weeks old. One of the shelter volunteers had taken him home to nurse him, and it was a miracle he had survived.

Paige had adopted him and named him Finn, after one of her favorite fictional characters, Huckleberry Finn. The little dog was white with freckled markings of brown and red over his body. Finn was her constant companion as she completed work for school every evening.

Amy joked that Finn was the only man in Paige's life. But it was true. She had terrible luck where men were concerned. She was always falling for men who were 'emotionally unavailable', as Amy put it. She had dated sporadically through college and afterwards, but at this point in her life, Paige was through with the whole mess. At least for now. She was finishing her master's degree in education and had a job she loved, even if Principal Morton disapproved of her youth and "new-fangled ways'. Now she had Finn. What else could she possibly need?

An image of Quinn popped up in her mind. His warm brown eyes and hard body were frequent thoughts of hers. She sighed. Although he had been friendly enough today, she didn't get the I'm-interested-vibe. Shame really since she was more than interested. But she had her pride.

The ringing of her phone roused her from her thoughts. She knew it was Amy by the special ringtone. Even though they worked together every day, Paige and Amy spoke at least once in the evening.

"Hey there, Amy. What's going on?"

"So, I was wondering what one wears to a firefighter bar."

"A firefighter bar? What are you talking about?"

"Ugh, I knew you'd forget. We were invited, and agreed to go, so we are. This leads me back to my original question. What are we wearing?"

"Oh, I think he was being nice, Amy. I don't think he was interested in hanging out with me. I never even gave it a second thought."

"Well I'm going, which means you're going. Don't bother arguing. You know you're only going to give in. So, again, what are we wearing? Probably something casual and maybe a little slutty."

Laughter burst from Paige. "You're right of course. I always give in to you. But then someone has to drag me out of my otherwise boring life. Fine, I'll go. But I draw the line at slutty."

"You're no fun! But that's all right. I'll do the slutty, you go with your usual conservative."

The two talked for a couple more minutes before ending the call. Paige's thoughts returned to Quinn. He was handsome without being caught up in his looks. He had broad shoulders and his arms were muscular and well defined, but he didn't have a look that said the gym was his sole focus in life. She figured being a firefighter had a lot to do with the shape he was in.

But there was so much to him beyond the physical. He was smart and kind. He might even be a bit funny. An active sense of humor was high on her list. Despite her history, or maybe because of it, she was an upbeat person who firmly believed humor solved almost everything.

Although she had pretty much taken herself out of the dating game, she wasn't blind or stupid. He was a nice guy. And there was a lovely little zing she felt all the way to her toes when he had touched her. God knows it didn't come along every day. She would be a fool to ignore it. Maybe she'd give it one more try.

Finn yawned as she placed him back into his comfortable bed. She grinned as he opened his eyes to peer at her before settling back in again. She shut down her computer. Although she still had a paper to finish for her own class, tonight was not the night. She was tired, and she never did her best work in this state. The paper wasn't due until next week, so she could finish it over the weekend.

Paige walked into the bathroom to brush her teeth and wash her face. The jibe Amy had made about her fashion choices stayed with her. The truth hurt, as they say. She looked into her closet and pondered options for Smitty's. Being a kindergarten teacher did not lend itself to clothes suitable for a bar. She'd have to think about this.

Glancing at her phone, she realized it was getting late. She turned off the closet light and got ready for bed. The ugly wallpaper taunted her. But she'd have the last laugh. Buying her own home had been a great decision, and not just financially. She'd loved living with Amy in her friend's condo, but owning a home felt right. Her parents would be proud she put their money to good use.

Initially Paige had looked at some new construction. But one day, she had seen this small house. Far from new construction, her home had been built in the 1950s. The design had character. And it wasn't a 'cookie cutter.' The previous owner, a woman in her eighties, had died, and the heirs had wanted to sell immediately. The house was being sold as is, which meant there was a lot of TLC needed. But it also meant a lower price.

Paige wasn't afraid of hard work. She had no idea what she was doing, but she could learn. After all, she was an intelligent, educated woman. And there was always You Tube. To start, she had decided to tackle small jobs like removing wallpaper and painting.

More than ready to go to sleep herself, Paige changed into a long T-shirt, her usual nighttime garb, flicked on the ceiling fan, and slid into bad. She was asleep almost before her head hit the pillow.

Somewhere in the middle of the night, she dreamed about her car accident. Once again, the twisted metal trapped her. But she felt safe. Protected. Quinn was with her in the car, speaking softly to her. Although she couldn't see him in the dream, she felt his presence. He reassured her in his sexy, deep voice. Paige awoke in the morning with a satisfied smile on her face.

Walking into school later, she looked up when Amy called her name. She smiled at her friend and fell into step with her.

Amy grinned back at her. "So, what did you decide to wear tonight?"

She shook her head in response. "I haven't given it a thought since our conversation last night."

Amy groaned. "I *know* you. You cannot show up dressed like a kindergarten teacher. One of these days you're going to have to start putting a little effort into your appearance."

Paige grinned. "You're the slave to fashion, not me."

Her friend smiled then frowned. "And I have the credit card bills to prove it."

Paige laughed. "We're going to a bar. One filled with firefighters and cops and EMTs. I don't think anyone will faint if I'm not wearing designer shoes. Not that I own any." Clothes didn't even begin to approach her radar, much to her best friend's regret.

"How are we best friends? I give up! Promise me you'll wear something to remind him you're a woman."

The two women reached their respective classrooms. "I promise, but I doubt he's going to be there anyway. See you at lunch." She dug her keys out of her purse and opened her classroom door.

*****

Quinn was up on a ladder painting a wall in the living room and listening to Garth Brooks sing about unanswered prayers when his cell phone rang. Needing a break, he put down the brush and climbed down the ladder. He answered and clicked on speaker without looking at the screen. A.J.'s booming voice filled the air. "Am I picking you up or are you meeting me there?"

"Hey, A.J., I'm fine thanks," he answered with a chuckle before continuing. "Not sure what you're talking about, but unless it's painting, I'm saying no."

"What? You're kidding me, right? It's Wednesday night. As in the night we're meeting Amy and Paige at Smitty's. How can you not remember?"

"I remember. But I never said I was going. I told you I'm trying to finish up this house, so I can get it back on the market. Have a great time."

"Wait, don't hang up! What am I supposed to do with Paige? I really want to get to know Amy, and I don't want Paige to feel left out."

"You don't even know for sure if they're coming."

"Oh, they're coming." There was silence on the other end followed by a sigh of frustration. "You really aren't coming?"

"I'm really not."

"OK, then. I guess I'll be calling Jack. I'm sure he's up to an evening chatting with your cute friend."

"Jack? You're kidding me, right?" His hands formed into fists thinking about the other firefighter chatting up Paige. Jack was a great coworker and even better friend, but he wasn't suitable for Paige. She was a kindergarten teacher for goodness sake! Jack was the king of one-night stands. Jack played the field and made no bones about it. He changed women like Quinn changed his socks.

"So, you're meeting me there in an hour?"

He glanced at his paint-splattered clothes. "Yeah at least an hour. I have to finish cleaning up here and then take a quick shower." He clicked off, knowing A.J. had tricked him into going. He doubted Paige and Amy would show, but he couldn't take the chance. Paige had probably never been to Smitty's. Never been to a first responder hang out. They didn't usually get kindergarten teachers. Although everyone was nice and there to blow off steam, it could get a bit loud. She might find it overwhelming. And she was still recovering from a head injury. Seeing a familiar face would help. Besides, someone had to protect her from men like Jack.

Keep telling yourself that. He could tell A.J. whatever he wanted, but the truth was he was looking forward to seeing her again. Knowing it wasn't a good idea didn't stop him. He banged the paint can shut and cleaned his brushes before heading for the shower.

*****

Doubt crowded Paige's thoughts as they pulled into the parking lot. She turned to Amy in a last-ditch effort to change her mind. "I don't think this is a good idea", she began her campaign. "We don't know them, and besides they might not even come. Then we won't know anyone. Besides, it's a…" She stopped as Amy held up her hand.

"Let me stop you right there before you can utter the dreaded words. Yes, Mom, I know it's a 'school night'." She took one last look in the mirror. "We are not *in* school anymore. Well, you are, but you're an adult and you'll be done in a few weeks. We are the teachers. If we want to take a walk on the wild side and go out on a Wednesday night, then we can. Lighten up! This is going to be fun." With that last parting shot, she got out of the car, forcing Paige to follow.

"I get it. We're adults and can make our own decisions. I think maybe this isn't a good one. Well, it's a good decision for you, as A.J. wants to see you again. But Quinn looked less than enthusiastic when he heard."

"So, forget about him. Yes, he's hot. Yes, he saved your life. Yes, you need to get laid. But there are other fish in the sea, as they say. I'm sure there will be many here tonight."

By now they had reached the front door. Paige gave up trying to talk her out of this adventure, partially because it was way too late but mostly because Amy was right. She needed to have a little fun. Between teaching and her graduate program, Paige hadn't made much of an effort to have any kind of life over the past two years.

With new resolve, she straightened her shoulders and pulled open the front door. As the women stepped inside, the noise and the crowd overwhelmed her. After adjusting to the din, she was pleased with what she saw. The bar itself was long and somewhat U-shaped with a brass rail. It was also surrounded by patrons. The interior was done in a light wood, and the walls were decorated with various memorabilia from local fire, police, and ambulance companies. There were many tables scattered throughout and more booths lining two walls. Best of all, it boasted a small stage on which a band was now warming up. A minuscule portion of the floor in front of this was cleared for dancing.

Amy turned to her with excited eyes. "Looks like we got here in the nick of time. Let's grab a table while we can." She took Paige's hand and dragged her through the milling crowd to the one empty booth. As soon as they sat down facing each other, a harried waitress appeared in front of them. She was dressed in denim shorts and a bright red T-shirt featuring the bar's logo. A name tag read Patty.

"What'll it be, ladies? We have draft specials and a limited wine list." She pointed to a laminated menu on the table. "We also have some appetizers available. Do you know what you want yet?"

"I'll have a Diet Coke," Paige answered.

"Jack and Diet Coke please," responded Amy.

The waitress hurried off to fill their drink orders. Paige looked up as A.J. approached their booth. "That didn't take long."

Amy slid towards the wall and motioned A.J. to join them. She gave him a brilliant smile as he reached their booth. "Hey, there you are! I didn't see you when we came in. I thought maybe we'd been stood up." She laughed and winked at A.J. before sliding back into the booth.

A.J. took a seat next to Amy. "No, ma'am, and I'm pretty sure that's never happened to you."

Amy grinned and placed a hand on his arm. "You'd be surprised, Andrew. Anyway, this place is great! I can't wait to hear the band."

A.J. looked across at Paige. "Nice to see you again. Quinn is on his way. He was in the middle of painting. He should be here shortly."

Paige shoved her purse into the corner of the booth and then slid out. "Nice to see you again, A.J. I'm going to run to the rest room. Amy, watch my purse for me, okay?" She walked towards the rear of the bar where a sign announced the ladies' room. She knew Amy would thank her later for giving her a few minutes alone with A.J.

She had almost made it to her destination when a large, blonde man stepped directly into her path. He was very tall, and Paige had to look up to meet his eyes. His bulging arms sported several large tattoos.

"Evening, Ma'am. Why is such a pretty lady here all alone? I'm Jack, and I'm more than happy to keep you company." He grinned down at her as he spoke.

Paige fought the urge to groan aloud. She was sure it had worked on many others but not her. "I'm not alone. On my way to the restroom, but thanks for your concern." She was chagrined when he stepped further into her path as she tried to scoot around him.

"Aw, come on now, let me at least buy you a drink."

Paige was about to let him know, once again, she wasn't interested, when a warm arm encircled her waist. She knew it was Quinn without even looking.

"Hey Jack, are you bothering my girl?" He smiled but there was a fierceness to it.

Jack held up both hands. "I didn't know you were here. I certainly didn't know the young lady was with you. No worries." Jack smiled one last time at Paige and turned back to the bar.

"Sorry about Jack. He's a good friend, but he really likes the ladies. And usually they like him right back. He probably doesn't know what to do when someone shoots him down."

Although confident in her ability to handle herself, Paige was glad for his intervention. She grinned at him. "He's not my type. I'm sure he would have gotten the hint, but thanks for the help. Did you just get here?"

"Yes, in the nick of time. Did Amy come with you?"

Paige turned and pointed to the back corner of the room. "She's over there with A.J. I excused myself for a minute to give them a little privacy. Come join us."

Quinn placed his large, warm hand in the small of her back to guide her. Heat spread in all directions. The slight contact zinged through her like an electrical jolt.

Amy looked up as they approached the booth. Paige slid back in across from Amy and reached for her drink. She took a sip of her soda, thankful for its cool wetness. Being near him made her mouth dry. He may not be as big or muscled as Jack, but in her mind, he was much more handsome.

Amy turned to Quinn. "A.J. was telling us you had been painting earlier. Maybe you could give Paige some tips."

"Oh, do you have a painting project? How big of a room are you tackling?"

"I actually haven't started painting yet, and I have a whole house to do. Right now, I'm tackling the world's ugliest wallpaper, which will take me a long time. It's okay. I still need to decide on colors, which may take me forever."

A.J. leaned across the table and pointed to his friend. "He can help. He's an expert. How many houses have you rehabbed now?"

The band started up, making conversation more difficult. Quinn moved closer and leaned in to her. "It's a hobby really. I buy older houses needing some TLC, fix them up, then sell them again. It keeps me busy in my off time."

"Wow, I had no idea. Mine was owned by an old lady whose husband had died years earlier. She hadn't made any changes to the home in two decades. I had an inspection done, and the house itself is in good shape. But it needs a lot of work to update it."

"Tell me about this ugly wallpaper."

"You have no idea. Every room has a different pattern, each worse than the one before it. The kitchen is all done in avocado, straight out of the 1970s. The wallpaper has teapots on it, if you can believe. Really big, really ugly teapots." She drained her drink.

He flagged down the passing waitress. "Can I get a Corona, please?" Turning to Paige, he indicated her empty glass. "What are you drinking? This round is on me."

Paige picked up her empty glass and swirled the remaining ice cubes. "Diet Coke for me, thanks."

He repeated her request to the waitress who bustled off. "Not much of a drinker, huh?"

"I do on occasion, but soda's fine for me tonight. I haven't had any alcohol since the accident, and I don't miss it."

He nodded. "So, tell me more about this house."

She was surprised by his behavior. After barely speaking to her when she brought her students to his station, she had not expected this reception. She had been shocked when he stepped in and 'saved' her from his friend Jack.

"I haven't lived there long. Right now, I'm focusing on getting rid of the wallpaper. Once that's done, I can start thinking about painting. All I know is I want it to be bright and sunny."

"Colors to match your personality, then."

Paige's smile widened. "What a lovely thing to say."

The waitress came by and plunked down their drinks without a word. He handed hers over before taking a quick drink of his own. "I guess picking colors can be tough. I don't have that problem, since I'm putting the house right back on the market. I stick with neutrals. You know, off white or something similar."

Paige wrinkled her pert nose in obvious distaste. "Sorry, no judgment there, but I'd go crazy. I love color."

He gestured to her white capris and bright orange shirt, sporting an even brighter Margaritaville decal. "I can tell."

She looked down at herself and shrugged. She was never going to be known for her fashion sense. "Amy is always on me for not dressing more fashionably." She sighed and glanced across at her smartly dressed friend. "It's not that she hasn't tried, but I really can't make myself care about clothes and shoes and even make up most days."

"I wouldn't worry. I think you're fine the way you are. Bright, like a summer day." His gravelly voice held more than a hint of approval

Paige felt her cheeks warm at his compliment. "Thank you." She leaned in towards him and placed her small hand on his arm. His skin was warm and firm. Electricity coursed up her arm. She breathed in his clean, male scent and sighed.

Quinn covered her hand with his larger one. "So, Amy, how long have you and Paige known each other?"

Amy sat back and eyed him over the rim of her glass before answering. "Oh, since we were in the womb."

He sputtered, almost spraying beer across the table. Recovering and wiping his mouth on a napkin, he replied. "Really? Seems like there's a story there."

"Not really," she answered. "Our moms were friends and pregnant at the same time. I was born 6 weeks after Paige, so we really have been friends all of our lives." She smiled at her friend who returned the gesture.

The band switched to a slower song, and Paige heard the opening strains of Van Morrison's *Into the Mystic*. She grinned and turned to him. "Would you like to dance? I love this song."

He extended his hand towards her. "I'd love to." He helped her from the booth and once again guided her with a hand at the small of her back. Paige felt as though her flesh was on fire where his hand touched her. *What would his whole body pressed along hers feel like?* Quinn caught her when she stumbled. Probably better to keep her thoughts at bay while she was with him.

They stepped onto the crowded dance floor. He gathered her in his arms. She wrapped her arms around his waist and closed her eyes on the delicious feel of him pressed along the length of her. They drifted around the dance floor. Paige looked up long enough to notice her friend was dancing with A.J. To their left, Jack danced with a very young woman. She nodded her head to the left. "I've been replaced."

"I wouldn't take it personally."

Paige looked at Jack and his dance partner. The other woman was wearing skin tight jeans and a very low cut, sheer blouse leaving little to the imagination. They seemed better suited to each other.

"Oh, I don't. I've met plenty of guys like Jack before. Like I said, he's not my type."

He gathered her even closer to him and leaned down to whisper in her ear. "So, what is your type then, if Jack's not it?"

She grew silent, wondering how to answer. Then she took a half step back and looked up and into his eyes. "I like guys who want to be with me for me, not just a warm body." Her face warmed a bit as the inevitable blushed stained her cheeks. "I want someone who is kind and intelligent. Someone who takes life seriously but not too seriously. Someone who I can laugh with. "

"But you didn't mention what this mystery guy would look like."

Paige stepped back towards him and rested her cheek against his chest. She could hear his strong heartbeat, even above the din of the band. She hadn't given a physical description, because she was afraid she would describe him.

"Oh, I don't think it matters as much to women as it does to men."

"Really? So, he could be four feet tall, and you wouldn't care?"

She laughed. "It's not like I wear heels often."

He shook his head. "You really are not like most women I've ever met." The song ended, and Quinn took her hand, leading her back to the table.

After they were seated, and Paige took a drink of her soda, she looked at him directly. "So, is it a good thing?" she asked.

He smiled. "Yes, it's a very good thing. I meant you seem very straightforward. No games. Rare in this world."

"Is that what you're looking for? Someone who doesn't play games?" Her heart thundered as she waited for him to answer.

"Always a bonus," he began. "But I'm not looking for anyone." The words hung between them. He looked down at the floor.

"You're not looking right now? Or not at all?" Paige was more confused than ever. She enjoyed dancing with him, and the sparks between them didn't come along every day. But he was shutting down again.

He had the grace to look uncomfortable. "I, uh date, of course. Not in a while now, but I do. I'm not planning on getting married. Ever. Or having kids. It's not what I want."

Her heart squeezed at his confession, but she couldn't let him see her pain. So, she grinned at him. She placed her hand over her heart and declared, "You mean I shouldn't be expecting a ring anytime soon?" She lasted less than five seconds before bursting out laughing. "Don't worry, I haven't started dress shopping."

He took a drink of his Corona. "That's not what I meant, and you know it. I like to be honest with people. Honest with women, specifically. I don't lead them on. Most women I know, if not all, plan to marry and have kids someday. I don't.

I feel it's important to mention in the beginning of a relationship." Quinn stopped talking, as if he had realized what he had said.

The silence stretched between them as she absorbed the information. "So, is the beginning of a relationship, then?" For a moment, he looked so scared she had to feel sorry for him. She decided to let him off the hook.

"Wow, the look on your face was priceless!" She reached across and squeezed his hand. And tried to ignore the zing of attraction darting through her. "I've got to tell you, this has become a very strange conversation. So, to be clear, you and I are not dating. Nor will we be. Ever. You and I are not getting married and having 3.5 kids either. Have I got it right?" She grinned at him and reached for her drink.

She continued before he could say anything. "It's okay, by the way. I'm not dating right now either. Between work, fixing up my house, and my graduate program, I don't have a ton of free time. Besides, I always seem to choose the wrong guy. It's better I don't date for a while." The small, white lie ate at her. She was honest to a fault. He was exactly the type of man she would have gone out with, but that wasn't going to happen. There was no point in even entertaining the idea.

"Well good. I'm glad we understand each other. But we can be friends, right?" He looked away and reached for his drink.

Paige was amused at the fleeting expressions she had seen across his handsome face. Although he made it clear they didn't have a future, he seemed loathe to let her walk away altogether. Hmmm… She wasn't sure how it would work with the electricity crackling between them.

"So, you and I are friends, then? No dating or anything." Her mind wandered to the 'anything ' part, and an image of Quinn with his shirt off popped into it. This would be tricky. "I don't have a lot of guy friends. Well, Alex, but he's more like my unofficial, big brother."

His head came up at the mention of another man. "Alex?"

"He's Amy's brother. He's a few years older than us. We all grew up together, and I consider him my family."

"Huh," he grunted in reply.

Feeling as though they had already danced through a verbal minefield, Paige switched the conversation to more neutral topics. They were both from Windsor Falls but hadn't met due to the nine-year age difference between them. However, they knew a lot of the same people.

Awhile later, Paige glanced at her watch, shocked to see it was almost eleven. She looked around for Amy and spotted her friend at a small table for two, her head bent close to A.J. She sighed. Amy didn't look like she was ready to leave anytime soon. She really needed to get home and go to bed. She also had Finn to think about. She should have insisted on meeting Amy here earlier.

"What's wrong? That was a world-weary sigh."

She looked at him and shook her head. "Nothing so important. I should be getting home, but Amy drove." She pointed to where their respective friends sat. "It may be a while. No worries. I'll call a cab." She took out her phone.

He placed his hand over hers. "I'll drive you home, Paige. I need to go anyway. A.J. and I are on shift in the morning." He stood up and threw some bills on the table.

"Are you sure it's not too much trouble?"

"Not at all. You're on my way home."

She raised one blonde brow. "How do you know where I live?"

"Oh, I remember seeing your address on the accident report," he stated.

"Well, if you're sure." She waited until he nodded. "Okay thanks. Let me tell Amy I'm leaving." She picked up her small purse and walked away.

*****

Quinn watched her weave her way across the packed room. He appreciated the way her hips swayed as she moved. He shook his head. He needed to stop thinking about her body if this 'just friends' thing was going to work. It wasn't one of his better ideas.

He waited as she spoke with Amy. A.J. turned and looked at him with a huge smile on his face. *Great!* He would have some explaining to do tomorrow.

Paige headed back to him. He noticed the waitress had already come by and cleaned their table. A group of four was ready to grab it. He grabbed her hand and headed for the door. Once out in the parking lot with the door closed behind them, the silence was deafening. He watched Paige rub her left temple.

"Are you okay?"

"I'm fine. I didn't realize how loud it was in there until we came outside. I still get headaches from time to time. The doctor told me it was to be expected."

"Are you sure? Do you need anything?"

She placed a hand on his arm. "Absolutely! I don't get them all the time. A loud bar with a band probably wasn't the wisest choice." Her soft smile hit him right in the gut. "But it sure was fun. I'm glad I let Amy talk me into coming."

"So, Amy had to talk you into coming, huh?"

A light blush colored her face. He didn't know women still blushed. "It's not that I didn't want to come, but I usually don't go out much during the week. I always have prep work for the next day of class. Plus, I'm trying to finish up my final paper for my graduate degree. There's only so many hours in the day."

Quinn stopped next to a large, navy blue pickup. There were ladders in the bed and his painting business information stenciled on the doors. Paige laughed.

"What's so funny? Something wrong with my truck?" He wasn't thrilled with the defensive note in his voice.

Paige's eyes widened, probably at his tone. "What is it with men and their trucks? No, it was me being goofy. My mind wanders sometimes. I can't even blame the accident. I looked at your truck and thought how perfect it is for you. Then I tried to picture you in my car."

"Oh. What have you replaced Betsy with? Is it a Gunther?"

Her face lit up. "You remembered? No Gunther for me. This one is Zoey. I wanted something with a little zip to it, pardon the alliteration."

He shook his head as he opened the passenger door for her. "I still can't believe you name your cars."

"It's true. I do. Not everyone gets it, but Zoey doesn't mind." She grinned as he helped her into his truck. "Yours seems more like a Dave."

"Dave?"

"Yes, Dave. Dave is no nonsense, direct, to the point. Dave is also dependable. Like your truck. Like you."

He wasn't sure he liked being described in those words. Dependable? While it was a respectable quality, did it have to be in the top five? "Why are we having this conversation?"

"Well, you did start it."

Her laughter trickled between them in the darkness of his truck. She was right. He had started it. He pulled out into traffic and headed in the direction of her home. He didn't say anything else.

"Are you mad at me?"

He glanced at her before returning his eyes to the road. "No, I'm not angry. I'm tired. I've been putting in a lot of hours on the latest house, trying to get it ready to put back on the market."

"Where do you live? Are you living in this house you're rehabbing?"

He stopped at a red light, turning to look at her in the glow of the dash. "Yes, I live in it. I'll buy another when this is done and then move into it when this one sells."

"So, you're kind of a nomad. Only without the dessert and camels."

A bark of laughter burst from him. You never knew what would come out of this woman's mouth. He liked it about her. "Uh, definitely no camel. Not even a dog."

"I have a dog. His name is Finn. I had gotten him a week before my accident. I had no idea how great owning a dog could be."

"So, Finn is your dog. I wondered."

"Wondered? How do you know about Finn?"

"You said his name at the accident. I thought maybe he was your boyfriend."

"Well, he is the only man in my life." Her laugh was a delicious shiver up his spine. "Amy thinks I'm going to grow old with Finn, or whichever dog comes next. I probably will, but I guess it's better than growing old alone."

"Amy seems to have a lot of opinions."

"Yes, she does. Amy and I are as different as night and day, but we'll always be there for each other. You have no idea what she's meant to me."

He felt there was more to the story but didn't press. A few minutes later, he pulled up to her house. The porch light showed flower boxes on the railing with a riot of colorful blooms bursting from them and an old-fashioned porch swing. He could picture Paige sitting there on hot, summer evenings.

Quinn got out, walking around to her side. Opening her door, he offered her his hand. Electricity passed between them when they touched, just as it had on the dance floor. He could imagine the chemistry would explode if they made love. But it wasn't going to happen. Someone as wonderful as Paige deserved the whole package. Deserved the kind of commitment he wasn't willing to risk.

They walked to her front door, side by side, almost touching but not quite. He clenched his teeth at the subtle scent of her perfume. When they reached the front porch, he held the storm door for her while she looked in her purse for her keys. He felt like he needed to say something to her, but for the life of him, he had no idea what. The situation was ridiculous. He was attracted to her, and he really liked her. She was sweet and funny, honest and seemingly low-maintenance. He found her easy to be with. Couple all those things with the attraction that snapped in the air between them, and it seemed like a no brainer. At least on paper. But he needed to keep his distance because he liked her so much. He had told her how it was, and she seemed to respect it. So why couldn't he?

She unlocked her door. "Well, thanks again for taking me home. Amy never seems to need any sleep, so who knows how long she'll be there."

She looked like she might hug him but then thought better of it. Probably for the best. "No worries. I was happy to help. A.J. is the same way. I need some sleep before work in the morning." He hesitated, not sure what to do next. He wanted more than anything in the world to lean down and kiss her goodnight. But it would be a mistake. Taking a step back, he waved goodbye and walked away.

Chapter Five

Paige watched Quinn walk away, frustration coursing through her veins. He seemed as though he was going to kiss her goodnight but changed his mind at the last second. He didn't want a relationship, yet she caught what looked like yearning on his face when he left. She shook her head and went inside her house.

Frantic yipping from the kitchen greeted her. Stepping over the baby gate and picking up a happy Finn, she laughed as he kissed her face, straining to reach all of it. Paige took the excited puppy outside to do his business.

Once they got back inside, Paige put together a lunch for tomorrow and sat on the kitchen floor to spend some quality time with Finn. Between work and going to the bar, she had hardy seen him today. "So, Finn, you're a guy, sort of. Explain your gender to me please, because I don't get you guys. I like Quinn. I could like him a lot with the smallest encouragement, but he's keeping me at arm's length. He says he wants to be 'just friends', even though the attraction between us snaps in the air"

Finn sat between her legs, tilting his head back and forth, as if following the conversation. "Great! Now I'm reduced to asking a puppy for advice on my love life. No offense, Finn, but this is getting me nowhere."

She stayed there for another thirty minutes, playing with him. He loved to chase the ball and bring it back to her, dancing out of reach. They also played tug of war with a knotted piece of rope she bought in the toy section of a local pet shop.

Satisfied she had managed to tire him out, she kissed him and went into her own bedroom. The nights were staying warmer, so she left her bedroom windows opened a crack. She had always loved fresh air. Soon, she knew, the oppressive humidity of summer would not allow this.

Twenty minutes later, she was still awake. She blamed a certain gorgeous firefighter. She didn't have a ton of experience with men, but she had dated enough to know the chemistry between them wasn't ordinary. But he wasn't willing to even give them a try. Being friends with him might not be the best idea.

*****

Quinn walked into the station the next morning knowing he looked as bleary eyed as he felt. He had gotten into bed in plenty of time for a good night sleep. If only he had been able to. If only thoughts of Paige hadn't been running through his mind all night. If only the smell of her skin and hair hadn't tortured him.

"Hey, where'd you go last night?"

"Home. I didn't think you'd notice."

A.J. laughed. "Oh, yeah, Amy and I were getting to know each other. I kind of forgot anyone else was there."

The sappy look on his friend's face said it all. "So, you like her, I take it?"

"Of course, I like her. I'm going to marry her."

His mouth hung open, but he couldn't do a thing about it. "I'm sorry. Did I hear you say you were going to marry her?"

A.J.'s grin from ear to ear was answer enough.

"Does Amy know this?"

A.J. burst out laughing. "Of course not! Amy would think I was crazy or something."

He shook his head, trying to understand. "So, what does this mean?"

A.J. answered in a tone someone might use on a 3-year-old. "Let me see if I can make you understand. I love her. I knew from the second we met she was the person I was meant to spend my life with. It doesn't make any sense, but I'm not sure it's supposed to."

"So now what?"

"So now we get to know each other better. We're going to date like normal people do. But I know what the result will be."

The alarm rang, preventing him from asking more questions. Firefighters ran from all sides of the station to grab their gear and respond.

*****

At lunchtime, Paige grabbed the salad she had brought from home and walked outside to meet Amy. For the first time ever, Amy was the one who had run late this morning. She had watched her students until her friend showed up. Halfway through the morning, she got a text asking her to head out to the picnic tables for lunch. Apparently, Amy had something to discuss that she didn't want to say in the crowded teacher lounge.

Paige was happy to eat outside. The day was sunny and warm. As she waited for Amy to join her, she closed her eyes and leaned back on her elbows to soak up some rays. The warmth of the sun soaked into her tired body.

Amy plunked down across the table. "So, how was last night? It didn't seem as though Quinn was reluctant to spend any time with you after all. What's the deal? When are you seeing him again?"

Paige knew this was coming and still dreaded the inquisition. She had no idea what to think, so how was she supposed to explain it to Amy? "Talking to you might help me to understand this." She gave an abbreviated version of last night's events. To her credit, Amy did not say one word though the entire speech. However, her expressive face spoke volumes.

At last, she ran out of words. Amy continued to stare for a moment before responding. "He told you last night he's never getting married and never having kids? Really? You didn't find it a bit presumptuous?"

"Not really, although I can certainly appreciate his honesty. It bothered me. I like him. I like him a lot. And I think he likes me too. But he has this wall built around him. We had a wonderful time together, but he's not going to let me, or any other woman, get close to him."

"Is that what you want? To get close to him?" Amy picked at her lunch as she asked.

"Yes. No. I don't know. Ugh!" Paige broke off and gathered her thoughts. "It's frustrating because I really enjoyed being with him. And then there were the sparks."

"Sparks? There were sparks? Why I am hearing this now?"

Paige laughed at the look on her friend's face. "Did I not mention the sparks?"

"No, you didn't mention the sparks." The glint in her eye let Paige know she wasn't fooled.

"Well, every time we touch, it feels like an electrical current zinging through my blood. It's amazing!"

"A zing, huh? That's a whole level above a spark by the way."

Paige's heart sank. "So, you see my problem then. I had a great time, sitting and talking with him, and there were sparks to boot. But none of it matters because he's made it quite clear *this* isn't going to happen. Apparently, we're going to be friends. Just friends!"

"Wow," Amy replied in exasperation. "I'm not even sure what to say. Just friends, huh? Does he really think it will work?"

"I have no idea. But I know I was up longer than I should have been last night, thinking about him." She sighed. "On to more fun topics. Tell me about A.J."

The huge grin on Amy's face said it all. "He's fabulous! We danced. We talked. He walked me to my car at closing time. Then we stood in the parking lot for another half hour." She sighed. It had a much different tone than Paige's.

"Wow! Any zings?"

"Oh, there were zings all right. He kissed me goodnight, and I melted. If I wasn't such a nice Southern girl, I may have jumped him right there in the parking lot." She wagged her eyebrows to back up her words.

Paige laughed. "Well, at least one of us had good luck last night. When will you see him again?"

"I would say tonight, but they started a 24 hour shift this morning. It'll take some getting used to. So, I guess Friday night after work."

Paige was happy for her friend, but she couldn't help feeling a bit jealous. New relationships were always exciting. Maybe she should think about lifting her moratorium and trying to meet someone. She couldn't help thinking it was Quinn she would like to get to know better. But she was a realist. There wasn't any point in thinking about it.

The two friends finished their lunches and went back to their classes for the afternoon. Paige did her best to not think about him. She needed to get some work done on her house and finish writing her paper.

After school, she stopped at the grocery store before driving home. Balancing her purse and briefcase plus a couple of reusable grocery bags, she almost didn't see the flowers waiting for her on the front porch. The cobalt blue vase containing a large bouquet of brightly colored flowers sat on her welcome mat. Putting down everything she was carrying, she picked up the vase and held the flowers to her nose. The card was from a local florist. It read, "Thinking of You."

She opened the door and carried the flowers inside, placing them on the table in the foyer. They cheered up the room, which needed a lot of brightening. The small entryway opened to a decent sized living room. The many windows bathed the room in natural light. She had removed the wallpaper, hideous butterflies this time, several weeks ago. She was leaning towards a sunny yellow or warm peach but hadn't committed yet. The only furniture was an old hand me down couch from Susan, and a TV sitting on a cast-off end table. It looked as though college students lived here. It was getting old.

While many teachers worked some sort of job during their summer off, she had chosen to not do so this year. She would be finished with her graduate program, and she was looking forward to the time off to tackle the house.

Paige was pulled from her reverie by Finn's excited puppy noises coming from the kitchen. "Give me a second," she called to the happy puppy. She ducked back onto the porch to grab the bags she had left there and walked into the kitchen.

Finn, always happy to see her, jumped up and down to get her attention. She scooped up the enthusiastic puppy and carried him out to the grass. Kissing him on his silky face, she left him to do his business and terrorize squirrels.

She picked up the card from the flowers again and reread the words. Hmmm, *who* was thinking of her. Although she wanted to think Quinn had sent the lovely flowers, she knew better. This didn't fit into the 'just friends' category. But who else could it be? She'd have to wait until the mystery person revealed themselves. She tucked the card into a drawer and unpacked her groceries.

*****

On the other side of town, Quinn was peering into the station refrigerator, wondering what to make for dinner. He had cooking duty tonight, with A.J. cleaning up. The men and women of Station Fifteen all took turns with various chores, and now it was his turn to make the meals for their twenty-four-hour tour. He didn't mind cooking, but he wasn't creative about it. He decided upon burgers, again, and leaned in to grab fixings for a salad to go with it. He was rinsing lettuce when A.J. walked in from the bay.

"Let me guess. Salad and burgers. Again."

He threw a piece of wet lettuce at his friend and continued cleaning the rest of it. "It may not be original, but at least we know it'll be good. Feel free to jump in of you have a better idea."

A.J. held up both hands. "No way, man. I can barely handle cooking duty when it's my turn. Burgers sound great."

He gave A.J. a look.

"So, when are you seeing Paige again?"

"I don't know. Why?"

"I was curious. You guys seemed to hit it off last night. I thought maybe…"

"You thought what, A.J.?" He didn't bother looking up from what he was doing. He knew where this conversation was going.

"I thought you liked her enough to maybe change your mind. I thought you'd want to see her again."

He picked up a cucumber and a peeler and went to work on it. "I do like her, A.J., enough to not hurt her." He used a little more force than necessary on the cucumber.

A.J. took the vegetable and peeler out of his hands and walked to the sink. "I'll do this."

Quinn grabbed the hamburger meat from the refrigerator and placed it in a large bowl. He tossed in a few spices and mixed it all together. The two worked in a silence for a few minutes, but he knew his friend had unanswered questions.

"So, I explained to her we could be friends because I had no intention of marrying or having children."

A.J.'s eyebrows almost met is hairline. "How did it go?"

Quinn grinned in remembrance. "You'd be surprised. She took it very well."

"Really?"

"She made a joke about not having to rush out and buy a dress after all. But, basically, she was fine with it. I drove her home, walked her to her door, and left."

"And you're okay with the situation?"

He wasn't, but A.J. didn't need to know. "Yes."

"So, you left without making any plans?"

"Yes."

"Huh." A.J. finished peeling the other cucumber in silence.

He had no idea when, or if, he would see her again. He had only met her because she happened to have the accident when he was working. Would they have met otherwise?

He walked outside to fire up the grill. His life was fine before they had crossed paths. He'd never lost sleep over some woman he couldn't have. What was different now? Paige was the difference. There was something about her drawing him to her. Making him want to forget his rules.

He stretched his hands over his head and tipped his face to the sun. He loved these late spring days when the temperature was warm but bearable. Before long, the summer heat and humidity would crush him.

What was it about her? She was pretty, but the world was full of pretty women. She had an appealing small town, girl-next-door quality to her. She was intelligent and kind. She was funny to the point of being irreverent. And she gave as good as she got. Even in the brief time he had spent with her, she made him feel alive. Not so alone.

She had a happiness about her, shining brightly like a light. Which was what reaffirmed his decision. He wouldn't be the one to put it out. He had seen firsthand, lived it, what being married to a firefighter did to a woman. He refused to be the reason the light went out of Paige.

*****

Early Saturday morning, Paige dressed in old shorts and a T-shirt left over from her college days. Her blonde hair was pulled into a ponytail, and she had a beat-up Appalachian State University Mountaineers hat on her head. She caught her image in a mirror as she passed and laughed. Although she wasn't big on appearances and certainly lacked Amy's fashion sense, even she had to admit she looked frightful. Ridding her home of nasty, old wallpaper was hard and messy work. Luckily, Finn never seemed to mind her appearance.

Paige was high on a ladder spraying the offending wallpaper with water to loosen it when she heard a knock on her front door. Assuming it was Amy, she yelled for her friend to come in. She turned to greet Amy and was surprised to see Amy's brother, Alex, instead.

"Hey Alex! What brings you by so early in the morning?"

Alex Windsor stepped into the room and waved to her. "Ah, I thought I'd come by and see what you were up to, Paige. I haven't been here in a while."

Amy's older brother was a fixture in Paige's life. Alex was a successful attorney on the verge of making partner in his family's firm. Over six feet tall with short, blond hair and green eyes, Alex had grown into a handsome man. Even if he was like a brother to her. He had an endless line of girlfriends, one more beautiful than the last. She and Amy had a secret game of grading each and taking guesses on how long they would last.

She climbed down off the ladder. Stopping a few feet short of Alex, she eyed his clothing. Casual Saturday morning to him meant perfectly creased chinos and an expensive polo shirt. "I was going to hug you, but I can't risk messing you up." She leaned up and kissed his cheek instead. "Can I get you something to drink?"

Alex smiled down at her and shook his head no. "I wanted to see what you've done with the place." He looked around the living room.

Paige caught his expression and laughed. "I know it doesn't look like much, but I'm getting there. I haven't had a lot of time yet. I like to refer to it as a work in progress."

"You know I'd be happy to lend you a hand, right?"

"Now, Alex, you and I both know 'lending me a hand' really means paying to have someone else do it."

His smile revealed perfect white teeth. "Tell me again why it's wrong?"

"We've been over this time and again." She smiled at him. "I love your generosity and desire to help, but you're missing the point. I want to do this myself."

"I know you're the poster child for independence. We both know you *can* do this by yourself. I'm offering to help the process along a bit."

Paige walked into the kitchen to grab a bottle of water from the refrigerator. "Are you sure you don't want something?" she tossed over her shoulder.

A knock sounded at the front door. "This time it will be Amy, can you let her in?" Paige yelled to Alex from the kitchen.

Paige was walking back into the living room, bottle of water in hand, when she saw Alex and Quinn staring at each other. Surprise and wariness colored both of their faces.

Why was Quinn here?

She grimaced, remembering how she was dressed. Although she never thought much about her appearance, she was still a female. With a pulse. She knew exactly how horrible she looked. Too late to do anything about it now.

"Quinn! What a surprise!" She held the water bottle tightly, as though it was a lifeline. She realized the two men were still standing there, sort of staring at each other.

"Quinn Adams, this is Amy's big brother, Alex Windsor. Alex, this is my, uh, friend Quinn." The two men shook hands, but to Paige it seemed a bit forced.

"Sorry, I should have called first." Quinn backed towards the front door. "I had some free time today, so I thought I'd see if you needed some help with the enemy."

Paige burst out laughing. She turned to a confused looking Alex to explain. "The other night I was lamenting to him about the hideous taste the previous owner had."

"I thought maybe she had been exaggerating, but I see now she might have actually been conservative in her estimation. This is truly awful wallpaper."

Alex cleared his throat. "Well, Paige I have a tee time. I'll see you later." He leaned down and kissed her cheek, giving her shoulder a familiar squeeze. He turned towards Quinn. "Nice to meet you."

"Amy's brother, huh? He seemed very much at home here."

Paige hid a smile. Maybe he wasn't quite as unaffected as he would have her think. "Alex is one of my oldest and dearest friends. After Amy of course. We all grew up together."

"If you say so. Anyway, like I said, I had some free time."

Paige stood where she was and looked at him. *What to do?* She liked him. More than she should. But he had made it clear he wasn't interested in anything permanent. And she was never one for casual affairs. Did she really want to try to be friends with Quinn? Did she really want to risk starting something doomed from the beginning? Taking his help today meant spending time with him in close quarters. On the other hand, life was short and without guarantees. No one understood better than she did.

"Well, as you can see, I have a lot to do in this house. I'll never turn down free help. Where do we start?"

"Let's have a look."

Paige led him on a tour throughout the house. She loved her home, but she knew she saw what others didn't. She knew what Alex saw; work to be done and bills to be paid. Even Amy, who was her biggest fan, thought Paige was in over her head. How could she make him understand?

The first floor offered a living room, dining room, kitchen, and a small room that would double as her office and library. She opened the door and turned to smile at him. "So, right now, this room is small and dark." She waved a hand at yet more hideous wallpaper. "But look at those built-in bookshelves! I had to have those."

He glanced around the room. "Whoever owned this house was trying to make it ugly. Once you remove the paper and paint, I think you'll see an enormous difference. Also, I would strip the paint on the bookshelves and see what's underneath. You might be pleasantly surprised."

Paige could have hugged him. Finally, someone got her. Someone saw what she saw in this house. "Exactly! You have to look beneath the surface in here. Let me show you the rest of the place."

She led him up the stairs and down the hallway, showing empty rooms on either side of the hall. "I know it needs a lot of work. I know it's hopelessly outdated. I know I'll have to spend a lot of money before I'm done. But I also know I fell in love the moment I saw this house."

She opened the door of her bedroom and held her breath. Quinn walked in. And right out through the French doors to the second-floor balcony. She did a little victory dance as she joined him.

"Now you see why I had to have this house."

He turned in a small circle, taking in the view. A grin on his face. "This is fabulous."

Without thinking, she launched herself at him. For one moment, her body was in full contact with his. The simmering heat between them boiled over. Then she took a step back and out of his arms. She would have pulled out her shirt and fanned herself if she hadn't already acted like an idiot. Desire raced through her body. But as much as she enjoyed it, she couldn't keep throwing herself at him.

"Uh, sorry. I got a bit carried away." She paid very close attention to the green polish on her toenails.

He shoved his hands in his back pockets. "No worries, Paige. It's not every day a gorgeous woman throws herself at me."

He thought she was gorgeous? Paige had never thought of herself that way. Cute? Yes. But never gorgeous. "I was so thrilled someone finally understands. I saw the balcony and I knew. I pictured a couple of chaise loungers and a good book on a warm evening."

"Funny, I pictured you reading on the porch swing downstairs."

"You did?"

He nodded. "When I dropped you off the other night when I dropped you off. I thought 'Paige will love this in the summer.'"

He'd pictured her on the porch swing? Paige smiled and led him back into her bedroom, shutting the porch doors. She turned to say something but caught him watching her. Words flew out of her head. They stood there, only a few feet apart. Heat pooled low in her belly. Then she remembered where they were. Her unmade, queen-sized bed beckoned from feet away. She tried to *not* think about it. The last thing she needed was an image of him in it. Naked.

"You're probably wondering why it's so barren in here. Nothing much other than the necessities." She also had a small dresser and her mother's antique Cheval mirror in the corner.

Quinn's gaze grew hot, as though maybe he was thinking about the bed as well. "Makes sense since you're rehabbing. Easier to do if you're not tripping over all your stuff."

"Exactly."

They moved into the master bathroom. A large, old-fashioned claw foot bathtub dominated the room. Now she had images of candles, wine and strategically placed bubbles. *Go downstairs already.* In the corner was a modern shower stall as well. She had already stripped this room of its horrifying wallpaper.

"I see you started in here."

"When you spend your days with twenty-five six-year-olds, no matter how much you love them and your job, you need a haven."

Quinn cleared his throat. "So, all you need is a color, right? Have you narrowed down any choices? We could either start in here and paint, or I could help take down more of the ugliest wallpaper ever."

There was no way she was spending any more time up here with him. "I'm already set up downstairs. I can't handle staring at the decor for one more second. Over the weekend, I can at least strip most of it off the walls. I've put off painting until the wallpaper's gone throughout the house."

"So, you're a one woman wrecking crew?"

"Amy offered to help. But she's not into getting messy. She means well."

"What about your friend, Alex?"

Paige laughed at the thought. "His idea of helping is to write a check. He can't understand I really want to do this myself."

"So, he means well also?"

Paige smiled. "Yep. They both do. But I'm not counting on either of them. It's challenging work and takes a lot of my time. But there's a satisfaction, or rather there will be, in looking around and knowing I did everything."

"I know exactly what you mean. I love taking an old, neglected house and turning it into someone's home."

She squealed in delight. "I knew you'd understand. Like you get why I love this house."

They went back down the stairs, Paige leading the way. She gestured and pointed to other things she wanted to do.

He grinned at her. "OK, then, let's do this. I'm going to go outside and grab some of the equipment I brought. Then we can get started on the downstairs. I'll be right back."

Paige picked up the vase of flowers she had received the other day. She needed to move them out of the path of destruction. Carrying them into the kitchen, she stuck her nose in once again to enjoy the wonderful scent. Placing them on the kitchen table, she went back out to the living room and climbed back up her ladder.

*****

Quinn couldn't help the foolish grin spreading across his face. He gathered tools from his truck. Paige might not dress to show it off, but she certainly had a nicely shaped body. When she had hugged him a few minutes ago, their bodies had been pressed together in all the right places. He grew hard remembering. He shook his head at the memory. She wasn't going to make this easy for him.

He walked back into the house to find her already hard at work at the top of a ladder. Not wanting to startle her, he cleared his throat. "I'm ready to take on the beast." With a grin, he got to work on the opposite side of the room.

They worked together for a few hours without much conversation, the radio tuned to a local country station and providing background noise for them. He noticed she sang along frequently, with more enthusiasm than talent. She didn't seem to care she couldn't carry a tune, and he didn't either.

Shortly after noon, Paige stretched and put down her scraper before climbing down off the ladder. "We might be winning the war, but my muscles are screaming. I guess I'm not used to this kind of manual labor." She walked into the kitchen and he followed her.

He stopped to stare at the flowers on her table. Someone, most likely a guy, had sent them to her. The muscles in his stomach clenched. The idea bothered him more than he cared for. "Nice flowers," he muttered.

"I guess they're not from you, then."

"You thought they were from me?"

"No, I was joking."

"Oh." His stomach knotted further.

"I don't know who sent them. I came home from work on Wednesday and found them on my front porch."

Quinn looked back at the now suspicious flowers. He had been hoping she bought them for herself. "You really have no idea? Doesn't it bother you?" He grew a little worried thinking about some random man sending her flowers.

Paige turned back to him and laughed. "I hardly think I have a stalker. I love flowers, and it was lovely to come home after a busy day and find them there. Maybe I'll never know who sent them. It doesn't matter to me."

"You can't be too careful. You're an attractive, young woman living here alone. And now you're getting mystery gifts. You need to take this seriously."

"So, you think I'm attractive?" Paige smiled at him, melting his insides.

He groaned. "That's your takeaway message? Of course, you're attractive, Paige. But I'm serious about being careful. You should always be aware of your surroundings."

"I know you mean well, and I am not naïve. Even living in a small town, I am careful. Thank you for caring."

"I was only giving you the standard lecture I give to my sister, Lauren. She didn't always listen either."

"I didn't know you had a sister." Paige opened the refrigerator and grabbed the fixings for sandwiches. "Turkey or ham?"

"You don't have to," he protested.

"It's a sandwich, not a commitment," she teased him.

"I meant you don't have to feed me."

"Well, I'm hungry after the past few hours of hard labor. I can only imagine you are too. So, turkey or ham?"

"I'll take turkey, thanks. Can I help?"

"I got this. Maybe you can grab some plates and fill glasses with ice. I have tea and sodas in there. Take your pick. I'll have a Diet Mountain Dew."

Quinn washed his hands thoroughly, drying them on a paper towel before tending to the tasks she had given him. When she was done making sandwiches, they carried their meal outside to the table on the back patio. The large, colorful umbrella offered a welcome refuge from the scorching sun. They sat and dug into the light meal.

"So, you have a sister named Lauren. Tell me about the rest of your family."

"Lauren is my only sibling, nine years younger than me and an interior designer. You'd like her: about your age, doesn't approve of my 'nomadic lifestyle', and so appreciates it when I give her safety tips." He laughed at the expression on her face.

"I don't have any biological siblings, although I consider Amy and Alex to be family. Alex is forever lecturing Amy and me as well. So, I can imagine how much she appreciates your *advice*." She shook her head and reached for a bag of potato chips.

"I've heard you refer to Amy as family before. I imagine there's a story there." He took a huge bite of his sandwich and sat back with his attention focused on her while he chewed.

"It seems strange, after all these years, to be explaining it again. I always think everyone knows."

"Knows what, Paige?"

She finished chewing and blew out a big breath. "My parents were killed in a car accident when I was twelve. Amy's parents took care of me. My mom and Amy's mom, Susan, had been best friends their whole lives. They are my family." She picked up her soda and took a large gulp.

Her words hit him like a kick to the stomach. He couldn't believe what he was hearing. "I had no idea. I'm so sorry."

She put down her soda and placed her chilled hand over his warm one. "Please don't be. It was a long time ago, and I was so lucky to have them. Otherwise, I would have ended up in the foster care system. I've seen firsthand with one of my students what a disaster it can be."

Turning over his hand, he gripped hers and squeezed in a show of silent support. She had lost so much and yet remained one of the most positive people he had ever met.

"Wow, Paige, you have an amazing way of looking at the world."

"It's a choice I make every day. Losing my parents was awful, I won't tell you it wasn't. But I was lucky in so many ways. We had a great life right up until the day they died. I never doubted how much they loved me. And each other. And Amy's family had always been so close to ours. They had an arrangement since the day my Mom found out she was pregnant with me, in case the worst ever did happen. I have always been loved and cared for."

"You're so upbeat about everything."

She shook her head. "I'm not some Pollyanna. I know, more than most, bad things can happen. I miss my parents every day, and I would give anything to have them in my life; even for one more day. But it's not possible, and there's nothing I can do about it. What I can do is enjoy my life. I can be happy. I know they would want me to be."

He thought about their experiences with loss, similar yet different. She had somehow come out of hers with a better attitude than he had. And she had lost *both* of her parents. But it didn't change how he felt. He still risked his life being a firefighter. He wasn't willing to put her, or any other woman, in the same position his Mom had held. He didn't want to have children, only to possibly leave them without a father.

She got up from the table and gathered plates. "I didn't mean to darken this lovely day."

He popped the last bite of food into his mouth and grabbed both glasses to help. After chewing and swallowing, he turned to her. "You didn't. I was thinking about what you'd gone through. I still think you're amazing, no matter how you try to explain it all away."

"Thank you. It means a lot to me. But don't think you get out of more work. We finished stripping the living room, but you're not off the hook."

He opened the sliding glass door. Paige led the way into the kitchen. Even with her less than glamorous clothing, he could appreciate the figure hidden beneath. He watched the gentle sway of her hips and pert butt. He may have resolved to not get involved with her romantically, but he was still a man. He'd have to be dead to not appreciate the view in front of him.

"Oh, I know how much work is left, Paige. After all, I've already done this to two houses. What's next? Kitchen?"

"Sure."

Chapter Six

Paige rinsed their dishes and placed them in the dishwasher. She wiped down the counter and grabbed her spray bottle. Quinn grabbed the scoring tool to make small holes in the ancient wallpaper. She followed behind, spraying the paper. When all the surfaces had been treated, they moved into the living room to wipe down the walls.

"I really admire what you're doing."

"Thank you. I know others may not understand, but I fell in love with this house the moment I saw it. Sure, it would have been easier and more practical to buy new construction, but I wanted something different."

He stopped what he was doing and dropped the rag. He turned to Paige with an odd little smile on his face. "So, you're saying you go after what you want."

Paige's heart pounded at his words. She wiped suddenly sweaty palms on her shorts. It didn't seem as though they were talking about houses anymore. "Yes. Life is short."

He took a few steps closer to her, stopping within arm's reach and looked into her eyes. "So, you'd be okay with me doing the same? Going after what I want?"

Paige licked her lips and nodded her head, incapable of speech. Her heart threatened to burst from her chest.

He reached out and caressed her cheek with a work roughened hand, sending a thrill down her spine. "Well, as long as you're sure." He closed the gap between them and covered her mouth with his.

Paige moaned deep in her throat, the sound muffled by his mouth on hers. She had imagined this moment for weeks. The reality was so much better. She moved closer until there wasn't any space left between them and wrapped her arms around his back. Her hands moved restlessly over his hot skin.

It was his turn to groan. The sound made her crazy with wanting to be closer. To touch him everywhere. To taste him everywhere. He must have felt the same. He grabbed her butt in both hands and lifted her to her tiptoes, pulling her tighter against him. His erection pushed against her belly.

Time stopped. There was only the two of them and all the places their bodies touched. Each point was alight with a flame burning them both. It consumed her.

H released her mouth. Before Paige could form a protest, he moved his attention to the sensitive underside of her jaw. His lips teased the area before he moved onto her ear, flicking his tongue around the tender flesh he found there. Quinn bit down ever so gently. She rewarded his efforts with another, louder moan of pleasure.

Paige arched her neck to give him better access and fisted her hands in the material of his T-shirt. She attempted to pull the shirt over his head when he broke contact and took a small step backwards. He placed his hands on her shoulders as if bracing himself.

"I shouldn't have done that. Do you want me to apologize? Because I'm not sorry."

"There's nothing to apologize for. I wanted this as much as you did. But I'm confused."

Quinn ran a hand through his short hair. "I've wanted to kiss you since the hospital room."

She gave a nervous laugh. "When I was wearing a shapeless gown and bruises on my face? Are you kidding me?"

"I saw the beautiful blue eyes and the otherwise flawless skin. I saw the cheerful woman who loved life."

Paige was momentarily speechless, which wasn't an everyday event for her. "Well then I can tell you I felt the same way. You stood there in my room with that smile and those arms. Whew! I never had a chance."

He raised an eyebrow at her. "Really? You felt it too?"

"I sure did, especially dancing with you at Smitty's. I've never felt so protected and attracted at the same time. I wished the song could have lasted forever."

He paced the room. "But this doesn't change anything, Paige."

"I never assumed it did. Although I don't understand your position, I respect it. I wasn't trying to change your mind. But you kissed me."

He took her hand and led her to the couch. They both sat, and he turned to face her. "I should have explained. I lost my Dad. Like you, I was twelve. He was a firefighter, and he died in the line of duty. It was the worst day of my life." His eyes clouded.

Paige reached across and placed her hand on his. "I'm so sorry. Why didn't you tell me when we were talking about how I had lost my parents?"

"I'm not sure. I was so focused on what you were telling me. I can't help feeling you dealt with your losses better than I did mine. You have such a wonderful attitude."

"I have Amy's family to thank. No one ever questioned a thing. I moved into their home the day my parents died. They welcomed me with open arms and never looked back. How many people would?"

"It wasn't all them. Yes, what they did was incredible. But most of the credit goes to you. Like you said, Paige, it's a choice you make."

"But it was more. There were many times when I could have given into the sadness and the loss. Why me? Why did I have to lose both of my parents? Amy's mom was there with me every step of the way, making sure I didn't become bitter. I owe them a lot; more than I could ever repay."

He stood and paced around the room. "My situation was different. Even before my dad died, my mother was affected by his career choice every day. Every time there was a working fire, she panicked. It was like she didn't breathe until my dad came home safely. Then one day he didn't, and she was shattered."

"Yet you became a firefighter."

"I was twelve when he died. I had already grown up in the firehouse. It was a part of who I was. They were already my extended family. It's hard on my mom, but it's who I am."

"I may not understand what the life is like, but you can't tell me there aren't firefighters with families."

"Yes, of course, there are. That's their choice. This is my choice. "

Sadness roughened his voice. It cried out to Paige. Longing coursed through her. To comfort him. To make it better. She jumped off the couch as well and crossed the room until she was standing right in front of him. "Of course, it's your choice. I already told you I respect it, even if I don't understand it."

"Then why are you so angry?"

Those simple words shook her. "I'm not angry. I may respect your choice, but I don't have to agree with it. You have your opinion, and I have mine." Brave words, considering her stomach rolled at the thought. He was serious about it and not likely to change his mind. *Why do you care when you barely know him?*

"Well you don't look like your usual, happy self."

"As I said before, I'm not a Pollyanna. I have a full range of emotions." She dragged in a ragged breath. "I feel like there could be something between us, but you're cutting yourself off from the world. Your choice, but I cannot be a part of it."

He dragged a hand through his hair. "Why are we even talking about this?"

Now it was Paige's turn to be frustrated. "You kissed me. You started this."

He stepped a few paces away and remained silent.

She closed her eyes. Then she muttered something under her breath.

"Did you say fudge cookies?"

"Why, yes I did." She held her chin up, even though she felt like a fool. Great! She didn't think he heard her.

"Really? Fudge cookies? Care to explain?"

"I am a kindergarten teacher. I can't go around cursing when I'm with my students. If I say things I'd like to say here, I might slip up in the classroom. So, I try to always say things like 'fudge cookies' when I feel like saying something else. I have a whole list of alternates."

"Like?"

She shook her head. "I'm not going to tell you all my secrets."

They were back to a better place, away from the tension. But she didn't know what it meant. This whole situation was puzzling. "So, to be clear, what are we doing? Are we friends? Are we more?"

"I don't know what to tell you. I'm not trying to be difficult. I'm very attracted to you, as you know. But I'm not in it for the long run. It doesn't seem fair to start something. I should not have kissed you."

"Why do you think I need protection? Is it the firefighter thing? I'm not an 18-year-old virgin. I am perfectly capable of having a relationship without having my heart broken. Who says this has to be all or nothing anyway?" Even as she said the words, she was pretty sure this was a bad idea. But the idea of not seeing him again was worse.

He looked at her for a long time before answering. His voice was rough when he did. "It's not a good idea."

She stopped just short of grinding her teeth. "You know what? You're right. This is too hard. And you're too stubborn. Maybe it is the firefighter in you. I don't need protection." She poked his chest with her finger. "What I need is people in my life who know what they want and aren't afraid to go after it. You're not really living, if you're wasting your life being so careful. But it's your choice." She turned away from him. "Maybe you should go."

She remained rooted to the spot, determined to not let him see her cry. She heard him gathering his tools. After what seemed an eternity, she felt his hand on her shoulder.

"I'm sorry, Paige. I was only trying to spare you."

She nodded, words too difficult. He walked out of the house, and she stood there for several moments until she heard his truck pull away. Then she closed the door and walked into the living room. Paige picked up a picture of herself with her Mom. She moved to the couch and curled up in the corner. Hot tears slid down her cheeks. In the picture, they were sitting next to each other in the back yard. The sun was shining, and her mom looked so young and happy. It had been taken not long before the day of the accident. Her Mom had only been thirty-four. It was times like this when she wished her parents were still with her.

She self-indulged for another few minutes before wiping her eyes. What was the matter with her? Why was she crying over a man she barely knew? It was silly and unlike her. Quinn was a great guy with whom she might have had a real connection. But they would never find out. He wasn't willing to give them a chance. She hadn't known him long enough to weep over him. *Maybe she had,* whispered a small voice in her brain.

There was a knock at the door. She swiped at her face one more time and stalked over to answer it. Alex stood there. *Great, just what she didn't need.*

His eyes widened at the sight of her. He walked into the house and closed the door behind him. He took her face in his hands and tipped it up to look at him. "What's wrong, honey?"

Paige gave him a watery smile. "Nothing worth mentioning. Being a silly girl. What brings you by for the second time today?"

He cleared his throat. "I was wondering what you were doing for dinner. I thought we could go to the club."

She stifled a groan. The last thing she wanted to do was go to the club. Being a Windsor meant dinner at the club was an ordinary event. Paige had grown up in the lifestyle, swimming there in the summers and had even learned to play golf and tennis. It didn't appeal to her as an adult.

"Thanks, Alex, but I'm a mess." She gestured to the old, ratty clothes she was wearing.

Alex smiled at her. "Well, obviously, you need to change. I meant later."

Which was why she didn't care to go to the club. She wouldn't dream of going how she looked now, but she didn't need Alex talking to her as though she was a small child.

"What I meant, Alex, was I don't feel like going out." She gestured with her arm. "I have stuff to finish here, and I still have a paper to write." She hid a smile at the expression on his face. Alex wasn't used to women saying no to him.

"You don't have time for dinner with me? My parents will be there."

"Not even for your parents, Alex. This is my last class, and I have a 4.0. I'm not going to slack off now." All she wanted was to clean up the mess they had made in the living room and kitchen and then take a long hot bath before working on her paper.

Alex bounced the car keys in his hand. He didn't turn to the door. "I see you got my flowers."

Paige looked at the flowers in question and then back at Alex. "Those are from you?" She didn't mean to sound so shocked, but Alex was the last person she ever would have thought to send them.

"Yes, they're from me. You seem surprised."

Shocked was more like it. "Thank you, Alex. It's not that I don't appreciate them, but I am surprised. What's the occasion?"

"Does there have to be an occasion to send flowers to a beautiful woman?"

She hoped the shock at his words wasn't playing across her face. "I guess not, but you've never sent me flowers before."

"Well then I should have." He crossed the room, closing the distance between them. Taking her hand in his, he smiled down at her. "You know how much you mean to me."

"You're my family. Of course, you mean a lot to me as well."

"Please don't tell me you think of me as a brother, Paige. Because I'm not. What I feel for you, have felt for a long time, is anything but brotherly." Alex lowered his head and kissed her.

*****

Quinn stood outside of Paige's door with his hand frozen above the bell. The sight of Alex kissing Paige stopped him in his tracks. He had gotten most of the way home before realizing he had left his tool belt at her house. Although reluctant to return so soon after their argument, he needed it to get some work done at his house. Now all he could think about was seeing another man kissing Paige.

Screw this. Stalking back to his truck, a mixture of anger and jealousy rolled over him like a wave. He jammed his keys into the ignition and drove away faster than necessary. He backed off on the gas pedal when he realized the danger. He'd go to the station and get in a good workout. At least no one would get hurt.

*****

Paige pushed on Alex's chest, creating some space between them. She took a moment to compose her thoughts before speaking.

"Alex?" She had known him her entire life. She had lived with him, or rather his family, for almost ten years. What could he possibly be thinking?

He had the grace to look chagrinned. "Paige, this isn't the way I planned to tell you. I thought we would start dating, and things would evolve between us."

"What things, Alex?"

"Our relationship, of course."

She felt as though she was tuning into a movie already half over. She had no idea of the plot. "Excuse me for seeming lost, but, well, I am a little bit, Alex. We don't have that kind of relationship. I consider you, and Amy, to be the siblings I never had."

"You're not my sister."

"Of course not," she mumbled. "But I've always considered you my big brother." She hated to cause him any pain. She loved him but as a brother.

Alex's face flushed. He turned toward the door. "I'm so sorry this comes as such a shock to you. I probably shouldn't have dropped this all on you at one time. Think about it for a little while. I know you and I could be great together, Paige. I'll call you tomorrow." Alex turned and left her home.

Feeling as though the rug had been pulled out from under her, she sat in the nearest chair. *Could this day get any more messed up?* The man to whom she was wickedly attracted was not interested in pursuing a relationship. But Alex, whom she thought of as a brother, was chasing her. Really? She was doomed when it came to dating.

Like most women she knew, she was a stress eater. This situation called for only one thing. Pop Tarts. She walked into the kitchen and looked for her emergency stash. There they were, in the pantry, tucked behind much healthier choices. Paige reached in and grabbed a silver foil packet out of the box. Carrying her prize to the table, she sat down and ripped it open. There was nothing in her life strawberry Pop Tarts couldn't fix.

She had taken the first delicious bite and sighed when Amy strode through the front door, calling out a hello on her way. She had never stood much on formality. She stopped in her tracks and narrowed her eyes, pointing to the wrapper. "Okay, what happened?"

Paige looked up mid bite. "What?" It might have been more convincing if not mumbled around a mouthful of food.

"I thought we talked about this. These have absolutely no nutritional value. You're a twenty-six-year-old, educated, professional woman who has been reduced to stress eating. So, I'll ask again. What happened?"

As always with Amy, Paige knew when she was beaten. She kicked out the opposite chair and motioned for her friend to sit. "It's been a crazy day."

She waved a manicured hand at the table. "I see. I need you to tell me why. Pop Tarts usually signals a man crisis. I'm assuming it was Quinn?"

"Yes. And then it was Alex."

Amy clapped her hands. "Did they fight over you?"

"Why would Alex and Quinn fight over me?" Paige noticed her friend was no longer making eye contact. "Amy? What aren't you telling me?"

Amy blew out a long breath before answering. "I can only answer the Alex part of this. You'll have to fill me in on Quinn. My brother approached me a few weeks ago about you. I guess he was testing the waters, so to speak."

Paige's mouth dropped open. "And you didn't tell me?"

Amy held up her hands. "I know, I know. I should have said something to you."

She nodded. "Then I could have avoided being sucker punched."

Guilt colored Amy's face. "I guess I didn't for a couple of reasons. I was as shocked as you apparently are. I had no idea. In all these years, Alex has never said a thing to me."

That made sense. "Okay, but you said, 'for a couple of reasons'. What's the other?"

"I thought it was such a wonderful idea. You're two of my favorite people in the world. The idea of you in a relationship and maybe getting married someday was amazing! I'm so sorry I didn't tell you. There's a third reason though. Alex asked me not to tell you. He wanted to handle this in his own way."

She leaned across the table and squeezed Amy's hand. "I'm not mad at you. I'm surprised. You know I think of Alex as my big brother. I've never felt anything romantic for him."

"I tried to tell him, but he's had these feelings for a long time, and nothing I said was going to sway him."

Paige felt even worse about the situation. "You know the last thing I would ever want to do is to hurt him."

"Of course, I do."

Paige felt her eyes growing damp yet again. "I'm so glad. I love you guys, and I'm so very thankful you've always been there for me. I just don't share his feelings."

She thought back to the brief kiss she had shared with Alex. She hadn't felt anything other than shock when he had kissed her. There wasn't any zing. Unlike the kiss she had shared with Quinn. The memory of *that* kiss made her knees weak.

Paige realized Amy was looking at her funny. "Alex is way off base. I don't feel the way he wants. I never did. I almost wish I did. It would be easier."

"Easier than what?"

"Easier than liking someone who has made it clear they don't want a relationship." Her shoulders slumped. "It's Quinn. I could really fall for him; tall, handsome, kind, smart, funny. But he's made it clear it's not a possibility."

"Okay, spill. Tell me everything."

Paige told her friend about his father dying in the line of duty and how it had affected him.

"So, let me see if I understand this," Amy began. "You guys like each other. And you have amazing chemistry."

Paige nodded morosely.

"But he'll never risk it?"

Paige nodded her head again, afraid to speak.

"Doesn't it seem like a lot of protest to you? He barely even knows you, yet he wants you to understand, up front, there's no future with him. That's a bit of overreaction. Unless…"

"Unless what?"

"Unless he's protecting himself, Paige. Maybe he's throwing up road blocks because he knows he already cares about you and is unwilling to risk it."

She almost grinned at the satisfied look on her friend's face. Amy loved to be right. "The reason really doesn't matter. The bottom line is he has this stupid rule and isn't likely to break it. I'm not going to get hurt pursuing something when I already know the outcome."

"Sounds smart. So why do you seem so sad about it?" She moved her chair next to Paige and squeezed her hand.

"Good question. I hardly know him. Why should I care so much?"

"I'm not sure it's supposed to make sense, Paige."

Paige laughed. "Well, then I haven't lost my mind after all." She leaned in and hugged her friend. "You're not upset about Alex, right?"

"While it would have spared us his 'flavor of the month', no I'm not upset. But you have to tell him."

"I did tell him."

"Well, you may have to tell him again. You know how Alex is, Paige. Very stubborn. In fact, you may have to tell him several times until he gets it. I wish you luck."

She groaned. Her friend was right. No one ever said no to Alex. She'd have to be the first.

Amy got up and walked towards the door. "Well, you have to write your paper, and I have a date. Gotta go!!"

Paige walked her friend out and closed the door. She put down fresh water and food for Finn. Her little dog was spending the day next door with her ten-year-old neighbor. Carly was dog crazy but didn't have one of her own. Finn was too much underfoot when Paige was stripping paper, etc. Paige paid the little girl a few bucks to 'dog sit', and everyone was happy. She would go pick him up in an hour or two.

She spent the next half hour cleaning up the piles of debris they had created and trying to *not* think about him. At least not *only* about Quinn. Paige was as stubborn as her adoptive brother, and normally she would go after what she wanted. Like she had with the house. But this was different. He had made himself more than clear. She would have to respect his wishes.

Under the rubble, she found Quinn's toolbelt. She debated calling him. Then remembered she didn't have his number. She'd leave it on her porch. He'd figure it out.

Finally, Paige was able to soak in a hot bath. She hit the music app on her phone. The haunting voice of Enya filled her bathroom. The soothing voice of her favorite Celtic singer was exactly what her frayed nerves needed. She tried to soak away the troubles of the day.

But thoughts of Alex left her head spinning. In all the years they had known each other, he had never given the slightest hint he was interested in her romantically. And Paige was glad. Although he was handsome and successful, Alex Windsor was not her type.

Alex came with rules. He ran in higher circles than Paige cared to. He was a powerful man who would only become more so. He had talked for years about his desire to enter politics. Being the wife of a politician held no interest for her. She liked her life as it was; simple and uncomplicated.

No, Alex was not the man for her. Above and beyond everything else, she simply wasn't attracted to him. And she wasn't willing to settle. Quinn was another story altogether. Thinking about their kiss and the shock of his hands on her curled Paige's toes under the bubbles. She sighed and reached for her glass of wine, taking a sip. She had not felt this level of attraction in a long time; maybe never.

While she wasn't naïve, she wasn't very experienced either. She chose boyfriends carefully, preferring quality over quantity. There had been one guy in high school and then several in college. She had rules of her own, such as not getting involved with co-workers. Although the female teachers greatly outnumbered their male counterparts, there were still a few single ones at her school. But she had seen firsthand what happened if it ended badly.

The water grew cold, so Paige finished and got out of the tub. She grabbed a plush, aqua towel and wrapped it around her body. The antiquated exhaust fan was sluggish at best, so she used her hand to clear a spot of the mirror. It felt so good to be clean. At least both the living room and kitchen walls were cleared now. No more hideous tea pots to haunt her.

She brushed her teeth and her hair, allowing it to dry naturally. She had always been grateful her hair had enough curl. All she had to do was wash it and throw in a little product. She had neither the time nor inclination for curling irons and the like. Paige trod into the bedroom and threw on some clean clothes.

Not bothering with shoes, she ran next door to retrieve her dog. Finn was fast asleep in Carly's lap. Paige grinned down at the little girl, seated on the kitchen floor. "It looks like you wore him out for me. Good Job, Carly."

Hearing his mistress's voice, Finn popped open one eye and then yawned. He stretched his small, speckled body before climbing out of Carly's lap and pouncing on Paige's feet. She bent down to pick up her sleepy puppy and handed money to the little girl. "Thanks so much, honey. I'll let you know when I need your services again." She smiled as Carly kissed Finn on the head.

Walking back to her own house, Paige placed Finn down in the grass to let him do his business. Smart puppy, he peed right away then followed Paige into the kitchen, making a beeline for his food bowl.

Paige grabbed her lap top and sat in a comfortable armchair. This paper wasn't going to write itself. Although she was tired and didn't feel like doing so, she got to work. Knowing this was her very last assignment for her graduate degree spurred her on.

Several hours later, she called it a night. She was pleased with the amount of work she had accomplished and saved her paper before shutting down the laptop. After taking care of Finn for the night, she retreated to her bedroom. She washed her face and brushed her teeth before curling up in bed with the novel she had been reading for her book club at Between the Pages. Jamie, the owner and Paige's friend, would kill her if she didn't finish. Thirty minutes later, she tossed the book to the floor in disgust. Normally a voracious reader, she couldn't focus tonight. And the reason had a name: Quinn Adams.

Giving up altogether, Paige turned out the lamp and crawled under the covers. Hopefully, she would be able to sleep. Thoughts of him, and his impossible rules, had plagued her ever since he left this afternoon. Forgetting him would be for the best. Anything else was asking for heartache. But the glowing numbers on her digital alarm clock mocked her. She lay there for quite a while watching their steady progress until she fell asleep.

Chapter Seven

Quinn put some leftovers in the microwave and pressed start. After a grueling workout at the station, he had come home and put in a few punishing hours on the house. Now he was exhausted, but the progress he made was well worth it. Although not in a huge rush, he had a timeframe in mind each time he bought a house for rehab. This project was coming along nicely. Before long, he could start thinking about finding his next project. He'd need a place to live after this one sold.

Taking his dinner out of the microwave, he grabbed a beer from the refrigerator and went out to the back deck to eat. The evening had cooled a bit. While it wasn't chilly, it was more comfortable than it would be in two more weeks. Because he was born and bred, he took advantage of the cool night. He sat on the only chair out there and ate his meal.

Cooking wasn't his thing, and his turn at the station was generally the only time he put any effort into it. On his days off, he usually got take out, buying more than he needed to have leftovers for a few days. Tonight's choice was barbeque from a small hole in the wall down the road. Hank's may not be long on décor, but the small, family run joint more than made up for that in delicious food. He took a big bite of his pork sandwich with slaw and moaned in appreciation.

After finishing his meal, he leaned back and placed his feet up on the porch rail. He stretched out his body, twisting and turning to ease the tired muscles in his back. Between Paige's house and his own, he had spent most of the day working. A long, hot shower before bed would further ease the strain. Otherwise, tomorrow's work shift would be more painful than necessary.

Draining the last drop from his bottle, he set it on the deck and leaned back, closing his eyes. He allowed himself to think about Paige. The memory of her kissing Alex haunted him. Especially since he knew how she tasted. But he had no right to feel angry at what he had seen. Wasn't he the one who had told her, several times, they didn't have a future?

More than anything, he didn't understand what he witnessed. She denied being involved with anyone, and yet mere moments after he had left, she was kissing another man. Maybe that's what upset him. He valued honesty above almost all else. She had seemed like a direct and honest person. He never thought she would lie to him.

After running through the gamut of emotions, he came back around to regret. Meeting her was like a breath of fresh air. She was beautiful and low maintenance, a rare combination he found delightful. He had never been a fan of women who played games. She had a freshness about her he liked.

Then there was the powerful attract between them. The memory of her today, in an outfit far from sexy, raised his blood pressure again. The kiss they shared could have gone on for hours.

Quinn shook his head in disgust and got up from his chair. He grabbed the empty bottle and his plate and went inside. Although it was still early, he would take a shower and go to sleep soon. Six o'clock came early, and he needed to have his wits about him at work tomorrow. He puttered around the kitchen for a few minutes, rinsing and loading his few dishes into the dishwasher.

When he was finished, he headed up the stairs, taking them two at a time. He stripped his dirty clothes off as he walked into his bedroom, throwing them into the nearby hamper and continuing into the master bathroom.

He stopped and looked around the finished room. He always started with the master bedroom and bathroom for his own comfort. He had installed a large garden tub and a separate, luxurious shower stall in the corner of the large room.

From experience, he knew paying attention to detail paid off in the end. The room was decorated in neutrals with sand colored tile and oil-rubbed bronze faucets. The vanity boasted a double sink with granite counter tops.

His favorite feature was the walk-in shower. It was roomy enough for two and enclosed by glass on two sides and a wall of tile on the others. There were built in shelves and a bench, all in the same tile. His sister Lauren had helped him to design this as she had done on all his projects. He was very appreciative. She had an eye for these things.

He reached in and turned on the water to as hot as he could stand. The dual shower heads sent hot water pulsating to all his tired muscles at the same time. He could have stood there forever. He thought back on the day and the whole problem of Paige. But no matter how he dissected it, he always came up with the same answer. There wasn't any way to keep her in his life without eventually hurting her. He had been honest with her and himself.

Reluctantly leaving the shower, he grabbed a thick towel from the bar and dried himself off. And gritted his teeth in frustration. He had done the right thing. But he didn't have to like it.

Not bothering with clothes, Quinn flicked on the ceiling fan and crawled into bed, kicking the covers to the bottom. They would end up there anyway. It had been a long and taxing day, both physically and mentally. He tried to tell himself she was just another woman. There would be others. She wasn't special. But as he drifted off, he feared it wasn't true.

*****

Paige leaned back in her chair and smiled to herself. At last, Memorial Day had arrived. It was the unofficial start to the summer, and she couldn't be happier. She opened her eyes to slits against the bright midday sun. The sky was a bright azure blue without a single cloud to mar it as far as the eye could see. The weather was perfect for the Windsor's annual picnic. Alex wouldn't have it any other way.

She turned her head as she felt someone drop into the chair next to hers. "So how are things going with your firefighter friend?" Alex sat there looking his usual perfect self in flawless clothes.

"I wouldn't know." She hadn't seen Quinn in over ten days. Before going to work on Monday, she had placed his tools in a box near the front door They were gone when she returned home.

"Really? I thought you guys were an item. He seemed rather possessive of you."

"We are friends, Alex. Actually, we're more like acquaintances."

"Well, all for the better. He wasn't your type."

She didn't bother to counted to tend while she gathered her patience. The conversation was ridiculous. This new *interest* of his was more annoying than flattering. He had stopped by twice in the past few days. 'Happened to be in the area,' rang hollow since they all lived in the same small town.

But she didn't like what Alex was implying, and her temper got the better of her. "Not my *type*? What does that even mean? And how would *you* know what *my* type is?"

Alex used his patented megawatt smile to calm her. It failed. But he was a bit too sure of himself to notice. "I didn't mean anything bad. But he's a firefighter." As always, his tone was calm and soothing. Alex Windsor never got upset.

Paige couldn't help herself and laughed. "You are such a snob, Alexander Patrick Windsor!"

Alex stood and took her hand in his own, pulling her up from the chair. "This is not a discussion I care to have in front of fifty people." Guiding her out into an empty spot in the far corner of the yard, he turned to face her.

"Paige, you can't really be so naïve. I'm sure he's a nice guy, and being a firefighter is a noble career choice. But he's not like *us*."

She looked around the lovely, manicured lawn and well-dressed guests. Paige then glanced down at her own expensively casual clothing. This was far from her usual weekend outfit, but she was expected to dress a certain way when attending a Windsor party. She would be the first to admit she was far happier in shorts and flip flops than the expensive sundress and less-than-comfortable heels she wore.

Removing her arm from under his smooth, manicured hand, she addressed him. "Alex, there isn't any *us*. And to be honest, as much as I love your family, I'd rather not be here. I'm much happier relaxing at a small, casual barbeque than I have ever been at these functions. I don't have anything in common with most of the people here."

"But you could. Once we're together, this will be your life as well."

She was tempted to stomp her feet in frustration. She blew out a long breath instead. "You're not listening to me, Alex. So, I'll have to use my kindergarten teacher voice."

She stopped and tossed her hair over one shoulder as she took a breath to settle herself. "There isn't any *us*, Alex, and there never will be. And it has nothing to do with Quinn. I am not attracted to you. I am not in love with you. I have only ever considered you my surrogate older brother. My feelings won't change. Please go back to your long line of highly suitable women and choose one." She slid off her heels and stomped away, a massive headache threatening to take hold.

Paige found Susan coming out of the kitchen. "I was looking for you. I'm not feeling great, and I'm going to go home a bit early if you don't mind."

"Oh, honey, I'm sorry. Can I drive you home?"

"No, thanks. I'm tired and have a headache. I'll be fine. Please don't worry about me."

"It's in the job description. You'll know one day." She enfolded her in a hug. "I'm sorry you're still getting headaches."

She stepped back. "I rarely get them anymore. No worries. It's probably the sun." And your annoyingly arrogant son, she chose not to add.

The older woman peered into Paige's face. "I saw you talking with Alex a few minutes ago. Did he say something to upset you?"

Paige could feel the warmth spread across her face. "No. We were chatting. But you know how Alex can be. He's very strong willed."

Susan laughed. "Yes, he is. Gets it from his father. But you're no slouch in that department. You can handle him. Should I ask what the conversation was about?"

"It's doesn't bear repeating. Really, it was nothing. I'll call you later in the week. Thanks for understanding." She left while she could, before anyone else stopped her to chat.

She got into her broiling hot car and tried to not think about the inane conversation with Alex. She left her door open and turned on the car, lowering all the windows and blasting the air conditioning until the temperature was bearable. Then she pulled away from their home.

She had inherited money from her parents on their death. Quite a bit of money. She had advantages most people did not. Working for a living was optional, but that's not who she was. Paige had been raised to appreciate what she had and to give back to others who were not as fortunate.

She'd finished her graduate degree and had spent all her spare time removing the last of the wall paper from her home. She had finished in a marathon session over the holiday weekend, only stopping today to attend the party. She felt a great deal of satisfaction in what she had accomplished. Except for the help Quinn had provided, she had finished everything else by herself.

In under two weeks, school would be out for the summer. she would have all the time in the world to paint and decorate. Through her friend Charlie Avery, Paige had met Sam Bishop, who owned a home and garden center. He probably regretted the introduction, since she haunted the place picking out paint samples. Each room in her home now had small squares painted on the walls as she tried to make her final choices. She had to admit it looked a bit odd, like a bizarre patchwork quilt on her wall, but the system had really helped her to eliminate most of the colors. She was down to a few finalists.

She also decided to start dating again. It had been over two years since her last boyfriend, and she was ready to try again. She didn't necessarily have to meet Mr. Right, but Mr. Right Now, might be nice. She needed a little fun in her life.

Her phone rang with Amy's specific ring tone. She touched a button on her dash for hands-free calling. "Hey, Amy."

"Where did you go?" Her friend's worried voice filled the interior of the small car.

"Sorry. I thought your mom would have told you. I left a bit early. I'm fine, just tired and have a headache."

"She did mention it, but I wanted to be sure you were alright."

"I'm fine. Nothing a good night's sleep won't cure."

"So, I was thinking about what you said; about being ready to date again. I have the perfect guy."

Paige groaned aloud. "I knew I shouldn't have told you. I'm perfectly capable of finding my own guy."

"I wanted to help."

"Thank you, but I'm not actively looking for someone. I'm just open to the idea. When someone comes along, I won't say no. Make sense?"

"I guess. Are you sure?"

"Yes, I'm sure. And for the record, Alex is *not* the right person for me."

"Oh no! What did my brother do now?" She laughed at her friend's disgusted sigh.

"Well, he cornered me at the party and essentially told me Quinn wasn't good enough for me."

"Wow! Alex can be such a snob."

"You think? I don't understand what's going on with him lately. He never showed the slightest interest in me, which was fine, and suddenly I'm the right person for him. Maybe Alex bumped his head?"

Amy laughed long and hard before responding. "As far as I know, you're the only one with a recent head injury. While I can't fault him for his excellent taste, I may have to have a little chat with him."

"I can handle him."

"Well, if you're sure."

"I'm sure."

"Okay, message received. I don't know about you, but I'm excited about summer break."

"I am too but probably for very different reasons."

"Let me guess. You're planning to become a full-time construction crew of one this summer. Do me a favor and let Alex pay someone to come in and paint."

Paige pulled into her driveway. "What's with you two? I am more than capable of painting this house myself. And I don't want to give Alex ideas."

"Yes, I know. You want to do it yourself. I've heard you a hundred times."

"If I was interested in having a hired crew, I would do it. As you know, I have more than enough money."

"That's exactly the point. You do have the money. Hey, you could hire Quinn!"

A funny little pain bloomed in her chest at the mention of his name. "Once and for all I am not hiring someone."

"Imagine I'm waving a white flag. I promise to never mention it again. Okay? I'm sorry."

She blew out an unsteady breath. "There's nothing to be sorry about, Amy. Let it go. I'll see you tomorrow." Paige disconnected the call and turned off her car. She didn't go in right away but leaned her head back and closed her eyes for a moment.

She missed him, but a clean break was for the best. He wasn't going to change his mind, and she wasn't going to set herself up for failure. Pep talk finished, she got out of the car and went into her house. As usual, a happy and excited Finn greeted her with puppy cries and kisses. She had grown very used to coming home to such a welcoming. It was hard to remember what life without a dog was like anymore.

Chapter Eight

Paige groaned as her alarm rang. She reached over, banging her hand on it to shut it off, or kill it. Then she remembered why she was awakening so early on a Saturday. Leaping out of bed, she pulled on shorts and an old T-shirt before heading to the kitchen. Today was her volunteer shift with a local charity building homes for families in need. She was excited about not only being to help a worthy cause but to also hopefully learn a trick or two about painting.

She greeted Finn before letting him outside and then changed the water in his bowl. Grabbing a yogurt and an apple, she went out to the back patio to eat a hurried breakfast. Finn sat at her feet hoping for a taste. She laughed at the expression on his cute, little face and gave in, slipping him some apple. Checking her watch, she was happy to see there was enough time to drive by De Luca's Bakery on her way. Bringing a couple dozen donuts might make up for her lack of experience.

Thirty minutes later, after purchasing enough refreshments for a small army, she arrived at the project site with exactly two minutes to spare. She pulled a baseball cap on her head and reached in for the boxes. Since she had more than she could carry by herself, she looked around for help. Her heart threw out an extra beat or two when she saw Quinn's truck pulling in a few feet down from her. Her palms grew sweaty. Since there was no avoiding this, she called out to him. The best offense is a good defense, her father always said.

"Hey," she called from behind the pink boxes. "Could you give me a hand please?"

Turning around, he strode across the short distance separating them. "Sure."

The sight of him sent a thrill coursing through her blood stream. Not a great start. Better to remember he was off-limits. "Thanks. I may have overestimated the number of hands I have."

He laughed at her joke. "I seem to remember you having the usual two. What do you have there?"

"Well, I figured bringing donuts might make them overlook my lack of any practical experience."

"I've been working with this organization for a few years now, and I can tell you they never turn down help. No matter how little practical knowledge you have." He reached forward and grabbed the top two boxes from her.

His hands brushed hers, and she felt it to her toes. "Thanks. This is my first time here. I'm a little nervous."

"How've you been?"

"Fine, thanks. Fewer headaches with passing time." She was thankful for the dark glasses covering her eyes. He was only wearing an ordinary pair of khaki cargo shorts and slightly worn navy blue fire department shirt. Both had seen better days. But the way he filled out his clothing made her heart beat a little faster.

Approaching the modest house, she was pleased to see at least two dozen people gathered. Just another reason to love Windsor Falls. People had given up their weekend to come out and help.

A tall, good looking man stepped up onto the front porch and waved at the milling group of people. "If I could have your attention, please." He waited as the others settled down and turned towards him.

"Good morning! For those of you who don't know me, I'm Frank Masters, and I am the organizer of today's event. First, thank you so much for coming out to help today. Your support is what makes this project a reality."

Frank broke off for a round of applause from the volunteers. "Folks, we are in the home stretch. Today we focus on interior work, mainly painting and carpet installation. I know we have some people here today with experience in these areas, while others are novices. It doesn't matter what you bring to this project. Most important is your willingness to help."

Frank waved to a family of four, standing off to the side. "I would like to introduce the new owners of the house we are finishing today. This is Hector and Maria Delgado and their two children Magdalena and Luis." The parents waved at the gathered volunteers.

"Miss Harrington, you came!!" The little girl, a student last year, ran over, hugging her around the waist.

She leaned down and returned the hug. "Magdalena, of course I came. I told you I would." She straightened up and approached the parents. "Senor and Senora Delgado, it's so nice to see you again. I'm so happy for you. This is going to be a lovely home for your family." They both murmured their thanks as the leader cleared his throat and called for attention.

"For practical purposes, I've broken you up into several small groups with each having at least one person having the necessary experience to help the others. The leader has a list of who will be with them and what you'll be doing today. OK, everyone, let's get started!"

Quinn pulled a piece of paper from his pocket. "I'm one of the 'group leaders', he explained.

She peeked over his arm and spotted 'P. Harrington' on the paper. "Reporting for duty, sir," she called to him. She stopped short of saluting.

"It seems you're stuck with me. Let's go find the rest of our team."

They spent the next five minutes finding the other four members of their group and then heading into the house. They had been given the three upstairs bedrooms to paint. The first was the master bedroom, and the other two were kids' rooms.

Since they had an even group of six, each room would be tackled by two group members with Quinn available for any help they needed. Paige was surprised when he chose her for the room he would be painting. Excitement zipped through her body even as doubts crowded her mind. Maybe spending the day with him was a bad idea. But she didn't want to make a fuss in front of the others.

The day was warm and not too humid, so all windows were thrown open to allow fresh air in as they worked. She was already busy taping the baseboards when he walked back in.

"I see you've been researching."

She looked up at him from where she was crouched down on the floor. "Between Google and YouTube, I'm practically an expert."

"Once we finish, we can tackle the walls. This is not a huge room, so we can get two coats done in no time."

Noticing an envelope on the window sill, she crossed the room and picked it up. Inside was a piece of paper folded in half. She unfolded it and read it aloud.

"Dear kind people, there aren't enough words to express our gratitude to you. It has been our dream for some time to be able to give our daughter, Magdalena, her own room. She is six years old and loves princesses and unicorns. She is very excited to sleep in her new room. Bless you all, Maria & Hector Delgado."

A sheen of tears coated her eyes. She cleared her throat. "I hope we're painting this room pink. That's what every little girl deserves; a pink room for a fairy princess."

"Did you have a pink room as a little girl?"

"As a matter of fact, I did have a pink bedroom. I had the same wishes and dreams as Magdalena when I was her age. Later, we painted it purple, and the walls were covered with posters of horses and boy bands."

"So, no pink bedroom for you now when you get around to painting it?"

Paige laughed. "No pink bedroom. I'm still making decisions, but I can safely say pink didn't make the final cut."

"Let's get started. I'll do the ceiling while you start on the walls." Quinn opened a can of soft pink paint and poured some of it into the pan. He handed this and a roller to her and pointed to the far corner of the room. "If you don't mind starting over in that corner, I'll start on this end. We can work around each other. This ceiling won't take me long, then I can help you with the walls."

"Of course," Paige murmured in return. She dipped the roller into the pan and started on the first wall. Although she was far from expert, she was pleased with her first attempt. Until she noticed the paint dripping off the roller and down the wall. "Oops!"

He turned and grinned at her. "Rookie mistake. No big deal. You have too much paint on the roller. Like many things in life, less is more." He set down his roller and joined her on the opposite side of the room. His hands brushed hers as he took the roller from her hand and demonstrated how to roll the excess paint on the upper portion of the pan. The electricity sparking between them still surprised her. And stole her breath. He turned back to the wall and used the mostly dry roller to smooth out the extra paint she had already placed on the wall.

"Much better. Now all you have to do is make sure you have the right amount of paint and keep going." He grinned at her and handed back the roller.

Paige tried to concentrate on what he was saying. But he was so close. And the scent of him nearly did her in. She really needed to get out more if his scent overpowered the paint fumes permeating the room.

Dragging her thoughts back to the topic at hand, she took the roller brush back from him. "I think I have it now."

"You'll be fine."

He didn't seem as affected by her as she was by him. "So, Amy and A.J. seem to like each other."

Quinn was reaching for the ceiling with his extended roller brush when he froze. "Oh, is that so?"

"Yes. Amy is spending most of her free time with him. She certainly seems smitten at the very least."

"I was wondering why I haven't seen as much of A.J."

"She's so happy. I admit, I'm a little jealous. It's made me rethink my recent moratorium on dating"

He jerked the roller brush. "Really?"

"Well, the past few months have been busy for me, between finishing graduate school and working on my house. With school done, I have more free time. It's probably time I got a life."

"Congratulations," he said. "On finishing school, I mean."

"Thanks. I'm so happy it's behind me. I have nothing but free time. And a whole house to paint, of course."

She stepped back to check her progress. She might not be the fastest, but at least it looked good. She rolled her brush in the paint tray again and went back to work.

"Tell me more about this moratorium you're thinking of quitting."

She was glad to not be facing him with her red-hot cheeks. What was she thinking? Was she really going to discuss this with him? The one guy she *wanted* to date but couldn't?

"Well, it's not like I'm going to join a dating website. I'll just be open to the idea. If someone comes along who interests me, then I'll consider it."

"So, who might interest you?"

"Didn't we already have this conversation?"

"You're right. You're looking for someone who is smart, funny, and kind. Looks don't matter."

Paige turned and stared at him. "You remembered?"

Quinn returned her direct look. "I remember everything about you."

She stared for a few moments before turning back to her wall. They would never finish the room if he kept looking at her that way. The intensity of his gaze made her wish for a different bedroom.

"Anyway, that's what I would want in a long-term relationship. But I'm not interested in the whole picket fence yet. Right now, I want to have fun. I want to spend time with someone who interests me. Someone who makes me laugh. Someone like you."

He was quiet so long, she wondered if he heard her.

"Are you asking me out?"

"What if I was? What would you say?"

The feel of his hand covering hers surprised her. He removed the paint roller from her hand and placed it in the pan. Then he back her up against an unpainted area of wall. Never breaking eye contact, he closed the distance between them and lowered his head to hers. Inches from her mouth, he whispered, "If this isn't what you want, you have about two seconds to let me know."

She answered by closing the gap between them and placing her lips on his. The heat simmering between them exploded. She groaned into his mouth, fanning the flames even higher. He took advantage of the opening to thrust his tongue inside her mouth, dueling with hers.

Her fingers needed to touch him. Anywhere. Everywhere. She placed her hands on his waist and moved them slowly up to his chest, splaying her fingers desperate to touch as much of him as she could. Even through his T-shirt, she felt warm skin and smooth muscle. She moved her hands higher to the skin of his neck, her fingers curling in his short hair.

Quinn broke the kiss before leaning his forehead against hers. "Wow," he uttered on a ragged breath.

"Wow indeed. Are you sure you're not interested?"

A laugh rumbled through his chest. "I never said I wasn't interested."

She ground her molars. "That's right. You are interested. But you're not going to do anything about it."

"Yes. You know why."

"I never asked you to protect me."

"You didn't have to. I already know the drill. That's not the life you want." He turned and walked back to where he had left his roller brush. He climbed back up the ladder.

She was left staring at his back. What was it with the men in her life lately? First Alex and now Quinn. Why did they think they knew what she needed?

"So now you know what I want? I wasn't aware you were psychic."

Without turning around, he answered her. "I mean in general. Women need more stability in their lives than being married to someone who might not come home at the end of his shift."

Afraid of what she might say, she clamped her mouth shut. She picked up her roller brush. "For the record, I do not appreciate having my decisions made for me."

The two worked in silence for a long time. She finally broke the silence. "I'm sorry I mentioned it. Don't worry, I won't be asking you again." She set down her brush and left the room.

Paige ran down the stairs and kept going until she was in the front yard. She took a seat under a tree and removed her baseball cap. Pulling the ponytail holder out, she shook out her hair. She was overheated, and she couldn't blame only the rising temperature.

What was she going to do about him? The bigger question was how she would handle her feelings for him. She liked him. A lot. In fact, she liked him a little more every time they met. And there was a huge attraction between them. But every time they got a little bit closer, he backed away.

She meant what she told Quinn. She was interested in dating again. And she was more than interested in dating *him*. But it wasn't going to happen. She wanted to have some fun, but her feelings for him were a bit too intense. She had to have to find someone else. And if that person didn't make her heart race quite as much, at least he wouldn't break it.

She looked up at the sound of a truck pulling into the driveway. Frank pulled into a parking space. He seemed nice, and he was attractive. If only he made her blood race even a little.

"Hey Paige," Frank called. "Can you give me a hand?"

She stood and wandered over to his truck. Looking in the back window, she was shocked at the amount of food she saw.

"Hungry?"

Frank laughed. "I am, but this is for everyone. A local deli donated all this to feed our hard-working volunteers."

Her stomach grumbled, and she laughed. "Well I guess you can tell I'm hungry. Let's go!" She opened the door and grabbed several bags of sandwiches while Frank lifted two cases of soda.

"The weather is perfect for an impromptu picnic, don't you think?" She placed the bags on a table in the yard.

"Absolutely! Why don't you go inside and tell everyone while I grab a folding table from the bed of my truck?"

Paige turned and jogged across the yard. She walked into the first floor and called to the various crews, telling them lunch was served out in the yard. Walking upstairs, she entered the master bedroom to inform those folks as well. She was met with high fives. She might not be the only hungry person.

She went back into the hall to see two guys coming from the other child's bedroom. "Did someone mention food?" asked the older man with gray hair.

She grinned. "I did. There's lunch donated from a local deli outside in the yard. You better hurry before it's all gone."

Paige took a deep breath and walked into what would be Magdalena's room. He was still on the ladder, using a brush to touch up a corner of the ceiling. She stared at his delicious backside before speaking.

"Lunch is here." Not waiting for a reply, she turned and left the room.

Chapter Nine

Paige grabbed a sandwich, chips, and a soda before taking a seat with Frank and some of the other volunteers. She needed to keep her distance from Quinn. Being 'just friends' was no longer an option. Time to take matters into her own hands. Find someone not afraid to take a chance. He didn't want to be in a relationship, so she would forget about him. Move on with her life. It sounded like a good plan, but she doubted it would be so easy.

Everyone in their small group exchanged names and took a seat in the shade of a tree. Frank turned to her and smiled. "So, Paige, tell us about yourself."

Not one for being the center of attention, she stifled a groan. "Well, I'm a kindergarten teacher. I was born and raised here. All very boring, I'm afraid." She smiled at the group.

"Nothing boring about small town pride. How do you know Quinn?"

She had taken a sip of her soda and nearly choked at Frank's question. "Uh, what do you mean?"

"Oh, I'm sorry. It seemed as though you two already knew each other."

"Oh, well, I don't really know him. We met when I was in a car accident. He was one of the firefighters who responded to the call."

"It's not much of a story, Frank," came a deep voice from over her right shoulder.

Knowing there was so much more to it than that, she told her version of events. "Like any true hero, he's making light of his role. What he isn't telling you is that he saved my life."

"That's nice of you to say, but you were never in danger of dying."

"True, but I didn't know it at the time. You may not have saved my life, but you made a terrifying ordeal much easier to endure."

"Just part of the job description." Quinn tipped his head to her and turned away.

Paige turned back to the group and was not pleased to see the open looks of admiration on the faces of three young women sitting there. She turned to Frank. "Tell us more about your work with the organization." She settled in and unwrapped a sandwich as he talked about his work and the local families that had been helped. Although she was interested in what he had to say, she couldn't help wishing she was sitting with him. She pushed the thought away. Spending more time with him was a mistake. She knew it, at least intellectually.

*****

Quinn picked a spot alone across the yard from where Paige sat with the others. He ate his lunch alone, not tasting the food. He watched with growing envy as she leaned in to hear what Frank was saying. His gut clenched when her soft laugh was carried on the breeze. He loved her laugh.

He had no one to blame but himself. She was better off without him, and he was determined to stay away from her. She deserved a stable life, not one that included the risks inherent in his job. Besides, he had seen many firefighter marriages burn out over the erratic hours and not so great pay. He had no desire to join the ranks. Thoroughly disgusted with everything, he bundled up the remainders of his lunch and tossed it into the garbage can in the driveway. Without looking back at her, he walked into the house and got back to work.

A little while later, her soft "I'm back" split the silence. He stayed on the ladder with his back to her. He had known she had come back into the room, even before she had spoken. He had developed a sixth sense about her. It was becoming a curse.

"Did you enjoy your lunch?" As soon as the words were out of his mouth, he wanted them back. This is what he had been reduced to; inane conversation.

"Yes, thank you. I was starving. I'm not used to so much physical labor I guess. It was really nice of the deli to donate everything."

"I agree. Nice to know there are still good people in the world. You guys seemed to enjoy yourselves." *What was wrong with him?* He may as well have told her he listened to her entire lunch conversation.

He almost turned at her soft sigh. "They're a nice group of people. And I learned the entire history of the organization."

Quinn couldn't help but laugh. "Yes, Frank is somewhat long winded at times. But he's very dedicated to his cause as well."

"Yes, he is." Another long sigh followed. "He asked me out on a date."

He smothered a curse. "What did you say?"

"I turned him down. He's not my type."

"Huh."

"He's a nice guy, and I admire his dedication, but that's all he can talk about. Besides, there wasn't any chemistry for me. I didn't want to lead him on, so I said no. I might let Amy set me up with someone. She's been wanting forever to do so."

"Do you think that's a wise idea?"

"She's my best friend and knows me better than anyone. Why wouldn't it be a good idea?"

He thought for a moment before answering. This conversation had minefield written all over it. "I meant that, best friends or not, you guys are very different. She might not be able to pick the best person for you. That's all."

"Who could pick better than my best friend?"

"I could probably do a better job of it than Amy." *Shut up, Adams.* She was the first person in a very long time to whom he had felt so attracted. And he's offering to fix her up? With someone else? What was wrong with him?

"I'm sure you think you could, but I don't need any help. I'll find someone all on my own. Thanks anyway."

He didn't say anything for fear of putting his size twelve foot even further into his mouth. He concentrated on painting the corner. No one he knew was good enough for her. He couldn't imagine her being involved with any of the guys from the station. The truth was he didn't want her involved with anyone else. But him.

Paige moved on to the next wall. Unfortunately, that brought her closer to him. The tension became unbearable to him. He was aware of every movement she made. The light citrus scent of her shampoo carried to him on the breeze from the open window. It made him want to run his hands through the luxurious thickness of it.

Quinn came down off the ladder slowly and placed his tray and brush on the floor. He stretched out his cramped muscles. Her face was in profile to him, but it was enough to see the pink tint to her skin.

"Something wrong? You look a bit flushed." He tried to not grin. He liked knowing that he bothered her as much as she did him.

"It's warm in here."

"I'd love to know what you're thinking about right now. You have a very expressive face. I can almost see the wheels turning."

She turned to him and put down her brush. Her small hands fisted on her hips. "Do you really want to know? Then I'll tell you. I was thinking about how very attracted I am to you and how it's a shame this thing between us will never get a chance to go anywhere."

His blood rushed from his head to a much lower part of his body. Her sassiness was intoxicating. "That was, uh, blunt."

"You don't know me well. I'm a brutally honest person. Some might say to a fault. But life is short; too short to not tell the truth. So, I'm attracted to you. I would have gladly started a relationship with you. But you're too busy playing it safe. So, as much as I like you, you're clearly not the guy for me. But someone out there is." She picked up her brush and turned back to the wall.

He stared at her slender back. His blood ran cold at the thought of her starting a relationship with another man. But that wasn't fair. He couldn't expect her to remain alone the rest of her life because he wasn't willing to get involved. For the first time ever, he wondered if he was wrong. About everything. But then he remembered what losing his dad had been like, for himself and Lauren and his mom, and he knew he wasn't wrong. Though being right was a bitter pill to swallow.

Paige took her phone out of her pocket and hit the playlist before placing it on the window sill. The upbeat tempo filled the room. She resumed painting, humming along with the music as she worked.

Quinn took this for exactly what it was. There wasn't anything left to say between them, and she was trying to lighten the mood. Even if they had vastly different musical taste, he could appreciate the effort. Turning back to his wall, he too resumed panting.

The rest of the afternoon passed with very little interaction between them. They both stayed to their sides of the room. They were very successful at avoiding each other until the end of the day. They had finished painting and only needed to clean their brushes when Paige tripped over a section of bunched up tarp covering the new carpeting. She would have fallen if not for his lightning fast reflexes.

Time seemed to halt as he caught her. He grabbed her around the waist. This brought them face to face. Both seemed to be holding their breath. She straightened and backed away a step, forcing him to release her.

She ducked her head and laughed. "Thanks. I'm a clutz."

He didn't answer her but reached forward and tucked a few stray hairs behind her ear. Touching the smooth skin of her face was almost his undoing. She moistened her lips, sending his heart rate through the roof. He ached to touch his lips to hers and surround himself in her sweet taste. He moved a half step closer, giving her time to back away if that's what she chose to do.

She placed her hand in the center of his chest and gave him a sad smile. "Please don't. You'll only hurt me. We both know there isn't any future for us." She turned and left the room.

Quinn stayed where he was, listening to her footsteps until he couldn't hear them anymore. She was right and obviously stronger than he was. He was finding it very hard to walk away from this woman he barely knew.

*****

Paige walked out of the house and straight to her car. She lowered all the windows and turned up the A/C to full blast to combat the oppressive heat trapped inside of it. Not waiting for any relief, she pulled away from the curb and concentrated on getting home before she fell apart.

This thing with Quinn had to stop. She barely knew him, and they hadn't spent a lot of time together. But despite that, she felt an intense attachment towards him; a longing of sorts. Maybe it was because of the way they had met. It had been very emotionally charged, and despite the terror of the situation, she had felt safe and protected with him.

None of it mattered. He had been throwing up barriers since they met. He wasn't likely to change his mind, and she didn't need the pain. She needed to forget him, no matter how much she didn't want to. No more hanging out with him.

She drove home, still musing about him. Until recently, she hadn't even known he existed on the planet. Tears slipped down her face, and she couldn't decide if they were out of sadness or anger. Either way, she didn't have time for them. Willing herself to stop, she turned onto her street only to see Alex's car parked in front of her house. *Just what she needed.* She threw on an old pair of sunglasses and got out of her car.

Alex met her at the sidewalk. He hugged her briefly and kissed the side of her face. "Hey, Paige." He glanced at her clothing, and she didn't miss the brief disapproval in his eyes.

"Better be careful, Alex, I'm not exactly presentable."

He smiled his megawatt-I'm running-for-office smile. "Don't worry. It's just us."

She knew he didn't mean anything by it, but he had no clue how insulting his words were. Paige compared Alex to Quinn. On the surface, Alex was perfect. He was GQ cover gorgeous, came from a great family, and had a fabulous career. But she couldn't help thinking Quinn came out on top. There wasn't any effort to being with him. They could sit and talk, and laugh, without even trying. He certainly didn't care when she had been covered in plaster dust the day they had stripped her walls. His presence was enough to send her body into overdrive. Oh yeah, he didn't want to be in a relationship. If she could look past that one pesky detail.

She realized Alex was staring at her. "So, what brings you by?" She winced at the dullness in her tone. She loved Alex. But she loved him in the big brother kind of way. She'd had a tough day, and she wasn't up for turning him down. Again.

His smile dimmed. "There was a time I didn't need a reason to stop by."

She took a deep breath and tried not to sigh. "You know I'm always happy to see you, but I've had a tough day. I'm hot, dirty, and more than a little cranky." She collapsed into one of her porch chairs.

Alex followed her and sat in a chair next to hers, angling it so they sat face to face. He stared at her for a long moment before speaking. "Amy told me you had finished the coursework for your master's degree. I'm pleased for you. I thought I could take you out for dinner to celebrate." At her raised eyebrows, Alex grinned. "And not at the club either. Wherever you would like to go."

She stifled a sigh. He was trying to be nice, but she also knew Alex. He had an agenda. "That's very nice of you, but completely unnecessary." She gave him a tired smile as she leaned her head back and closed her eyes.

"It may not be strictly necessary, but I would like to. Finishing your degree is a big deal. How about you clean up and I'll take you out for a burger? You have to eat, right?"

She opened her eyes. "A burger? Really? You'd go for a burger with me?" She hesitated before giving in. She would probably regret this, but she didn't want things to be strained between them. "Okay, a burger it is. I need a quick shower first. Give me twenty minutes." She got up and opened the front door, leading the way into her home. "The remote is on the coffee table. Help yourself if you want a drink of something. I'll be right back."

She bolted upstairs and ran into her bathroom, stripping off her dirty clothes and tossing them into the nearby hamper. With a look of regret, she walked by the large bathtub and headed for the shower. Maybe later tonight she would have time to soak her sore muscles. Bur for now, Alex was waiting downstairs, and she only had a few minutes. Going out for a bite might not be the worst thing. It beat mooning over him all alone in her house. Alex would prove to be at least an interesting distraction.

Exactly nineteen minutes later, Paige was clean and dry and dressed casually in a pair of capris and another T-shirt. She skipped even the minimal makeup she usually wore. Alex needed to understand she thought of him as an older brother.

She found Alex where she left him, sitting on her couch, watching network news. He glanced at her, clicking off the TV and getting up off the couch.

"You weren't kidding when you said you'd be ready in a few minutes." He examined her casual clothing. "Women I date are never quick about getting ready. They're also usually late for everything."

"Well, I'm not like your typical woman, and this is not a date." She smiled to soften her words. "Besides, I spend my days with 6-year-olds. I must be low maintenance. Shall we go?" She slid her feet into a comfy pair of flip flops, picked up her purse, and placed her phone into it before heading to the door.

"I am. Have you decided where we're going for your burger? Wherever you want."

She had considered taking him to Smitty's, for the shock value. She was quite sure the country-club dining Alex had never been to a first responder bar. But as much fun as it might have been, she didn't want to take a chance on running into Quinn. Or Amy and A.J. She wasn't sure what Alex knew about his sister's relationship.

"I know a great family-run restaurant with the best burgers around. Have you been to Cal's?" Paige gave him directions as he helped her into the car.

"I haven't, but I trust you. What were you doing today?"

She shook her head at the fact that he left out a comment about her earlier appearance. Alex might be trying, but he would never change. And she didn't want him to. Not for her. "I was helping finish a house for a family of four. Their daughter was one of my students, so I wanted to be involved. The looks on their faces was worth getting some paint on old clothes." She grinned at him "You can't get that by writing a check."

Alex grinned back at her. "That might be a bit too hands on for me, but I think it's great."

A few minutes later they pulled into the parking lot of a small family-style restaurant. Alex came around the side of his car, opening the door for her. She murmured her thanks and walked towards the front door. Once inside, she led the way to an open booth along the back wall.

"One of the other teachers told me about this place. Besides amazing burgers, they also have fabulous pancakes and waffles all day. Anything you pick will be great. I promise."

An older woman approached their table with menus. "Hi, I'm Debbie. Can I get you folks something to drink first?" After taking their orders for sweet tea, Debbie left, promising to come back for their food orders in a moment.

Alex looked over the menu as she pushed her closed one aside. "Already know what you're having?"

"Of course! I told you the burgers rule here. I'm having a cheeseburger and fries. I worked hard today, I deserve it. How about you?"

Alex closed his menu and place it on top of hers. "I meant it when I said I trust you. I'll have the same."

Their waitress returned with their drinks and took their food orders. Alex leaned back in the booth. "So, what are your plans for the summer?"

"I would think that was obvious. I have a whole house to remodel."

"And you're still determined to do this without my help?"

She burst out laughing. "As long as your version of 'helping' still means writing a check, then yes. But it's sweet of you to offer."

The bell over the door rang. He glanced towards the counter. "Hey, isn't that your firefighter friend?"

Warmth spread through her belly. She watched him take a seat at the counter. *So much for avoiding him.* She turned back to Alex and struggled for something to say. "Yes."

"Don't you want to say hello?"

Before she could answer, Quinn swiveled on the stool. Getting up, he crossed the restaurant towards their booth. Paige wished the floor would open and swallow her whole. This had disaster written all over it.

She forced a smile. "Hey, it's been, what, a whole two hours since I saw you?" Her voice sounded strained even to her own ears.

She turned to Alex. "You remember Quinn, right? He also volunteered today. Small world, huh?"

Ever the well-bred Southern gentleman, Alex slid out of the booth and extended his hand. "Yes, of course. Nice to see you again."

She watched as the two men shook hands. It gave her a moment to study them. Alex was the more classically handsome of the two, but she had always found his looks a bit too perfect. Never a wrinkle or hair out of place. Quinn had the all-American male look going for him. His hair was slightly rumpled, as if he had run his hands through it recently. He was still wearing the clothes he had on earlier, and he was sporting more than a few paint stains. But his eyes crinkled when he smiled, and the dimples bracketing his mouth sent a wave of warmth rolling through her belly.

Both men stared at her. Pulling herself out of her revelry, she motioned to the empty space next to her. "Would you like to stay and eat with us?" She crossed her fingers under the table. She didn't think she could eat with the tension coming off the two men.

He shook his head. "Thanks, but no. I called in take out on my way home." Glancing down at his rumpled shorts and T-shirt, he laughed. "Not exactly dressed for eating in public."

Alex flashed a triumphant look as he slid back into the booth across from her. "Well it was nice seeing you again. Any friend of Paige's is a friend of mine."

She could have kicked him.

Turning to her, Quinn smiled into her eyes. "Nice seeing you again." With a soft squeeze to her shoulder, he turned and walked away.

She watched him pay for his food and leave before turning back to face Alex. The strained but oh so polite exchange she had witnessed was a bit much. Neither man had any claim on her. Alex wasn't the right man for her despite his interest, and Quinn refused to enter a relationship, despite her interest. Yet they were both acting like she belonged to each. Men!

She was saved from dealing with this mess by the waitress appearing with their meals. She bustled off again, promising to return to top off their drinks. Paige took a large bite of her hamburger, watching her companion as she chewed. "You seem pleased with yourself."

Alex finished chewing before replying. "I'm not sure to what you are referring. I was merely being polite to your friend."

She knew he wouldn't be nearly as confident if he knew how much that *friend* set her insides quivering with a glance. Not to mention what his touch did. No, Alex would not like that at all. "You know we are only friends, you and I, right? I really do consider you the big brother I never had."

Alex set down his hamburger and took a moment to wipe his hands on the napkin. Reaching across the table, he took both of her hands in his. "You have made your point clear. But I'm not sure you understand mine. I'm not looking for the great love of my life. That's a bit messy for me. I'm looking for a partner, and I believe you would be a great fit. It may not be the most romantic thing in the world, but it's the truth."

Seeing he was serious, she replied as gently as she could. "That's very flattering. You have a lot to give someone, but not me. I want messy. I want to fall madly in love with someone. I don't need perfect. I need real."

"It's Quinn, isn't it?"

Paige blushed at the mention of his name. "I'm not going to lie to you, Alex. I have feelings for him. But it's not about him. He doesn't want a relationship. He's made that very clear."

"Well, that's his loss. I mean it. He's a fool if he can't see what's right in front of him." He picked up one of her hands and kissed it. "The offer still stands if you change your mind."

They finished their meals in a companionable silence. Alex got up to pay the check, while she sat in the booth thinking about Quinn. She was falling for someone who wasn't available. At least not emotionally. This whole situation was ridiculous. Why couldn't she feel this way about Alex? She had a wonderful man whom she adored and wanted to build a life with her. But she knew in her heart Alex was not right for her.

*****

Quinn drove home, kicking himself mentally. *Had he really left her with Alex?* Not that he had a choice. She deserved someone who could commit to her. But did it have to be Alex Windsor? That man was a too smooth for his taste. Surely, Paige could see he wasn't right for her. The real problem was that he liked her. Despite the devastating loss of her parents at an early age, she was the happiest person he knew. She enjoyed life and wasn't going to let anything stop her. Spending time with her made him happier. But more than anything, he didn't want to be the person who changed that for her.

Sighing, he pulled into the driveway of his latest project. Funny how he rarely thought of it as home. Home meant something permanent. And this house, like the others before it, was not it. He would live here until he sold it. Then someone else would buy it and make it *their* home.

Grabbing his take-out meal, he got out of his truck. He looked around at the landscaping he had done earlier in the month. The yard looked great with lush, green grass and flowers planted here and there. Yes, someone would appreciate all the effort he had put into this place. He would make a tidy profit and move onto the next project. Yet, somehow it wasn't as satisfying as it had been in the past.

Chapter Ten

Paige pulled into the parking lot beside Between the Covers, her favorite independent bookstore. She grabbed her purse and their book of the month and headed in for the monthly book club meeting. She was late. Again. The bell over the door rang as she entered on a run. "Sorry, everyone."

"Better late than never," exclaimed Jamie, the owner of Between the Covers.

"Good thing, as she's always late," grumbled Amy good naturedly.

"I know, I know. Someday, I'll be more organized. Just not sure when that day will be." She walked up to the refreshment table and poured herself a glass of white wine. "OK, what did I miss?"

"Nothing yet. We were busy taking bets on when Elizabeth is going to pop." Charlie Avery grinned as she said this. She laid a loving hand on her best friend's extended belly. "Baby Gabriel isn't due for two weeks, but Aunt Charlie can't wait that long."

Elizabeth leaned back in her chair, pressing a hand to her lower back. "As much as I want him to finish 'cooking', I'm so ready to not be pregnant. My back is sore. I have to pee every fifteen seconds." A serene smile lit her face. "On the other hand, I'm so thankful to have made it this far. I'm not complaining."

Everyone nodded in agreement. Long before they had met, Elizabeth had been married and pregnant. Sadly, she had lost both her young husband and unborn child within days of each other. She left Windsor Falls for ten long years, only coming back last summer. She reconnected with her childhood friend, Sam Bishop, and love blossomed.

Paige squeezed the other woman's hand. "We all know how happy you are. I can't wait to meet him either. Think of all those adorable little baby things I can buy."

Elizabeth heaved herself from the chair. "I told you it was every fifteen seconds." Her face contorted, and she reached out for the back of her chair. "Ah, Charlie, I may need a ride."

"Of course, silly. I drove tonight." She turned to the other women gathered. "Elizabeth is having trouble fitting behind the wheel these days."

"I don't mean home. We need to go to the hospital. Now. My water just broke." She turned to Jamie. "I'm so glad you have hardwood floors in here. Sorry about the mess."

"What?"

"Oh my goodness."

"What should we do?"

Everyone chattered at once, talking over each other, until the woman in question raised a hand. "No need to panic. There's plenty of time. He's only two weeks early, so everything will be fine. Charlie, I just need a ride. I'm going to call Sam."

She lowered herself back into the chair and pulled her phone from her purse. "Jamie, I'll buy you a new chair."

"Don't worry about that. Let's have this baby."

"No worries. It's not like I have a choice at this point. Now for the hard part; telling Sam. He's going to lose it." She dialed her husband and murmured softly into the phone. The sound of him freaking out could be heard across the room. After assuring Sam they'd meet him at the hospital, she disconnected. "Isn't he a hoot? Acts all tough but mention you're in labor and he falls apart."

Her love-soaked tone pulled at Paige's heart. For a moment, she allowed herself to imagine making that call to Quinn. *No use dreaming about things that would never be.* She cleared her head and helped the others escort Elizabeth to Charlie's car.

"Make sure you call us with the details."

Elizabeth lowered the passenger window. "I will. Wish me luck."

Paige stood next to Amy. "Someday soon that will be you and A.J."

"Yes. I can't wait." Amy turned to her, concern shining from her eyes. "That can be you too, you know."

"I know. Just not with Quinn." She looked down at her brightly colored toenails. Anywhere but at Amy. Seeing pity on her friend's face might send her into tears.

Several days later, tears gathered in her eyes as Paige watched the last of her students leave her classroom. The last day of school was always a tough one for her. She knew some of her colleagues counted down to this day with cheer, some from the very first day of the school year. But not her. While she loved having time off in the summer, she was always sad to see her students go home for the last time.

"Let me guess. You're crying."

She looked over her shoulder to see Amy lounging in the doorway. She blew her nose before grinning at her friend. "I know you think I'm ridiculous, but I love my students. I'm sorry to see them go."

Amy walked over to Paige and hugged her. "Of course you are. That's what makes you such a great teacher. But don't worry. In a few brief weeks, there will be a whole new bunch of monsters waiting for you to mold them into respectable human beings."

She shook her finger in Amy's face. "You can't fool me. You love your students as much as I do. Admit it."

Amy laughed. "OK, I admit it. I do love the little monsters. Cal asked me to marry him this morning at recess. But I am as much in love with summer and having weeks off to do whatever I want."

"Well, I can agree with that. I have such plans for the next two months. By the time school starts again, I hope to be done with the all of the major renovations on my house."

Amy stomped her size nine Prada. "What am I going to do with you? Summer is for lounging at the beach and reading trashy novels. It's most definitely NOT for working your fingers to the bone all day and getting covered in dirt." She gave a delicate shudder.

"You forgot to mention how I will destroy every fingernail. No manicures for me, I guess."

"As if you would ever agree to a manicure. How long have I been trying to make you over? I've about given up."

"I would say since we were both about five, and you'll never give up. Although you should. I'm hopeless when it comes to the girly stuff you love so much."

"I would have lost hope long ago if I didn't know about your secret love of very girly underwear."

Paige blushed at the mention of her vice. She had a thing for super sexy lingerie. She couldn't help herself and quite frankly had no intention of even trying. She loved all kinds of lacey, silky panties and bras. She had way more matching sets than necessary, but what was a girl to do? "You got me there."

"One day, you'll realize there's more to being a woman than your fabulous underwear. And when the day comes, I'll be ready."

She gathered her belongings in a box. "Don't hold your breath. I'm happy as I am. And I'm psyched to spend the summer fixing up my new home."

Amy held her up one perfectly manicured hand in defense. "We can just agree to disagree. But if it makes you happy, then go for it!"

"Exactly. This makes me happy. I take a lot of pride in knowing I will be doing all of it myself. It's an accomplishment. And now school is over for the summer and my graduate degree is done, so I have nothing but time to tackle things. I can't wait to get started."

Amy shook her head. "I give up. But at least promise me you'll start tomorrow. Tonight, we celebrate the end of another successful year of teaching. If nothing else, you survived another year of Mrs. Milton."

She grimaced at the mention of their by-the-book, old-fashioned principal. "That is worth celebrating. Okay, what are we doing?"

Amy grinned in triumph. "Come with me to Smitty's tonight. A.J. will be there along with a whole host of his delicious looking friends. Maybe you'll get lucky."

Paige was dismayed at the idea of going there. The last thing she needed was running into Quinn. She hadn't seen him since the diner. And even though she missed him, she didn't want to see him. It would only prove futile; and more than a little painful.

"I don't think so. I don't want to be a third wheel, and I don't want to see Quinn. You and I can do something another night. We have the whole summer."

"I wish you'd come, but I understand you not wanting to see him. If he's never going to commit to a long-term relationship, then you're better off without him." She stepped in and gave her another hug. "Well, I'm off to get my highlights touched up. Call me later."

"I will," she called to her friend's retreating back. She finished packing up her stuff and headed to her car in the parking lot. She drove home thinking about what to do next in her house. All the offending wall paper had been removed. It was time to get serious about color choices. She wanted her home to be bright and filled with light. The many large windows allowed for the latter, so she wanted warm, bright colors to complement it.

She opened the door to Finn's excited barking. She scooped up the puppy and took him out to the fenced in back yard to go to the bathroom. The days had been long for his young bladder, but now Paige would be home with him every day.

He finished doing his business and took off in excited circles around the yard. Finn was clearly happy to be outside in the sunshine. She stretched her hands to the sun, arching her back to relieve the stress from the last day of school. He finished running laps and flopped on his back at her feet, giving her a less than subtle hint to rub his belly. She did so with pleasure, sitting on the soft grass next to him.

Picking up the puppy and settling him in her lap, she thought about the weeks ahead. "So, Finn, it's you and me. Are you going to help me paint this summer?"

He swiveled his head back and forth at her words, making her laugh. She leaned in and kissed his furry face when her cell phone beeped, indicating a text message. Sure, it was Amy trying to convince her to go out tonight, she sighed and swiped her finger across the screen. An unfamiliar number popped up. Curious, she opened the message. *Hey! Are you home? It's Quinn.*

She gasped in surprise. With a less than steady hand she typed her reply. *I am. Just got home from work. Where are you?*

"I'm in your yard," a deep, masculine voice replied.

She startled and turned towards the voice, accidentally rolling Finn off her lap. Quinn stood with his hand on the top of it.

"May I come in?"

She stood and brushed grass from her clothes. "Of course."

Her puppy took off in a burst of speed towards him. When he reached Quinn, he threw his small body against his legs, barking happily.

He reached down and picked up the squirming puppy, getting his face washed in return. "He's not much of a guard dog, is he?" He set the puppy back in the grass.

Recovering from her surprise, Paige approached him. "You never know. He may lick you to death." She stopped a few feet from him and tried not to stare. Dressed in shorts and a T-shirt, he was six feet of delicious male. "This is unexpected. What are you doing here?"

He smiled. "Well, I have some time off, and I thought you might need some help with your house."

She tilted her head. "What about your own house? Don't you have a lot left?"

He blew out a breath. "The truth is I missed you. I know I've been acting like an idiot around you, giving you all kinds of mixed signals. I like you. I like being with you. You're funny and open, and you're easy to talk to. I haven't changed my mind about anything permanent. But I would like to be friends."

"I've missed you too," she whispered to him. She couldn't believe he was here in her yard. Her heart slammed in her chest, a warning to guard the vulnerable organ.

He played with the keys in his hand. "I tried to stay away, Paige. I really did." He reached out to tuck some hair behind her ear, his fingers brushing her face. "Something keeps drawing me back. I care about you more than I should considering we barely know each other. I want to spend time with you. I want to get to know you better. But I need to be sure you know nothing has changed. I'm never getting married and never having children. I love being a firefighter, and that's not going to change."

"So, no wedding dress then?" She laughed at his startled expression.

"Sometimes I forget you're joking."

"Here's the thing. Yes, I'm female, but I don't automatically want to marry you. I happen to enjoy sex as much as men do." She stopped at his raised eyebrow. "Well, okay, maybe not quite as much. What I'm trying to say is just because I might be interested in getting involved with you doesn't mean I'm naming our children. For all I know, you might snore."

Quinn shook his head. "I can see you're going to keep me on my toes." He stepped forward, closing the small gap between them and enfolded her in a hug. He lowered his head to hers and placed his mouth against her ear. "For the record, I've never had any complaints about snoring."

She shivered at the sensation of his lips on her ear. His warm breath tickled the sensitive skin on her neck, while the slight rasp of his stubble sent warm sensations down her spine. This was probably a bad idea. He had been honest with her, and she could very well end up brokenhearted. She could walk away now and keep her heart safe or see where this thing between them took her. She had a choice to make.

The feel of his body against hers sealed the deal. She stretched up onto her toes and placed her mouth on his. He leaned into the kiss. Wrapping his arms around her, he closed the gap between them. His keys made a jangling noise as they fell from his hand to the grass.

The flame that had always been there sprang to life. Paige opened her mouth to his, moaning in her throat. She had spent far too many nights lying in bed remembering this. But even her very specific memories paled in comparison to the reality. His lips were firm yet yielding to hers. His tongue met hers and warmth spread throughout her whole body, pooling in her stomach and lower.

She broke the kiss, a satisfied smile on her face. "So much for 'just friends'. I guess 'friends with benefits' is a better expression."

Quinn's face tightened. His eyes darkened. "That expression demeans you, us. You mean more to me than that." He dragged a shaky hand through his hair.

She took him by the hand and led him inside. "Let's sit down and have some tea. We can talk about it." She bustled around pouring two glasses and filling Finn's water and food bowls. The tasks gave her a few minutes to gather her thoughts and kept her hands busy.

Placing the glasses on the table she sat across from him. "I care about you. I haven't dated a lot in the past few years, and by that, I mean I haven't had more than a couple first dates. I am putting myself out there again. You and I have a chemistry." She took a moment to breathe deeply and hope her face wasn't flaming. "I'm not looking for forever. At least not right now. Do I want to eventually get married and have children of my own? Of course. But you're not that man. I am perfectly clear with your feelings on the subject. I promise to not try to change your mind."

He sat so still and quiet she feared she had pushed him too far. Then he reached for her hand. Turning it over, he traced the lines of her palm. Tingles of excitement ran up her arm. "So, you agree we should see what happens between us?"

"I do. But you have to agree to not fall in love with me." She said this with a broad smile and more than a little tongue in cheek.

"I'll try to remember."

"Why don't you stay for dinner? I have some stuff we can throw on the grill. If you don't have any other plans." She hoped she didn't come off as desperate.

"No, ma'am. I mean no, I don't have any plans for tonight. And yes, I'd love to have dinner with you. But wouldn't you rather go out?"

"No. Today was the last day of school, and I'm worn out. If you don't mind handling the grill, I can throw together a salad. I also have some Key Lime Pie in the fridge."

"Well, if you have Key Lime pie..."

"Great! Give me a few minutes to change. I got home about a minute before you arrived. Make yourself at home." She walked out of the kitchen and up the stairs.

*****

Quinn strolled around the first floor, taking in all she had accomplished. A grinning Finn shadowed him on the expedition. The old paper was down, and the walls looked prepped for painting. There were a few rough spots that needed some smoothing out, but he could help her. He wondered if she had picked her colors yet.

He walked over to the mantle to look at the pictures placed there. The frames were assorted sizes and colors. There was a formal wedding picture he guessed were her parents. He picked it up to look closer. She had her father's coloring, but she and her mother shared similar facial features. She had been a beautiful woman.

He replaced the frame and peered into another picture. This one was a less formal picture of Paige, Amy, and Alex. A teenaged Paige had her arm around Amy's shoulders, and the two young girls were smiling into the camera. Both were wearing bikinis. The way Alex was looking at her caught his attention. He was probably in college at the time it was taken. Alex stood next to Amy but turned towards Paige. His expression showed something other than fondness for his younger sister's friend. He turned as he heard her enter the room behind him.

"When was this picture taken?"

Paige walked further into the room and peered at the picture. "Right after Amy and I graduated from high school. We were having a family celebration. That's her parents' back yard and pool."

"Is that how long Alex has been in love with you?"

She gaped at him. "What? In love with me? Of course, he's not in love with me. He just thinks he is." She turned and walked into the kitchen.

He followed her, careful to not step on or get tripped by Finn. "Alex thinks he's in love with you?" The question came out sharper than he intended.

She closed the refrigerator door and set some produce on the counter before grabbing a bowl and a knife. "There are a couple hamburger patties in the fridge if you want to grab them and light up the grill."

He knew what she was doing but gave her a few moments. He went outside to light the grill. Leaving it to heat, he rejoined Paige in the kitchen. "So, you were telling me about how Alex isn't in love with you."

She turned to look at him and sighed. "It's not a big deal. Alex has been acting a little strange lately. He sent me flowers and then told me what my life would be like once we were together. Honestly, I thought he was kidding. Except he never kids." She ran a hand through her hair. "It's not like he got down on one knee and had a ring for goodness sake. How was I supposed to know he was serious?"

"And you said?"

"What do you think I said? I told him I don't return his feelings and left the party. I had a bad headache by then." She gave him a look that said she thought he might be a bit slow.

His forehead furrowed. "Help me out here. Alex asked you to marry him, and it wasn't a big deal?"

She resumed tearing lettuce for the salad. "Quinn, you have to understand. I've known Alex since I was born, literally. I have always thought of him as a big brother. Especially after my parents died, and I lived with his family. Alex is a Windsor. As in Windsor Falls. He has big, political aspirations. He needs the 'perfect wife'. Alex wants a 'partner'; his words. I'm not the right person. He's not looking for the love of his life. He and I view marriage differently."

"How do you view marriage?" He was dreading the answer, knowing what he'd hear. She would want everything he didn't want. Couldn't want.

"I'm fairly traditional. When I do get married, I want it to be forever. I want the person I marry to be my best friend as well as the love of my life. I want what my parents had. They loved each other from the moment they met until the moment they died. There was never anyone else for either of them. I want that. I'm not willing to settle for what Alex was offering me."

"What Alex is offering seems pretty posh. Lots of women would jump at it." What he didn't say was the other man clearly made way more than a firefighter. While he did okay, he was way out of Alex's league.

Paige put down the knife she had picked up to use on the vegetables with a loud thunk. "Is that what you think of me? I'd choose money over love? You don't know me at all if you do."

He had realized his mistake the moment the words left his mouth, but by then it was far too late. He placed a hand on her shoulder and tried to climb out of the hole he had dug. "I know you wouldn't. I should never have said that. I'm sorry. I know it's not a choice you would make."

She searched his eyes for a long moment before smiling. "Okay, then. The grill is probably ready for those burgers, if you don't mind. I'll bring out the plates and silverware."

"I'm off the hook?"

"What do you mean?"

"You forgive me, just like that?"

"Of course. Why wouldn't I? You said something you shouldn't have, and then you apologized. What else is there?"

He shook his head. "You're not like most women I've met."

She picked up the plates and headed for the sliding kitchen door. Over her shoulder she tossed, "Then obviously you've been hanging out with the wrong women."

"You may be right," he muttered to the empty room.

Chapter Eleven

They took their time eating, enjoying each other's company. Quinn watched her as she spoke, face animated, hands moving. She didn't do anything halfway. He loved watching her. She was the type of woman he could fall for, build a life with, if he was that man.

"Why so serious?"

He shook off those thoughts. "Nothing worth mentioning."

She smiled at him before gathering their dishes.

He stood and grabbed the salad bowl. He shook his head when she motioned him to stay. "I was raised right. My mother would skin me alive if I didn't help." He gathered their empty glasses. Walking to the door, he pulled open the slider for her and motioned for her to proceed inside ahead of him. On top of being chivalrous, he enjoyed the view.

"When do you work again?" Paige asked from across the room. Her back was to him as she rinsed their dinner dishes in the sink. He could stand there watching her all evening.

"I'm off tomorrow and then go back on Friday before having the weekend off."

She turned the water in the sink off. Turning, she reached for a towel to dry her hands. "Oh good. Have anywhere to be tonight?"

Everything inside him stilled. Including his heart. "No," he answered slowly and deliberately. "I don't have anywhere else to be." He took one step towards her, his eyes never leaving hers.

She threw the towel back onto the counter without breaking eye contact. Her smile called to him, lured him to the rocks like a siren. "Well then, what are you waiting for?"

He didn't need to be asked twice. Not wasting a second, he closed the gap between them and threaded both hands into her hair. Angling his head, he covered her mouth with his own. Like last time, the embers smoldering between them ignited.

She leaned into him, fitting her body to his. When she reached up to wrap her arms around his neck, her breasts molded to him. A soft sigh filled the air. He wasn't sure if it was hers or his. It didn't matter.

Encouraged by her moves, he backed her against the counter. Lifting her in his arms, he placed her on it and stepped between her open legs. He placed his hands on her thighs, enjoying the feel of her smooth skin.

She moved against him. "Wouldn't we be more comfortable upstairs?"

"We will be. Later. Right now, that's too far away." He lowered his mouth to the sensitive skin below her ear, nipping softly. When she gasped, he slid his hands up over her waist and under her shirt. His hands found her lace covered breasts. He felt the full weight of both before turning his attention to her nipples. Even through the material of her bra, they pebbled under his touch.

She threw back her head and moved on the counter. She gripped the edge with both hands. "Too many clothes," she muttered between clenched teeth.

"I can fix that." Releasing her, he brought his hands out from under her shirt. He grabbed the bottom edge and pulled it over her head. He sucked in a quick breath at the lacy bra he uncovered. Somehow, he hadn't expected it. The silky material was siren red, edged in lace against her velvety skin. The clasp nestled in between her breasts.

Using one finger, he traced the edge of her bra where it met her heated flesh. She sucked in a deep breath. He lowered his head and nibbled a trail along her collarbone and then down into the valley between her breasts. When he heard her gasp, he raised his head. His hot gaze seared her. With a quick movement, he flicked open the clasp, revealing her creamy breasts. Two hearts beating wildly was the only sound in the room.

Quinn leaned forward and flicked the pink, puckered nipple on her right breast with his tongue. She ran the fingers of both hands into his short hair, pressing his mouth harder against her breast. He rewarded her by scraping his teeth over the tightening bud. She released his head and gripped the counter until beneath her.

He raised his head and smiled at her before turning his attention to her other breast. A deep moan escaped her. The sound went straight to his groin. He needed more of her. He straightened and placed both hands on her backside, hauling her to the edge of the counter.

"You're still overdressed." Quinn placed his hands within the band of her shorts and pulled them down her legs before dropping them to the floor. She squirmed and made a motion to cover herself with her arms.

"Am I making you uncomfortable?"

"No."

A raised eyebrow was his only reply.

Red washed her cheeks. "Well, okay, maybe a little. Remember when I told you about my dating moratorium?" He nodded. "It's been a little more than two years since..."

"Since?"

"Since I've found myself in this position." Paige muttered something under her breath.

He tried very hard to not burst out laughing. "Did you say, 'shish kabob'?"

"Yes, I did. I told you I try not to curse to avoid doing it in front of my students." She tried to slide off the counter.

Quinn stepped in closer, trapping her with his body. "I'm sorry. I shouldn't have laughed. I'm surprised. You're a beautiful woman. I figured you had suitors lined up around the block."

"Well, other than Alex and Frank, it's mostly six-year-olds. They're always falling in love with me."

He brushed a hand down the length of her back. "We don't have to do anything you're not ready to do. Say the word, and we can sit on the couch and watch TV." Although he meant the words with every fiber of his being, he prayed she would not choose that option. He was already rock hard from touching her breasts.

She sucked in a breath and placed one small hand on his shoulder. "I'm ready. But I'm a little out of practice. I want this to be good for both of us."

Quinn's heart swelled at her words. She was worried about him? He took the hand she had placed on his shoulder and moved it to the front of his shorts. Her eyes widened. "Honey, put that thought right out of your head. I'm already enjoying this. Now tell me you're sure."

She smiled and nodded. He waited the length of a single heartbeat before leaning in and once again teasing her nipples with his mouth. He gave each equal attention and then planted kisses down her chest and abdomen, using his tongue in the indentation of her belly button. The small gasps coming from her encouraged him to move his mouth even further.

Gently hooking the edge of her matching red panties on two fingers, he eased them down to her knees. She was now fully exposed to him; his for the plundering. Giving her one last molten look, he lowered his head to the apex of her legs.

He darted his tongue into the very core of her. He flicked the small, tight bud several times, each eliciting a throaty moan from her. This was what he wanted, but he needed more access. He pulled back and effortlessly pulled her panties the rest of the way off her legs. Now with her legs free, Quinn nudged them apart wider. Crouching down, he slid one big finger inside her, bathing it with the wetness he found.

He glanced up at her. Paige was a goddess with her head dropped back and her honey-colored hair cascading around her. He grew harder by the moment. The feel of her internal muscles clutching at his fingers was almost enough to send him over the edge. He held on to his sanity with sheer will. There would be time later. He added another finger. Moving them faster, in and out, until he felt her fly over the edge.

"Hi there," he murmured when she opened her eyes again. Quinn enjoyed seeing the flush on her cheeks and a fine line of sweat right at her hair line. He had caused those.

She smiled, slowly and fully. "Well, hello yourself. That was, uh. I'm not quite sure how to complete that sentence. Why don't you pick a word?" She drew in a deep breath, her breasts rising and falling with the effort. Her opened bra still hung on her shoulders.

He grinned. "Amazing? Earth shattering? Fabulous? Should I go on? I could think of others."

She slid down to the kitchen floor in a slightly drunken manner, her legs a bit wobbly. She placed one finger over his mouth. "You could. Or you could come upstairs with me for round two. I think you're up." With those tantalizing words, she walked around him and out of the kitchen, heading for the stairs.

` Quinn hesitated for a moment while the full meaning of her words sunk into his addled brain. Gathering his wits, and her underwear, he chased after her.

*****

Hearing him in hot pursuit, Paige ran the rest of the way, beating him by mere seconds to the bed. She halted long enough to drag the opened bra off her arms and toss it onto the floor. Turning towards her bed, she pulled down the covers and sat down, patting the mattress next to her. "Come sit by me."

Stopping only to shed his shirt and shorts in record time, he did. The mattress dipped as his weight settled. He stretched out fully and pulled her down next to him, gathering her in his arms. Then he lowered his mouth to hers and kissed her. She could taste both him and herself in their kiss. Her toes curled.

Coming up for air, she pushed him down onto his back. "My turn to play." Raising herself up on to one elbow, she glanced down at his bare chest. She had imagined what he would look like without his shirt many times. The reality was so much better. He was in very good shape, with ridges of muscles throughout his chest and abdomen. His very distinct six pack made her think she should spend more time in the gym. A light covering of hair on his chest travelled downward, painting a trail that disappeared into his boxers. Her eyes widened when she saw the unmistakable proof of his desire barely contained in those briefs.

"I like it when you look at me."

The husky timbre of his voice went right to parts south. She reached out and traced one fingernail around his chest, tweaking a flat nipple.

His breath hissed. "Maybe we should move things along a bit."

She grinned at him. "Oh, I don't think so. You had your fun. Now it's my turn." The slender fingers of her left hand trailed from his chest to his abdomen, making the muscles she found quiver. She raked her fingernails back and forth across his abdomen for a moment, watching him writhe on the bed.

Pleased with his reaction, she slid her hand into his underwear and wrapped her fingers around the shaft of his penis. Glancing at his face, she saw Quinn had closed his eyes and his jaw was clenched, as if he fought for control. With a soft laugh, she moved her hand up and down his shaft. A harsh noise ripped from his throat.

With a growl, he pulled her hand out of his boxers. "I have a better idea." With those words hanging in the air, he flipped her onto her back and loomed over her.

"If you don't mind, I'll take it from here."

She reached across to the bedside table and opened the drawer. Grabbing a condom, she held it aloft like a trophy. "Need one of these?"

"Just happen to have those handy?"

"Don't worry, they're brand new. After all, I ended my dating moratorium."

After sheathing himself, he kissed her on the lips, stroking the flames of desire between them to a higher level. He slid a finger inside her, discovering she was more than ready for him. Quinn settled in between her legs, making sure the brunt of his weight rested on his arms on either side of her.

Her pupils dilated with desire. Tossing her head back and forth restlessly, she begged him. "Please hurry!"

He lowered his body until the head of his penis nudged her gently. She spread her legs further and wrapped them around his hips and lower back, silently begging him to enter her. He didn't hesitate, plunging into her hot, moist depths.

She felt the tension building but couldn't quite reach that place when he pulled back and entered her again, faster this time. He sighed aloud as she gripped him from within.

"Keep that up, and we're going to be done before we really started."

"There's always round two," she gasped, raising her pelvis to meet his next thrust. She dug her nails into his back, crying out in release. Their hips met in several more thrusts before he collapsed back on the bed, panting with the effort to breathe.

She heard a muffled 'wow' from the area of her left shoulder, where his head had come to rest. She took a couple of deep breaths before replying. "Wow doesn't even begin to cover it."

He started to shift his body off hers, but she stopped the thought by wrapping her arms around him, holding him to her. "Stay there for a few more moments, please."

He raised his head to look at her. "I wasn't going very far. Maybe three inches to the left. I don't want to squish you."

"I think I can take it for a moment more."

"There's nowhere I'd rather be."

They stayed as they were for several more moments before he kept his word and shifted off her and onto the bed. He gathered her in his arms, her cheek resting on his chest.

"What are you thinking? I can practically hear the wheels turning in your head."

"I was trying to decide if you would look better in a black or grey tuxedo." She laughed out loud at his answering gasp. "Gotcha," she cried.

He gathered her close and squeezed her, growling in her ear. "Funny, aren't you?"

"I was only joking. Don't worry. One night together hasn't made me set my cap at you." She turned in his arms, curling on her side.

"I knew you were joking."

She reached behind her and patted his chest. "Sure, you did. I won't hold it against you if you want to sleep in your own bed." Her voice drifted off at the end.

*****

Quinn watched in disbelief as Paige's breathing evened out. Within moments she was fast asleep. He lay on his back, staring at the ceiling. The sun had long set, and moonlight filtered in through the sheers on her windows. Her parting words were exactly what he wanted to hear. Weren't they? So why did his stomach ache? It was his practice to never spend the night. There was too much emotion involved. Sex was one thing. Sleeping together was quite another.

A beautiful woman had taken him at his word and begun a physical relationship with him, no strings attached. *Shouldn't he be ecstatic?* Then why was she asleep and he was lying in the dark trying to make sense of it?

He turned toward her and raised himself up on one elbow to better see her. Her blonde hair was spread out over her pillow like a silken fan, tousled yet alluring. She was wearing nothing but a corner of the sheet and moonlight. Reaching down, he smoothed back a chunk of hair that had fallen into her face and tucked it behind her ear. She stirred, and he held his breath, hoping he hadn't awakened her. But a moment later she settled down again.

Something in the moment scared him. Or maybe it reminded him of who he was. He wasn't the guy who stayed to watch a woman sleep. To protect her, and himself, he needed to leave. And right now. Paige was dangerous to him in a way she would never understand. He had understood from the moment he met her that she could be the one who could change his mind. If he was willing to do so.

But nothing else had changed. He was still a firefighter. He was still the twelve-year-old boy whose father didn't come home one day. He was still the man who would never cause that pain in a woman he loved. Knowing he wasn't willing to change his beliefs, Quinn did the only thing he could do. He got out of bed, found his clothing, and left.

Chapter Twelve

The early morning sun woke Paige long before she would have liked. She knew Quinn was gone before she even opened her eyes. She was sleeping when he left, so she had no idea how long he stayed. But her bed felt a little emptier without him in it. *Stop it.* She had started this, knowing all the rules when she did. There was no point in crying foul now.

Stretching, she smiled at the little aches she felt throughout her body. There were certain, long unused muscles protesting last night's events. Still, a twinge here and there was a price worth paying for mind blowing sex.

As much as she would have preferred to stay in bed and rehash the details of last night, a high-pitched howl from downstairs reminded her of other obligations. Finn had an uncanny ability to know the exact moment she was awake; no matter what the time. She hopped out of bed and threw on some old, comfortable clothing before heading downstairs to let her puppy outside.

An hour later, after eating a leisurely breakfast and asking Finn for advice on her love life, because that's what all twenty-six-year-old, sane women did, she took him next door. After much debate, and many small sample cans, she had chosen Summer Winds for her kitchen. The pale, buttery yellow was calming yet bright enough to cheer her on gray days.

Hitting the country music playlist on her phone, she cracked the first can. After months of steaming and scraping away the horror of the old wall covering,

Paige was pleased to finally make a difference. By the end of today, with a little luck, she would complete one room.

Hours later, she placed the paintbrush she was using in the tray and sat on the floor with her back up against the cabinets. *Who knew painting was so exhausting?* Not this girl. They made it look so easy on the million YouTube videos she had watched. But she was a rank novice. One whose arms ached. She smiled at what she had accomplished so far. The entire kitchen now had one coat done. It may not have been the most efficient job, and it was far from perfect, but she had done it herself.

This was where Amy found her ten minutes later.

"Amy! How long have you been here?" A chagrinned Paige struggled to get up off the floor, all kinds of muscles protesting now. After the second attempt, she decided the floor was fine.

Her friend pushed her designer sunglasses to the top of her head and perused the scene before her. She knew what Amy was seeing and laughed. She must be horrified. Debris littered every surface. Pale yellow paint speckled the drop cloth covering her table. And Paige.

Amy sat on a clean kitchen chair and looked at her friend. "You've had sex! You've had sex and didn't tell me about it," she accused with a smirk.

"Yes. Yes, I did," she crowed in response.

"I'm assuming it was Quinn."

"Of course it was Quinn. Who else would it be for goodness sake?"

"Just checking. So, how was it? I want all the juicy details. And I mean juicy."

She hesitated before answering. As much as she loved Amy, she didn't feel like sharing.

"I take it by your silence, you're not going to share. No worries. I didn't expect you to. Besides, since I'm also currently having the best sex of my life, I don't need you to do so."

Paige laughed. "So, you and A.J., huh?"

"To quote you, 'of course' it's Andrew. I'm not a slut."

"You like him! If I wasn't so tired right now, I'd get up and hug you."

"I love him." This came in a serious tone, new to Amy.

She stared into her friend's face and saw the truth written there. "Yes, I see you do."

"Mama always said I would know. I never understood, but she promised me it was the truth. She knew about Daddy the instant she met him." Amy's eyes held a new softness to them. Her friend was a beautiful woman who was used to, and bored by, men falling at her feet. Paige had not predicted A.J. being the one who was different.

That was enough to get her up off the floor. She leaped up and hugged her friend, practically dragging her out of the chair. "Oh, I'm so excited for you! What color will I be wearing?"

"Well of course you'll be wearing peach. Haven't we been planning this since we were six years old?" The two best friends hugged and laughed about this.

They had indeed been talking about their respective weddings since they were children. Amy, being a member of the town's founding family, would have a huge splashy wedding at her parents' home. There would be a bazillion attendants, all wearing peach, and Paige as her maid of honor. Paige, on the other hand, had always described a small, intimate affair with close friends and family. Amy would be the sole member of the wedding party. The color had changed a million times, but the location had not. The ceremony would have to take place in her beloved Blue Ridge Mountains.

"How does A.J. feel about all of this? Has he met your family?"

Amy lowered her eyes. "Uh, not exactly."

She nodded. She got it. Being a Windsor, in Windsor Falls, came with a certain responsibility. Although Paige was not a Windsor by blood, she had been raised as one since age twelve. She knew all about the pressure.

"I guess you haven't told Alex about A.J."

"What do you think?"

She grimaced in response. "Don't get me wrong. You know I love your family, including Alex. But he is a bit of a snob."

"'A bit' is being generous. I love Alex. But I am not blind. He is very wrapped up in 'being a Windsor'; much more than my parents are. He's going to have a fit."

"Yes, he is. I know because he and I already had this conversation about Quinn. Back before there was a conversation to have. You'll handle him. I'm not worried. And your parents are down to earth and want you to be happy. But does A.J. know?"

Amy's smile fled. "Yes. No. Maybe? I'm not sure." She threw up her hands. "He knows my last name of course. The rest of it never came up."

'The rest of it' was a tidy trust fund in the millions and the responsibility that went along with being a member of the founding family. While none of this stuff mattered to Amy, sadly it mattered to others. She had suffered many a suitor who was more interested in her family name, and its money, than in Amy herself.

Amy tossed her blonde hair over one shoulder. "I don't think he'll care. He's not like that."

"Good to hear. You've always been able to see people for what they are. If you say A.J. is okay, then he is."

"Oh, he's more than okay. But that's not what we were discussing. And you know it." Amy laughed and pointed her finger at Paige. "We were discussing Quinn. I can't believe he changed his mind so quickly. But then again, if anyone could change it, you could."

She held up her hand. "He hasn't changed anything, Amy. He was honest and up front. He doesn't want a long-term relationship. He never wants to get married and have kids. I'm not wearing blinders. This relationship between us is about the present and having fun. The mind-blowing sex is a bonus."

"And you're okay with that?"

"Yes." If the word felt like a lie, she'd learn to live with it.

"Really? Because it doesn't seem like you."

"Maybe, this is the new me. Anyway, I said I wanted to have some fun this summer. Who better to have fun with than a hot firefighter? You of all people can understand."

"Oh, I understand. But it's a lot more than fun and games for me. And I'm afraid it is for you as well."

"You're right of course. This isn't me, not even a new me. But I like him. I tried staying away. He tried staying away. It didn't work for either of us."

"As long as you know what you're doing." The doubt in her voice hurt Paige's heart.

"I'm not stupid. I know this won't end well. He has been more than clear from the beginning. It was my choice to accept those terms or not. I chose to live a little and see how it goes."

"I hate to say it, but this sounds like a recipe for hurt. I worry about you."

"I know, and I'm so thankful. Intellectually, I know this is a bad idea. I know I should end it now and be satisfied with one amazing night. But I can't."

"That part I do understand. I couldn't walk away from Andrew at this point. Maybe Quinn will…" She stopped at the look on Paige's face.

"Please don't say it. He will not change his mind. And I'm not going to try to change it. This was my choice. When it's over, we both walk away. No hard feelings."

"So, what's next for this place? I like what you've done so far."

A weight was lifted from her shoulders with the change in conversation. "After today, I'm almost ready to take up Alex on his offer to pay someone to do it. I had no idea how hard this would be. But it's okay. I have the whole summer. And it will be so worth it. I'm more than a little tired of living in a construction zone."

"I can imagine. This would drive me crazy! If I was living here, I would have hired someone to do it all at one time while I was away on an island somewhere." She wrinkled her nose, making Paige laugh.

"You would. Luckily for me, I don't mind a little dirt and disaster. The prep work is done. I've chosen most of the colors. I'm still not sure about my bedroom and bathroom, so I started painting down here."

"I may not agree with how you're doing it, but I know the result will be fabulous." Amy gathered her keys and purse and stood up to leave. "And now I'm off to meet Andrew."

"Having dinner?"

"After dessert," her friend replied, a wicked gleam in her eyes. "I've been shopping."

Paige smirked. They shared a love of sexy lingerie. Amy was a bit more adventurous than she. "Lucky A.J.! He'll never know what hit him. Have fun."

"Oh, we will." With a last wave, Amy left the house.

She groaned as she surveyed the disaster. While she enjoyed the conversation with Amy, she never should have stopped working. Glancing at the clock, she realized she only had a few minutes before she was due to pick up Finn from next door. She closed the paint can and washed the brushes. She moved the puppy gate and Finn's water bowl to the laundry room to avoid having a paint covered dog. She was too tired for anything else tonight. She would change clothes, pick up Finn and collapse on the sofa with leftovers and a movie or good book.

*****

The muscles in Quinn's arms quivered with effort. He squinted against the burning as sweat poured down his face and into his eyes. He was out of sorts today, making all sorts of mistakes at the house. A brutal workout might clear his mind. He placed the bar on the rack and breathed deeply. But the hairs on the back of his neck stood at attention. Someone was watching him. Glancing around the room, he spotted A.J. lounging in the doorway of the station's gym. Not in the mood for polite conversation, he ignored his friend and got back to it.

A.J. strolled over to the weight bench and looked down. "You should have a spotter when you lift."

Knowing A.J. wouldn't leave, he completed one last repetition before placing the heavy bar on its rack. He stood up, grabbing a towel to wipe the sweat off his face, before addressing A.J.

"Was there something you wanted?" He tried to not wince at the harshness of his tone. He had been in a peculiar mood ever since leaving Paige's bed the other night.

A.J. smirked. "Someone's in a foul mood this morning. Maybe you should try getting some. It's good for whatever ails you."

"Are you telling me Amy has fallen for your smooth lines already? She seemed smarter." He added a little smirk of his own.

"You know better. I already told you. I'm going to marry her."

"I know what you said, A.J. But, I didn't take it seriously. You met her like a minute ago."

"Have I ever said this before?" The joking tone was gone.

Quinn wiped his eyes and took a long, hard look at his friend. "No, I can't say you have. Have you asked her yet?"

"No, not yet. I'm waiting for the right time and place to give her this." A.J. produced a small velvet box from the side pocket of his gym bag. Quinn didn't need to look inside to know what was in there, but A.J. popped the lid anyway. A single diamond set in gold winked at him in the overhead light.

"I'm not sure what to say, A.J."

A.J. closed the box and secured it back in his bag. "I was hoping for congratulations from my best friend. Too much to ask, I guess." He left the room without another word.

He hurled the sweaty towel into the hamper. A.J. had every right to be angry. But he was having a tough time being happy for his friend. A mass of contradicting thoughts ran full speed around his head. He had never been able to get past his conviction you can't have it all. If you chose to be in this profession, you didn't get to have a family as well. But he also knew very few shared his opinion.

Walking into the locker room, he stripped off his soaking gym clothes and stepped into the shower. He shampooed his hair and thought about A.J. and Amy. Of course, he wished them well. But he couldn't help feeling terrified for them. Did Amy have any idea what her life was going to be like married to a firefighter? He doubted it.

He finished and turned off the shower, reaching for a towel. Jealousy ate at him. He wanted what A.J. had. That thought immediately led to ones of Paige. He couldn't keep the image of her asleep in her bed out of his mind. They had shared an incredible passion; one he had never felt before. He should be thankful and walk away. He never should have started down this path with her. He knew better. Yet he couldn't seem to help himself.

The next morning, Quinn drove the engine back to the station. They had finished up on an accident scene involving several cars. The injuries were minor, with no one requiring medical care. Since his thoughts were centered on a certain woman, he was lucky the job had been minor.

"Are you going to tell me what's wrong? Or do I have to guess?"

Startled out of his thoughts, he glanced at A.J. in the passenger seat. "I have no idea what you're talking about." He turned his eyes straight ahead, concentrating on the road.   "Really? You've barely spoken to me other than on the scene."

He tried not to wince at his friend's words. He knew he was being a jerk today, and it wasn't A.J.'s fault. He blew out a long breath and loosened his grip on the steering wheel as they came to a red light. "Yeah, sorry. I'm a bit off today."

At his friend's raised eyebrows, he smiled for the first time. "Okay, more than a bit."

"Care to share your feelings with the group?"

He burst out laughing at his ridiculous friend. "Been watching Oprah reruns again? You know we warned you."

The two men laughed aloud in the cab of the engine. The light turned green, and Quinn moved through the intersection.

"I may have gotten myself into a situation I shouldn't have."

"Oh? A situation? What does that mean?"

He blew out another breath before continuing. "I told Paige I would never get into a long-term relationship. She said she understood. I was honest with her. Yet, somehow I still feel like a jerk."

"Why do you feel like a jerk? Did I miss something?"

"I started a relationship with her even though I knew it wasn't a good idea. She's not like the other women I've dated. There's something fresh and open about her. She says she understands, but I don't think she does."

"Wow! You used the 'R' word. You never use that word. You don't have 'relationships'. You have sex with women who get the rules from the start. Why is Paige different? And notice I'm being a gentleman and not asking for all the gory details."

"There's something about her. She's sweet and adorable yet hot at the same time. She teaches kindergarten of all things. And she's funny and irreverent and doesn't take herself, or me, too seriously. She's like the first day of spring; sunny and open. Just being with her makes me happy."

"Is that a bad thing?"

"One day I will ruin all I love about her."

"I don't know how to get through to you. It doesn't have to be true. I believe firefighters can have a normal family life. If I didn't, I wouldn't be about to ask Amy to marry me."

"You're never going to 'get through' to me. It's how I feel. It's what I know. I'm not going to change. I wish you luck, but it will never be me."

"Never say never."

"I just did!"

"So back to the original topic. What happened?"

"I went over to her house, knowing I had no right to be there. And then I stayed for dinner. We had a great time, and I could still have done the right thing, but I didn't. Couldn't."

They reached the station house, and Quinn swung the huge engine around and backed it on to the apron. Now was a good a time as any to clean the truck. It would take hours of labor. Perfect for keeping his mind off Paige.

He jumped down and headed into the station to stow his bunker pants and jacket. He stripped down to shorts and a tee shirt for cleaning detail in this heat.

He was not surprised to find A.J. on his heels when he went back outside, dragging a hose with him. He started wetting the truck as his friend peppered him with more questions.

"When was this?"

"Two nights before our shift. Why?"

"Hmmm. So, you had dinner. And then you stayed. What happened in the morning? Was she making demands you weren't ready for?"

"There wasn't any morning after," Quinn bit out.

"How could I forget? You never stay. You might give a woman *ideas*."

"That's right. You know I don't. I'm honest from the start."

"Oh, you're honest. To a fault. So, what's different this time?"

"I wish I knew."

"How was it when you talked to her again?"

He could feel the warmth creep up his neck. There was no need to answer.

"You haven't spoken to her since? She hasn't called? Texted?"

"No." Quinn was more than a little embarrassed to think about the number of times he had checked his phone. He wouldn't be mentioning that little fact to A.J.

"Sounds to me like everything is normal. This is how you roll. Yet you've never been so miserable about it."

"Get the silly look off your face. There's no reason to be pleased at my expense. This doesn't mean anything. It doesn't change anything."

"You keep telling yourself that." A.J. slapped him on the back and walked back into the station, leaving him alone with his thoughts.

Well, hell. A.J. brought up all this stuff and then walked away. There weren't enough hours of physical labor to keep thoughts of Paige at bay. He cursed and started the long task.

Chapter Thirteen

Sunday morning, Paige let herself back into her home after dropping Finn next door. At this rate, Carly would be able to buy herself the new bike she had been talking about and anything else she might want. But the money spent was well worth it. Trying to paint with Finn's "help" was not an option.

She looked around the first floor. She had gotten a lot accomplished. The kitchen was done, and she had moved everything back into place. Her critical eye caught a few small flaws, but overall, she was pleased with the effect. She had transformed the room into a warm and cheery area.

She had also managed to finish the living room, although she still needed to paint the ceiling. She had chosen a soft blue for this room. The old, dusty curtains had been the next thing to go. Without anything on the windows, natural light poured in. Eventually she would pick new ones, but for now she enjoyed the daylight.

Despite the physical labor, she had not managed to put Quinn out of her mind. She missed him. She tried not to, but there it was. Thanks to Amy, she knew he had worked Friday and had the weekend off. After that, she had no idea of his schedule. She wondered what he was doing.

A knock sounded at the door behind her, and her heart gave a brief, wild leap. Even though she was sure it wasn't him, she couldn't help wishing she'd find him on her porch. She opened the door to find Amy instead. She swept into the house, grinning from ear to ear. Before she could say hello, Amy thrust her hand into her face. Her left hand. A gorgeous diamond winked at her in the light.

Amy jumped up and down, squealing, so Paige joined in. This went on for a little while before Paige picked up Amy's hand to view the ring more closely.

"He did good."

"Yes, he did. I know I should say the ring doesn't matter." A grin lit her face. "But I'm not going to lie. After all, I am the one who will be wearing this every day for the rest of my life."

"Absolutely right." She looked at the ring again. "He knew what to pick, Amy. This ring is exactly what I would have said to get."

"So, you had nothing to do with this?"

Paige shook her head. "I would tell you if I had. This was all A.J. Good for him!"

The ring was sleek and modern in design, which reflected Amy's style. The diamond was a marquis shape and probably well over a carat in size. It was beautiful and sparkly all on its own, not needing any further adornment, also like Amy.

She was beyond thrilled for Amy. But a pain settled in around her heart. There wouldn't be any happy ever after for them. Shaking off the gloom, she returned her friend's grin. There would be time for those thoughts later.

"So, have you set a date?"

"Not an actual date, but we discussed a fall wedding. I may have to rethink the peach dresses for a more autumnal color." Tears streamed down Amy's face. She laughed through her tears. "I'm a mess!" The words were no more out of her mouth before she burst into sobs.

She led her friend to the couch and pushed her down. Placing her arms around Amy, she held her and rubbed her back. "What's wrong?" Amy was tough, not a crier.

Amy pulled back and made a sound, half laugh, half hiccup. She swiped at the black mascara pooling under her eyes. "Note to self. Waterproof mascara for the wedding."

"Okay, now you're rambling. Please tell me what's wrong."

Amy took a deep breath. "I love him, in a way I never thought I could love someone. I know it's corny, but I knew. The second I met A.J., I knew he was the one I didn't even know I was waiting for."

"Wow, Amy, I'm so happy for both of you. But what's with the tears?"

She sighed and wiped at her eyes again. "I'm so happy about marrying him. In fact, I'd do it today. But he hasn't met my family yet. They don't even know there is an A.J. Mama's going to kill me!" She broke off on another wail.

Paige continued to rub her back. "She is not going to kill you. She may be a bit surprised." Amy pulled out of her embrace and stared. She laughed at the look of incredulousness on Amy's face. "You're right, she's going to be very surprised. But she's also going to see how much you love each other."

Shaking her hair back from her face, Amy blew her nose. "You're right of course. She's going to be fine. She'll see how much I love him, how much he loves me, and she will be fine."

"So why don't you look less worried?"

"I don't want to do the whole 'Windsor thing' anymore. I don't want to invite three hundred people, when only seventy-five of them mean anything to me."

Paige had grown up on the fringe of being a Windsor in Windsor Falls. She knew what Amy meant. "There's a lot of pressure being you."

"Exactly! I knew there was a reason you're my best friend. I don't want a huge fancy wedding. I'm fine with getting married at my parents' home, but I want it small and special. More than anything, I want to be married to A.J. Am I crazy? We barely know each other."

"No, Amy, you're not crazy at all. You want what you want. You and A.J. should decide on what kind of wedding you want and then tell your mom and dad. Present everything to them. You're engaged, and this is the kind of wedding you want."

"Just like that?"

"Your family loves you. They only want what's best for you."

"I wish they had already met A.J. It would make this so much easier. But we have been so caught up in being together. There hasn't been much time for the outside world."

"Your parents are going to understand. They fell in love the moment they met. They also watched my parents do it. They're going to be okay with this. I know it."

Amy wiped the last of the tears from her face. "Even though I want a small, intimate wedding, you will still be my maid of honor, right?"

Paige squealed and hugged her again. "Of course!"

"I'll talk to A.J. and get things settled between us and then bring him to dinner at my folks. You'll come, right?"

"I don't think you'll need me, but I'm happy to be there."

"It's not about *need*. I *want* you there. I'll call you with the details." She hugged Paige one more time before leaving.

She spent the next two hours working harder than she ever had in her life. Painting a ceiling was brutal. Her arms ached from trying to hold the extended roller above her head for so long. She was balanced on top of the ladder, resting the offending brush and her tired arms when she heard a knock at the door.

"Door's open," she called from her perch. She had her back to the door and didn't bother to look, assuming it was Amy again. She felt a tingle down her spine. It wasn't Amy. She grimaced at her appearance.

Quinn walked into her house. "Hey."

She smiled down at him. "Hey, yourself. What brings you by today?"

"Well, I figured you could use some help. And I haven't talked to you since..."

"Since we had sex."

He grinned at her. "Yes, we haven't spoken since we had sex. I wanted to see how you were. I wanted to see *you*."

She stayed where she was, afraid she would throw himself into his arms if she came down off the ladder. She had agreed to this arrangement, but it was harder than she imagined.

"If you're serious about helping, then absolutely. Ceilings suck!"

He laughed out loud. "Did you curse? I thought you didn't do that?"

"I generally don't. But ceilings do suck!"

"Yes, they do. How about you work on the trim, and I'll finish it for you?"

She groaned. "Yes, please. My tired arms thank you." She handed him the brush and climbed down the ladder, muscles complaining the entire way.

"Feeling your age?"

Paige stuck out her tongue. "Age? I believe you have a few years on me. But I'm feeling something, and it's not pleasant." She stepped off the bottom step and stopped to stretch out her cramped muscles, head to toe. She finished and turned to find him looking at her with a funny expression on his face. "What? Do I have paint on my nose?"

He shook his head, closing the distance between them in a few small steps. Standing almost on top of her, he reached down and caressed her jaw with both hands before lowering his mouth to hers. In the last second before he did, she watched his brown eyes darken to almost black. She stood on tiptoe to close the gap.

Once again, the flames of desire roared. The light clothing they both wore frustrated her. She wanted to feel his skin pressed to hers. Bunching her fists in his T-shirt, she pulled it up and over his chest, exposing the broad plains of muscled flesh. She broke the kiss and moved back a step to remove his shirt completely. Looking around the living room, she remembered removing all the curtains. That wouldn't do. Not for what she had in mind.

"How long do you think it will take us to get upstairs?"

"Not long," he answered and scooped her up. He headed for the stairs, taking them two at a time. They reached her bedroom in moments. He leaned in for another searing kiss before letting her slide slowly down the length of his body. Their skin burned with the intimate contact.

"You still have your shirt on. That hardly seems fair." His voice had both lowered and roughened, sending warm tingles across her skin.

"Easy enough to fix." With lazy, deliberate movements, she grasped the bottom hem of her shirt and raised it slowly upwards, exposing skin as she went. She pulled it over her head and tossed it onto the floor, revealing a silky, blue bra.

He reached for her, but she stepped to the side. She grabbed one of his wrists and led him to the bed, pushing him not so gently down on the mattress.

He moved to the center of the bed and stretched out on his back. "Is this where you want me?"

She let her eyes wander the length of his gorgeous body and smiled. "That will do for now."

The heat in her eyes left no doubt of her intentions. She sat next to him and picked up one hand. Turning it over, she placed the smallest of kisses in his palm before raising his arm over his head. She did the same for the other. Both of his hands now rested against the wrought iron of the headboard.

"Not planning on tying me up, are you?"

"Now what fun would that be? If I tied your hands, then you wouldn't need any control. No, I want you to keep them there because I asked you to do so. I want you to lie there and enjoy."

Without waiting for a response, she leaned in and kissed him. She didn't hold anything back. Her tongue traced the outline of his firm lips before dipping into his mouth to tease his. It felt very erotic to be kissing him so deeply without any other area of their bodies touching.

She deepened the kiss further until small moans filled the room. She wasn't sure who made them. After a few moments, she broke the kiss and trailed her mouth down his jaw planting tiny kisses as she went. She nipped the sensitive skin under his jaw, causing him to fist his hands around the spokes of the head board.

Paige sat back, letting her eyes wander the length of him. "Getting to you, am I?"

"You know you are. You always do. Look further south, and you'll see exactly how much you 'get to me'."

She turned her head and did as he asked. He was only wearing a pair of cargo shorts, and the material was stretched trying to contain him.

He shifted on the bed and started to move his hands down.

"No, you don't. I'm just getting started with you."

He growled low in his throat. "I'll get my turn too you know."

She gazed at him and with a purely feminine smile replied, "I'm counting on it."

She raked her nails over his chest before focusing on one nipple. She lowered her mouth to suck on it. Encouraged by the noises he made, she scraped her teeth over the nipple. It puckered under her attention. She turned to the other nipple to do the same.

Satisfied she had his full attention, she slid down his body, darting her tongue into his naval. The wiry hair tickled her nose. She followed the trail of dark hair to where it disappeared into his shorts. The front of which was now tented.

Paige struggled with the button before getting it opened. She eased the zipper down, taking care to not scrape him with it. Quinn lifted his hips to help her. She pulled the shorts off him, leaving only the soft cotton of his boxers between them. She slid her hand under the band and cupped the length of him. She was rewarded by his quick hiss of breath.

She smiled at him. "Like that do you?" She drew his boxers down over his hips, freeing him. His erection sprang to life. She gently traced one finger around the swollen tip, spreading the drop of moisture beaded there.

His hips moved on the mattress. His hips pushed into her hand. A muttered oath sprang from his lips.

She took this as encouragement and continued her torture. She never broke eye contact as she lowered her head toward him. He stilled, and she closed her lips around him. His body tensed. She smiled then took his entire length in her mouth, inch by inch. His hips raised off the bed even as his breathing grew harsh.

"I think you can agree I've been very patient." Without waiting for an answer, he grabbed her by the upper arms and flipped her onto her back.

Quinn reached into the bedside table to grab a condom. He tore open the packaging with his teeth and started to sheathe himself, but Paige's small hand on his wrist was enough to stop him.

"Let me." She was a little clumsy but got the job done.

When he was fully covered, he stretched out beside her and placed one large hand on her knee. "I hope you appreciate how compliant I was. It wasn't easy for me." His hand flattened over her thigh and moved upwards. Her flesh heated everywhere he touched her.

"Oh, I do. I know it was *hard* for you."

"You're about to find out how hard." His fingers crept higher, pausing at the curly hair. He looked into her eyes and slid a finger into her.

"Please." She lifted her hips off the bed and ground her pelvis into his hand.

"Relax. It's my turn now."

Relax? Was he crazy?

Quinn raised up on one elbow, continuing to tease her. He now moved two fingers in and out at a maddeningly slow pace, as if he had all the time in the world.

Paige clenched the sheets on either side of her and moaned. She had started this game, but it was a lot easier when you were not on the receiving end. But, oh, how wonderful it felt. The tension built higher and higher within her.

"I need you. I need you in me now."

"Nothing would make me happier." He knelt between her quivering thighs. Nudging them further apart with one knee, Quinn entered her with one, fast stroke.

Eyes locked on hers, he pulled back and plunged in again and again. Her eyes drifted closed. "No, honey, keep them open. I want to see you."

She opened her eyes and saw his face above hers. He panted as he plunged into her warm depths once again. She lifted both legs and gripped him, driving his shaft even deeper into her. The sensation was overwhelming, and she tumbled over the edge. She gasped as sensations raced through her, almost too much to bear. She clenched him from within, dragging him with her to completion.

His breathing was ragged, but he smiled. He collapsed onto the bed next to her. She trailed her fingers down his chest, clinging to the warm, slightly damp flesh. She loved the feel of him but feared he would feel smothered. He was clear about his intentions.

He rolled to his side. He got up and walked into the bathroom. Much to her surprise, he walked back into the bedroom and got back into the bed with her. Lying on his back, he pulled her tight against him and pillowed her head on his shoulder.

Paige didn't say a word but enjoyed the closeness. She wasn't going to risk anything by pointing it out. Instead, she snuggled down close to him. "Well, that went okay."

"Okay?"

She giggled in response. "You're right. It was probably more like not bad."

"Well, if was only 'not bad', then I guess I'll have to try harder." She shrieked as he pounced on her. Those were the last intelligible words for quite a while.

A long while later, she pushed the damp hair off her face. He disappeared into the bathroom. She stared at the ceiling, watching the fan whirl. This was the closest to perfect her life had ever been. If the person making her so happy was anyone other than Quinn, she would be complete. But he wasn't going to be her happy ever after. She would have to settle for happy right now.

The man in question came back into the bedroom and glanced down at her. "In my humble opinion, we blew 'not bad' out of the water. Any better, and I'd be dead."

"Ditto."

"Well, I worked up an appetite. Why don't we go grab some dinner?" Very unselfconsciously, He moved about the room picking up various items of his clothing and putting them on.

Paige envied his confidence. While she was in decent shape, considering her binge eating of Pop Tarts when stressed, she wasn't anywhere near his level. Sighing aloud, she got out of bed and walked into the bathroom to clean up. She tried to walk at a normal pace and be subtle about it. She failed.

"You do know I've seen every inch of you, right? Tasted most of them too. Surely, you can't be shy now."

"I'm not shy," came her muffled reply from the bathroom.

"It seemed like it."

Another few muffled words escaped, drawing him to the open doorway. "What did you say?"

She averted her eyes and mumbled something again, this time into the towel she was holding.

He reached out and spun her towards him. "Try telling me so I can actually hear you."

With her face flaming, she stated, "I said I'm not shy. I'm just not as confident as you are. There. Are you happy now?"

Quinn placed one hand under her chin and tilted it up to look at her directly. "You are beautiful. Don't ever doubt it."

She tried to duck her head, but he wasn't having it. "I'm serious. Tell me why you don't know this already."

Because she had always been brutally honest, both with others and herself, she answered him. "Gee, where would I start? My thighs are larger than I'd like. I've battled with the same ten pounds forever. Basically, I need to be a bit taller for my weight. Then I'd be perfect." She laughed to try and cut the tension.

"I wouldn't change a thing about you. You're beautiful; inside and out."

Paige stared at him. And felt her heart thunk inside her chest. When he looked at her that way, she felt beautiful. "Thank you. Every day I tell myself I'm going to run or go to a gym, but it never seems to happen. Somehow there's always something 'more important' to do." She glanced down at his perfect body. "You obviously make the time."

"I do, but I don't enjoy it like some of the guys at the station do. I run and work out regularly because I must. If I can't handle the physical challenge of the job, someone could die. Also, we have an amazing weight room in the station. I work out when we have down time."

"That's convenient. I know myself better though. When I have down time, I'm watching some DIY show on TV, not going for a run."

"You could always go running with me, if you wanted."

"Nice of you to offer, but I wouldn't want to slow you down." She moved around him to her dresser, opening a drawer and picking out fresh, matching lingerie. She dressed as quickly as she could, throwing on a sundress over the lingerie. She turned to see him watching her with more than a little heat in his eyes.

"Are you trying to kill me?"

"Kill you?"

"I'm going to die of malnutrition because we are never getting out of this room." He lunged towards her.

Paige held up her hands up in defense. "Oh no. You promised me dinner. Dessert is for later. Let's go."

Chapter Fourteen

Quinn took her to The Smoke Pit for barbeque. Paige shared his love of hole-in-the-wall restaurants with great food. Another point in her favor, not that she needed any. They sat and laughed and ate until he thought they would both burst. For a tiny woman, she could eat. He loved this about her. Nothing annoyed him more than taking a woman out to dinner and watching her pick through a salad all night.

"So why teaching?" They sat sipping sweet tea, neither in a hurry to leave.

"My mom was a teacher. She loved her students so much." A dreamy expression came over her face. "And they loved her right back. Mine wasn't the only art work gracing our refrigerator when I was young."

"Do you like what you do?"

"I love it. The kids are adorable; for the most part. There are always one or two terrors, but the rest make up for it. I like teaching young children. I feel like they're a clean slate when I get them. I have a chance to make a difference."

"I'm sure you do."

"What I didn't understand before I started was how much more than teaching is involved."

"What do you mean?

"There are so many other issues. Some of my kids come from broken homes or those with very limited income. I have hungry kids and kids who are not as clean as they should be. Others come wearing clothing that doesn't fit or has holes in it. It breaks my heart."

He knew she didn't let those issues go unnoticed. "So, I imagine you find a way to help."

She reached up and toyed with a lock of her hair. This was a tell for her. "I do what I can."

"Let me guess. You feed some. And maybe you donate clothing to others. Am I right?"

"Yes," she said on a sigh. "You're right. I can't *not* do anything. I make sure there is always food in my classroom closet along with extra clothing. A lot of them are gently used items I collect from friends with kids. Wearing clothes that fit right and aren't torn or dirty raises their self-esteem. It's the least I can do." She cleared her throat.

Quinn got it. It was how he hated being called a hero. Paige did what she could to help and was happy to do so, but she didn't want anyone drawing attention to it. He changed the topic to lessen her discomfort.

"So, it looks like we will be going to a wedding soon."

She leaned forward and grinned. "I know right! Were you as shocked as I was?"

"It does seem very quick. However, A.J. did tell me he intended on marrying Amy after their first date."

"What? You mean at Smitty's?"

"Yep. He told me at work the next day."

"What did you say?"

"I don't remember, but probably something like 'You're crazy.'"

She rolled her eyes at him. "Of course you did."

His eyebrows raised at her tone. "What does that mean?"

"Well, you've made it very clear how you feel about marriage, so…"

"So, what? Just because I'm never going to get married, doesn't mean I can't be happy for my best friend. And I am happy for A.J. And for Amy of course as well. But I do think it's a bit quick. Don't you?"

"I did have some concerns. It hasn't been very long. But when I hear Amy talk about A.J. and see how happy she is, I know it's right."

His lips tightened. "I think they're rushing things. Why does it have to be this Fall? It feels forced"

"I know you don't get it, since you're not planning on getting married. But Amy has met the person she wants to make a life with. And she wants their life together to start as soon as possible."

"This has nothing to do with how I feel. But let me ask you. Would you feel the same way?" Acid churned in his stomach while he waited for her to answer. He was afraid to hear. One day, and probably not too long from now, she was going to wake up and realize he was not the person she needed. And even though that was his plan all along, it still hurt to think of her with someone else.

"I don't know, since I haven't been in her situation. I do know this. My parents fell in love the moment they met. And so did Amy's parents. They both had wonderful marriages. Her parents still do. So maybe how long Amy and A.J. have known each other has nothing to do with anything."

Well, hell. He had nothing to say to that. "Okay, that's fair, I guess. I still don't think it's a great idea."

Paige drew a hand through her hair. "You've made your feelings very clear. Maybe we can agree to disagree. But do me a favor please. Don't share your opinion with either A.J. or Amy. They're happy, and they deserve to be." Her voice held a slightly chilly note.

The waitress brought the bill. Quinn reached for it and his wallet at the same time, wondering how this night had gone to hell so quickly. He threw down enough money to cover the bill and a tip. "Are you ready to go?"

"Yes." She picked up her purse and placed the strap over her shoulder.

He stepped back and motioned her to proceed him. "Would you like to go to a movie?"

"No thanks. I'd rather go home if you don't mind."

"If you're sure." The short drive to her home strained his nerves. Before long, he pulled up in front of her house. She got out of the car as soon as he stopped, not allowing time for him to come around and open her door. She was pissed.

He hurried to catch up with her, walking her to her door. "I'm sorry." He wasn't sure what he was sorry for. All he had done was express his opinion. Women!

She smiled, but it didn't reach her eyes. "Thanks for dinner. I'll see you."

He didn't want the night to end this way. He spun her around and backed her into the wall. Without warning, he covered her mouth with his and pressed his body up against hers.

After a long moment, he lifted his head. "I want you to remember this about tonight. Not a silly argument." He walked away into the darkness.

*****

Pressing a less than steady hand to her trembling lips, Paige watched Quinn go. She stood there long after the roar of his truck silenced. Only Finn's yipping from inside the house roused her. Sighing, she unlocked the door and went inside to get the puppy.

Always ecstatic to see her, Finn covered her face in doggy kisses when she scooped him up and carried him out to the back yard. She sat in a patio chair and watched as Finn ran puppy circles around the yard, searching for just the right place to relieve himself. *If only life were so simple.*

Dinner had been going so well. Until the topic of Amy and A.J. came up. He could deny it all he wanted, but his views on the subject were skewed by his own opinions on marriage. Yes, it was quick, but they were in love. Why couldn't he be happy for them?

She knew why, and it darkened her mood further. Another painful reminder of how stupid she was for getting involved with him. This could only end one way, and it involved heartache for her.

Finn threw his small body against her legs. She shook off the gloomy thoughts and picked up the puppy. She held his soft, wiggling body to her, a shield against the chill she felt inside. They had spent most of the day together. She would learn to be happy with that.

*****

Quinn pulled up in front of Aidan Fitzgerald's home and shut off his truck. Not sure he was in the mood for poker night, he sat in the darkness for a moment. *What had just happened?* One minute they were having a fun time at dinner, then everything went to hell. Shrugging off his black mood, he got out of the car and walked up the sidewalk. He stopped and looked at his friend's home. Built of wood and stone with plenty of windows, Aidan's home fit perfectly into the woods surrounding it. But then he was an architect in a family of builders. He wouldn't expect anything less.

He could hear the animated conversation within before he even opened the front door. This was what he needed to cheer him up. Take his mind off Paige. He knocked once on the door before entering, not that they would hear him. None of his friends stood on formality.

"Hey! I thought you weren't going to make it tonight." Aidan stood and came around the table, clapping Quinn on the back. "What can I get you? Beer or a beer?"

He laughed, glad he had decided to come. "I'll take a beer, thanks." He approached the table, taking a seat between Sam Bishop and A.J. "Hey, Sam, I didn't expect to see you. How's the baby?" He had met the other man over a decade ago, when Sam had been involved in a horrific crash with Connor Fitzgerald, who had been married to Elizabeth at the time. Sam had sustained serious injuries, while Connor had died on impact. The tragedy had bonded the two men.

Sam's grinned. He whipped out his phone. "Never ask a new father that question."

He took the phone and scrolled through dozens of pictures of the newborn Gabriel. "He's adorable. How is Elizabeth holding up?"

"Great! I don't know how she does it. She insists on getting up with him every time since she's off for a few months. Even insisted I play poker tonight."

"She was getting rid of you," snickered Donovan. "Let me guess. Charlie was coming over. We have three kids. Been there, done that. She's telling Charlie how you're doing everything wrong."

Sam's face fell. "She does give me that look sometimes."

Donovan nodded before gathering the cards and shuffling them. "No worries, man. Just another rite of passage. You have it worse, being married to a doctor."

He took a pull from his beer. "I'm just happy to see you. Thought you'd be too busy changing diapers." The other men laughed, and he joined in, tamping down the ache in his chest. An image of a pregnant Paige flashed through his mind.

Another round of laughter and good-natured ribbing ensued. Donovan gathered the cards and shuffled before dealing them all another hand. "Speaking of domestic bliss, don't you have anything to share with the group, A.J.?"

His gut tightened. This was exactly the topic he didn't want to discuss. This had ended his dinner early. He pasted a smile on his face and turned to his friend.

"I do indeed," A.J. responded. "Amy has agreed to be my wife."

Cheers and more than a few comments on his 'impending doom' followed. Coming here had been a mistake, but Quinn couldn't leave now without raising a few eyebrows. He joined in the congratulations.

A.J. took all the ribbing in stride, smiling and laughing along. "Say what you will, but the most beautiful woman in the world is going to marry me. Nothing you say can ruin my good mood."

Several hands later, he excused himself and walked into the kitchen. He grabbed a beer from the fridge and turned to see Aidan looking at him.

"What, do I have something in my teeth?"

"More like something stuck in your craw. What's up with you tonight? You seem off."

He liked Aidan, but he wasn't in the mood to bare his soul. "Just tired I guess. I've been putting a lot of time into finishing the house."

The other man nodded. "If you say so."

"I do. Let's go join the game. I'm feeling lucky." He grinned and wished his words were true. Thinking of how the evening with Paige had ended, he was feeling anything but lucky.

*****

Paige looked in the mirror one last time and smoothed an imaginary wrinkle from her sundress. Glancing at her watch, she realized she was, once again, running late. She couldn't even blame early morning this time. With a final pat to Finn, she grabbed the bunch of flowers sitting on the hall table and walked outside to her car.

The drive to the Windsor home only took a few minutes. Most things were a short drive in Windsor Falls. Just one of the many things she loved about her hometown. Tonight, Amy's family would meet A.J. She was along for moral support if needed. She had tried to persuade Amy to at least mention the engagement to her mother ahead of time, but Amy wasn't having it.

A week had passed since the doomed evening with Quinn. She hadn't spoken with him. She had made a lot of progress on her home. Amazing what frustration did for motivation. She was pleased with the way it was turning out. She had finished the living room and moved on to her bedroom, skipping the downstairs office. She was anxious to get the area completed.

The only down side to painting was, although it was physically taxing, it didn't take much mental prowess. It left way too much time to think about him and their situation. She tried to remember how the conversation about Amy and A.J. had spun out of control so quickly. She had her opinion. He had his. That should have been the end of it. But she feared it hit a little too close to home and brought up the situation between them.

She was falling in love with him. She knew it, dreaded it, and yet was helpless to do anything about it. He wasn't going to change his mind about them. If anything, their ridiculous fight certainly showed his resolve. He was exactly who he told her; someone unwilling to commit. When he broke her heart, she'd have only herself to blame.

She turned into the circular driveway of her childhood home. It was time to put on her big girl panties and get over herself. Tonight was about Amy and A.J., not her. It would do her good to remember. Plastering on a smile she didn't feel, Paige got out and walked up to the front door. Before she could reach for the handle, Susan Windsor came out and engulfed her in a hug.

"Hello, honey! It's so good to see you. Come in."

She returned the hug and walked into the house. Despite its size, the home was warm and welcoming. She had been happy here after her parents' death. Her mother's childhood friend was the next best thing to having her own mother back.

She handed the flowers to her. "These are for you."

Susan accepted the flowers and exclaimed over them. "Oh, irises! My favorite! How lovely, Paige."

"Well, of course I know they're your favorites. You only mention it every birthday, anniversary and every other national holiday."

The two women shared a laugh. "I certainly do. I know what I like and am not afraid to ask for it."

"Another of your many wonderful qualities."

Susan led the way into the kitchen. Paige looked around fondly, remembering all the hours she had spent here doing homework in her teen years. The room was warm with a huge table around which they had gathered for so many meals. There was a formal dining room as well, but she found it stiff. It was only used for holidays and dinner parties. This room was the true heart of the home.

"How many hours do you think you spent trying to teach me to cook in this room?"

The older woman turned and smiled at her. "Oh, probably far too many to count."

"Too bad none of those lessons stuck."

Susan laughed and came toward Paige, placing a hand under her chin. "I wouldn't say that. You can feed yourself, can't you?"

"True. I have survived on my own cooking. But I only make the simple stuff. Everyone raves about your Chicken Pot Pie and homemade gravy. I've never been able to master either."

"It takes patience and practice, and sadly you lack at least one of those."

"Also, true. I don't have the patience to spend the hours that you do in the kitchen. And because I don't, I sorely lack in practice as well."

"Even as a young child, you were always flitting about, afraid you might miss out on something."

"Guilty."

"You are also the warmest, happiest person I know. Especially considering how much you've lost in your young life. You light up a room and make others around you feel better just being in your presence. Yours is a real gift."

Paige grimaced thinking about this very conversation she had with him. Despite their similar losses, they held very different views on the world. That difference, her ability to risk her heart and his refusal to, would ultimately be her undoing.

"Was it something I said, dear?"

She thought about faking a smile but knew the tears brimming in her eyes would give her away. "Oh, I've done such a stupid thing." Hot tears slid down her face.

Susan rushed in and gathered her in a hug. After a few moments, she led her to the table and pulled out a chair for her. "Tell me what's troubling you."

She was horrified by what she had done. She brushed at the tears on her face and thanked the heavens above for water proof mascara. "Today is not the time. Today is about Amy, and she and A.J. will be here any second."

"Nonsense," Susan scolded. "She isn't here yet, and you have a few minutes to tell me what's making you so unhappy."

She shifted in her chair. "I'll give you the Cliff's Notes version. I fell for a man who is emotionally unavailable. What makes it worse, and me even more stupid, is he warned me from the very beginning." She sniffed, fighting off the next wave of threatened tears.

"Oh, Paige, I'm so sorry. But loving someone who isn't right for you doesn't make you stupid. Just human." She reached out and stroked the younger woman's shoulder.

"Well, human or stupid, it still hurts." She squared her shoulders. "But today is about Amy. What can I do to help?"

"Well, you could set the table if you want. Everything you need is in the dining room. I would have loved to eat outside, but it's hotter than you know where out there today."

"Agreed. I'm happy to do that for you. Besides, I like A.J. I'd hate to poison him with my cooking." She laughed and walked towards the formal dining room. Looking back over her shoulder she glanced at the woman who had given her so much over the years.

"Thank you, Susan, for everything."

"No thanks needed, dear. Okay, enough mushiness. Tell me about A.J."

She was saved from answering by the opening of the front door. Amy swept into the kitchen with her usual imitation of a tornado, looking both cool and chic. Paige rushed over and hugged her best friend.

Amy pulled A.J. by the hand, dragging him to her mom. "Mom, this is Andrew. Everyone else calls him A.J. Andrew, this is my mom, Susan Windsor."

A.J. stepped forward and handed Amy's mother a bouquet of irises. Both Susan and Paige burst out into laughter, leaving the others in the dark. The confused looks on their faces made the two women howl even harder.

After a few moments, Susan composed herself. "A.J., I'm so sorry. You must think I'm terribly rude. I am sure Amy told you that irises are my favorite flower.

I'm not shy about it. Paige was kind enough to bring me some as well." She turned and pointed to the vase in the center of the gleaming mahogany dining room table.

A.J.'s smile faded.

"A woman can never have too many of her favorite flowers. I'm so pleased to meet you. Welcome to our home. Amy's father should be right back. He ran to pick up something for me. And Alex, Amy's brother, should also be here soon. Paige, why don't you take A.J. into the family room? I placed some drinks in there on the bar. Amy, will you help me with the salad?"

She murmured her agreement and led the way into the hall. She glanced over her shoulder and grinned at Amy. Her friend was about to be grilled. "So, A.J., I haven't seen you in a while. How have you been?"

A.J. grimaced, running a finger around the inside of his shirt collar. "Great. Until now." He leaned into her and lowered his voice. "You know Amy's family well, right?"

"I should, since they raised me from age twelve onward."

"Oh, right, I forgot. Are they going to like me?"

She took pity on him. The poor man's skin was almost green. "Anyone can see how much you love Amy. And how much she loves you. Be yourself."

The sound of voices and the front door opening and closing broke into their conversation. Paige poked her head out of the room at the noise. She turned back to A.J. "I guess we're about to find out."

He took a deep breath. "How bad could it be?"

"I'll give you a hint. Being a Windsor in Windsor Falls has its plusses and minuses, from what I've seen. Amy's parents are pretty laid back and don't get caught up in all of it. Her father wants her to be happy, and he will side with his wife."

A.J. looked a bit reassured, but his relief was short lived.

"Alex, her brother, is another story. He's very concerned with appearances. He's going to be pleasant but superficial because he doesn't believe a firefighter is good enough for his sister. Alex is a bit of a snob. He means well but can be narrow minded. Luckily for you, Amy isn't."

"Well I knew when I fell in love with a woman whose family founded this town, my background might be an issue. We love each other. We'll figure out the rest."

"So, you must be Andrew." Alex came into the study, a scowl marring his handsome face. Paige gave A.J. a look that said, 'I told you so.' She gave A.J. credit for not flinching.

A.J. crossed to Alex and stuck out his hand. "And you must be Alex. Amy has told me so much about you."

Alex hesitated, staring the other man down, before shaking his hand. "Funny, she hasn't mentioned anything about you. Why do you suppose that is?"

"*This* is exactly why, Alex, and you know it!" Amy stalked into the room, eyes blazing, and stood by A.J.'s side. Placing her arm through his, she faced Alex. "You will behave, Alexander."

"Yes, you will Alex," came the booming voice of Amy's father, Michael.

The elder Windsor had a presence that had more to do with his personality than his pedigree. "Andrew, I'm Michael Windsor, Amy's father. But you can call me Mike." He extended his hand.

"It's a pleasure to meet you sir. Please call me A.J.." He shook Mike's outstretched hand.

A.J. cleared his throat. The pallor on his face made her nervous. "Sir, things happened a bit backwards, and I take responsibility for that." He took hold of Amy's left hand, raising it for the family to see. "I regret not talking with you before asking Amy to marry me."

Anything else he might have said was drowned out by the collective exclamations of her family. Only Alex was notably silent. Amy's mother hugged and kissed her and then A.J. Paige felt relief this was finally out in the open. She could only imagine how Amy felt.

Mike smiled, transforming his rugged face to handsome, and slapped A.J. on the back. "Water under the bridge son. Welcome to the family. Why don't we go grab a drink, something a bit harder than tea, while we wait for dinner?" He led

A.J. and Amy to his study while Alex trailed after them. Amy turned and stuck her tongue out at her brother.

She sighed. "That went well!"

"Yes, it did," agreed Amy's mother. "I suppose you already knew?"

"I'm sorry. I begged her to tell you. She was nervous for some reason, not sure y'all would approve of A.J."

Susan dabbed at her eyes. "I'm so pleased for her. Just a bit surprised since it all happened so fast. Mike needed to see Amy was serious about this guy. He knows she has a good head on her shoulders. Alex, however, is..."

"Alex. Eventually he will come around when he sees his sister loving a firefighter won't ruin the family name."

Susan shook her head. "Sometimes I think Alex wishes we lived on a huge plantation in the 1800s. He's so focused on 'being a Windsor', whatever that means."

The two women moved back into the kitchen. Paige agreed with Susan's description of her son. Alex believed things should be a certain way. Of course, he meant *his* way. She giggled thinking about his issues with Quinn.

"What's so funny?" asked Susan.

She debated for a moment then decided to tell her. She described the rather bizarre conversation between her and Alex about 'his intentions'. She expected Susan to laugh as well. She didn't.

"So, you never knew then, all those years?"

Paige's mouth fell open. "You did? I had no idea. I hope you know I would never hurt him."

"Of course, you wouldn't, darling girl." Picking up pot holders, she removed a baking dish from the oven. "Alex has always been very reserved, different than Amy. Alex keeps his cards close to his chest. But I've known, probably since you girls were seventeen or so, how he felt about you."

"How did I not know?"

"Because he never said a thing, and you were busy being a teenager, as you should have been. You can't help who you fall in love with, honey. The heart wants what it wants." A serene expression crossed her face. "My grandmother used to say that. It's for the best, dear. You and Alex would not be a good mix."

"Oh." She turned away to hide the hurt Susan's words caused.

The older woman took one of Paige's hands in her own and squeezed. "Nothing would make me happier than the two of you being married. If you were right for each other. But you're not. You are far too open and warm for Alex. I love Alex more than life itself, but sometimes I wonder where he came from. He's so closed off to emotions, especially love."

"I tried to explain that to him. I want a crazy, messy love. He seemed horrified and tried to assure me I don't."

Susan laughed. "That's my Alex! I believe one day he will meet his match, and she will change his mind about love." She smiled. "In fact, I'm looking forward to it. Poor Alex thinks he can control whom he loves. Enough talk! Let's eat. We have some celebrating to do. Will you bring everyone to the dining room and send Amy in to help please? By now, she probably needs a break from Alex."

Several hours later, she was back in her car returning home. The night had been a success. Even stick-in-the-mud Alex had been cordial. He loved Amy, so Paige was confident he would come around. She sighed thinking back on the evening. She wished, not for the first time, things were clear cut for herself and Quinn. She turned on the radio and began to sing along to a pop hit. Wishing for things that could never be was pointless. And painful.

Chapter Fifteen

Quinn sat on Paige's front porch swing and thought about all the ways he was a fool. The list was depressingly long. Right now, she was having dinner with Amy's family. He had A.J. to thank for this bit of information. She hadn't spoken with him since the night their dinner ended badly. She hadn't asked him to accompany her.

He sighed and set the swing in motion with his foot. The night was hot and muggy, but the motion of the swing brought a small breeze. Alex Windsor was at the dinner. *He should be at dinner.* Going to it with Paige, and meeting her surrogate family, is what a boyfriend would do. What someone in a relationship would do. Wasn't it? That's not what he wanted. *Or was it?*

And there was the issue. Did he want to be with Paige or just *not* want Alex to claim her? He had been trying all along to keep her in a little box in his mind. She was someone with whom he hung out from time to time. Someone that he had sex with. She wasn't someone with whom he had a relationship. Was she? And he didn't want one anyway. Did he?

He dragged a hand through his hair. It had always been so clear with the other women in his life. They kept him company, but they never got too close or became too important. He flinched thinking about it. Was he that guy? Is that what he still wanted? His best friend was right now meeting his new fiancé's parents. Did he wish for that with her?

The questions warred with the memory of his father's death. Even so many years later, he could picture the devastation on his mother's face. He could remember the exact moment he realized his father was never walking in the front door again. Why would he ever want to risk putting her through it?

He didn't have any answers. But he couldn't go on treating Paige the way he was. She was a beautiful woman with a lot to offer. Any man would be lucky to have her in his life. She wasn't going to settle for what he was offering for very long. His reverie was cut by the sweep of her headlights in the driveway. Quinn stood and walked to the edge of the porch, waiting until she got out of the car and calling out to avoid startling her.

Paige turned at the sound of her name. "Hi."

The uncertainty in her voice cut him to the bone. He had no one to blame but himself.

"How was dinner? Did Amy's dad and brother give A.J. a hard time?"

She stepped up on the porch and walked to the door. "I have to let Finn out. Why don't you come inside? I'll tell you all about it." As she placed her key in the lock, the small dog could be heard yipping from the kitchen.

They went inside, and Paige walked through to the kitchen, scooping up the puppy. As always, he tried to cover her entire face in kisses. She laughed and opened the back door to let Finn out. Quinn figured he'd sunk low when he was jealous of a dog.

"Would you like a drink?"

She seemed sad and unsure of herself. He had done that to her. He cleared his throat. "I'm sorry."

"What are you sorry for?"

He tried not to grin. Of course, she would not make this easy for him. "Well, I'm sorry about the other night and how it ended. I don't want to argue with you." He took a deep breath before continuing. "And I'm sorry for how I've been treating you. You deserve better."

She gripped the counter with both hands. "I missed you tonight. I kept thinking you should be there with us. With me. But then I remembered we don't have that kind of relationship." She smiled, but it didn't reach her eyes.

"What if I wanted it to be?"

"Do you? Because I'm not sure if you're asking me or yourself."

"You know the reason I feel the way I do about relationships. It hasn't changed."

"Then why are we even having this conversation?"

"I don't know." He dragged a hand through his hair. "Nothing hasn't changed except I miss you. I've never missed anyone before." He waited for the panic to set in at his own words, but all he felt was relief. He had told her how he felt.

She smiled at him. She seemed about to say something when Finn yelped from the other side of the kitchen slider. She turned and let him into the house. Finn made a beeline for Quinn, pouncing on his feet.

"Hey there, little man." He picked up the puppy and tucked him into his arms. He rubbed Finn's speckled face. "Have you been taking care of Paige for me?" Finn barked as if he was answering.

She laughed then emptied and then refilled Finn's water bowl. She got a dental chew out of the pantry for him. Taking him from Quinn's arms, she put him behind his gate to settle him in for the night.

He watched her, wondering what she would do or say next. He was hanging by a thread with her. All his own fault.

She was dressed more formally tonight than he had ever seen her. She was wearing a sleeveless summer dress but no shoes. He noticed she had kicked those off as soon as they had entered her house. Her wild curls were gathered in some complicated way on the top of her head. But even with several pins, wayward strands had escaped on either side of her face. He reached forward to wrap one around his finger.

She took his hand and led him to the stairs. Without a word, she ascended them, pulling him along after her. At the top, she turned and walked into her bedroom. No lamps were on, but the moon bathed the room in a soft, white light. She flicked on the overhead fan.

Quinn turned to face her. "Are you sure?"

"I've missed you, too."

It was all the answer he needed. He covered her mouth with his and drank greedily. She was warm and soft and tasted faintly of berries. He deepened the kiss, twining his tongue with hers while he buried his hands in her hair.

She moaned, pressing her body against his. Then she broke the kiss and took a step back.

He watched her move to the dresser. "Should you be so far away?"

She grinned at him and took decorative pins out of her hair. "These look pretty, but they don't feel so good when they jab you."

Her arms were raised to her hair, and their movement pulled the material of her dress tightly across her chest. Quinn took advantage. Tugging his shirt off as he crossed the room, he stepped behind her. With her arms still raised to her hair, he turned her to face the Cheval mirror in the corner.

He placed his lips on her neck, nibbling the soft skin. She drew in a quick breath. Never breaking the contact of his lips on her neck, he reached around with his left hand and cupped her breast. Through the thin, silky material of her dress, he teased her nipple to full attention.

Their eyes met in the mirror. He splayed his right hand across her belly and then down to her hip. He dragged the hem of her dress slowly upward until it was bunched around her thighs, giving him access to the soft skin he found there.

He nipped her ear lobe with his teeth, biting down with just enough force to elicit a cry from her. She stopped removing the pins from her hair and dropped her head back, arching her neck. She moaned as his hands worked their magic.

"Open your eyes, Paige," he commanded. "Watch what I'm going to do to you."

She did what he asked, watching in the mirror as he slid his hand up her thigh to the edge of her panties. But he didn't stop there. Her skin flushed with warmth.

"You're going to like this." He slid his hand over the brief material. He could feel how moist she was. He hardened at the sensation, his erection nudging her from behind. She moaned louder, and he slid one finger under the band of her panties and stroked her curls.

"Please, Quinn."

"Tell me what you want."

Her eyes met his once again in the mirror. "I want to feel you, all of you, inside of me."

"Anything for you." He slid one finger deep inside of her, coating himself in the dampness there. Slowly he moved his finger in and out, foreshadowing what would follow.

She moaned louder and moved her hips in time to his finger and then gasped as he slid in another.

Quinn withdrew his fingers and pulled her panties down her thighs, giving him more room. The brief scrap of material slid to the floor. He palmed her mound and once again inserted his finger, teasing the small, sensitive bud. At the same time, he pulled down one strap of her dress and slid his other hand under her bra, cupping her bare breast. He teased the nipple, rolling it between his thumb and finger.

She tangled her fingers in the hair at the base of his neck and arched her pelvis further into his hand. She closed her eyes tightly. Her knees quivered.

"Open your eyes. You're almost there. I want you to see what I see."

She did as he asked. He stroked her harder and faster, pulling a cry from her throat. She shook in his arms as the orgasm ripped through her. Quinn continued to hold her to him in front of the mirror. "Don't ever doubt yourself again. You are a beautiful woman."

He spun her to face him and kissed her with all his pent-up longing. Watching her reach those heights almost sent him over the edge. The need to bury himself inside of her was almost painful.

He backed her to the edge of the bed and broke the kiss. He smiled at the satisfied look on her face. He hooked a finger under the other dress strap, lowering it off her shoulder. At the same time, Paige reached out and opened the button on his cargo shorts. She lowered the zipper, reached inside, and brushed her hand over the hard ridge of his erection.

He placed his hand on her wrist. "Careful. Too much and I'll never make it inside of you."

She grinned and removed her hand. She took a step to the side. With a little wiggle, the material slid down her body and pooled on the floor at her feet. She was standing in only her bra.

He removed his shorts and briefs in a single movement. His erection sprang forward and nudged her belly. He reached between her breasts and opened the clasp of her bra, freeing them. Her breasts were the perfect size and firm with pink nipples begging to be kissed. He leaned in, teasing first one and then the other with his tongue.

"Hurry. I want you with me this time. In me."

His eyes darkened to melted chocolate. "I'm right here with you."

Paige pulled the duvet down to the bottom of the bed. She reached into the drawer of her nightstand and pulled out a condom. She tossed it at him, hitting him in the chest.

"I like the way you think." He tore open the foil and sheathed himself.

Quinn watched her get into the bed. She lay on her back in the middle, her glorious hair spread across the pillows. She was more than ready for him. He kneeled between her open legs and kissed first one thigh and then the other. He trailed his lips to her very center and teased her with his warm breath.

"Hurry! I want to feel you inside of me."

The plea in her voice was all he needed. He lowered himself and thrust inside of her in one move. He felt her muscles quivering around him. Paige raised her hips and opened her legs wider, and he sank in all the way. The fit was perfect. Reaching down, he gathered her close to him and rolled onto his back. She rode him, her breasts high and her hair flowing around her shoulders.

She gave him a sultry smile. He grew impossibly hard with the friction between them. He thrust his hips upward to meet hers. He placed both hands on her breasts, caressing them and teasing the nipples.

Paige quickened her pace. Her breathing grew erratic. With a final cry, she spiraled out of control.

Quinn thrust one final time before bursting inside of her. He pulled her down gently until she became a blanket on top of him. The ceiling fan whisked, drying the sweat from their cooling bodies. Their breathing was the only sound in the room.

After a few moments, she made a move to slide off him. Quinn stroked his hand up and down her back, keeping her in place. "Give me a minute." She lay her face on his chest.

"I missed this, too." He murmured into her shoulder.

"It's only been a few days."

"Doesn't matter." He could feel her smile against his chest.

"Let me go get rid of this." Quinn gently slid her off him and down to the bed. He walked into the bathroom and disposed of the condom. After cleaning up, he rejoined her in bed.

She stirred and smiled at him sleepily. "You're like a drug. I can't get enough, but then you knock me out." Her voice trailed off near the end.

He gathered her close and pulled a sheet over the two of them. He stroked his hand lightly over her skin as her breathing deepened. She burrowed into his chest and sighed. "Hmmm, nice. I wish you could stay."

Her words haunted him. She was stating a fact, not asking for what she wanted. He knew it was because of him. Paige was a woman who always went after what she wanted, but he had put up roadblocks.

He lay in the darkness and continued to stroke her skin long after she fell asleep. He felt comfortable, content even. The thought of leaving her tore at him. He had never felt the urge to spend the night with a woman. But she wasn't any woman, as he was beginning to understand.

Defying everything he believed in, he slid further down on the pillow and wrapped her in his arms a bit more tightly. Staying one night wouldn't kill him. His eyes grew heavy, and he closed them. He breathed in her scent, a mixture of light citrus, musky sex, and something uniquely her. He could get used to this.

*****

Paige came awake by degrees and realized something was different. She opened one eye and saw Quinn sprawled on his back next to her. She smiled. Against all odds, he had stayed. She took advantage of the situation and allowed her eyes to roam.

He was a beautiful man, although she was sure he would prefer the term rugged. His shoulders were broad and heavily muscled. His chest was lightly covered in hair that tapered down to his waist. Well defined muscles outlined his thighs and calves. Nothing about him was little.

He stirred, and she held her breath. She longed to trace every inch of him with her hands, but she was reluctant to wake him. She didn't know when she would have this opportunity again. As much as she loved waking up with him, he probably wouldn't share the feeling.

Sighing, she got out of bed. She walked naked into the adjoining bathroom and turned the shower to as hot as she could stand. Her muscles ached from their lovemaking last night. She stepped into the steamy shower and reached for her shampoo as she wet her hair. She hummed to herself, happiness bursting from her very pores. Last night had been amazing. She tingled all over as she remembered the sight of them in her mirror. She had hardly recognized herself. She wasn't shy about sex, but she had never been quite that wanton either. Seeing his hands on her, touching her in ways she had dreamed of since meeting him, had been a fantasy come true. Even remembering it now made her grow wet between her legs.

The shower door opened, and he joined her. She smiled at him. "I was just thinking about you."

His cocky grin answered her smile. "Were you now? What were you thinking?"

"I was remembering watching us in the mirror last night."

"I take it you enjoyed that."

"You know I did. A lot." She reached for the shower gel and poured some into her hands. "Let me show you how much."

She rubbed her hands together to lather the soap. She started with his broad chest, spreading her hands over it and washing every inch. Quinn groaned and widened his stance as if to brace himself. She reveled in the power she held over him.

"Am I doing this right?"

He took one of her hands and moved it lower. "What do you think?"

Her smile promised heaven. Without a word, she dropped to her knees on the tile of the shower and placed her mouth over his tip. Flicking her tongue against it, she reveled in the shudders racking his body. He backed up against the wall and placed his hands on her shoulders, kneading the soft flesh. A groan ripped form his throat as she took more of him into her hot, wet mouth.

She sucked before releasing him then ran her tongue along the length of his shaft and cupped his balls in her hand, squeezing.

He grasped her upper arms and attempted to raise her to a standing position. But she stayed where she was. Tilting her head back to look him in the eye, she smiled. "Relax and enjoy." With those words, she placed her mouth back on him. He threw back his head and groaned.

This time she didn't resist as he raised her to her feet. The air had grown steamy from the hot water and heat between them. Paige reached between them and wrapped her hand around him. His muscles tense. With a few strokes, he groaned and came in her hand. The water continued to rain down over them.

"That was a hell of a thank you."

"I wanted you to know you were appreciated."

"A person could get used to this."

She didn't answer. She loved the time they were spending together, but she knew better than to count on it. She smiled at him and then reached around to shut off the water. He followed her out of the shower.

"Did I say something wrong?"

She handed him a towel. "I can't allow myself to 'get used to this'." She tucked a towel around her and left the bathroom.

She stood in her walk-in closet under the pretense of finding something to wear. In reality, she was hiding from him. Giving herself time to recover. She was having a hard-enough time keeping her emotions out of this thing between them. She wasn't interested in trying to change him. But when he casually threw out such statements, what was she supposed to think?

Paige had entered this *thing*, whatever it was, knowing he would never commit. This was supposed to be a fun, summer *thing*. But Amy had been right. She wasn't built for casual flings. She sighed and blindly reached for a pair of shorts and another of her endless T-shirts.

Grabbing a set of underwear, she pulled on her clothes before returning to the bathroom to deal with her hair. She found Quinn still standing there, staring into the foggy mirror.

"The exhaust fan needs to be replaced. It may be out of my area of expertise."

"I could do fix it for you."

"I might take you up on that." She reached for a hand towel and swiped the mirror to see. Ignoring him as best she could, she flipped her hair upside down to brush it before securing the wet strands into a bun. Her hair was not meant for North Carolina humidity. There was no point in trying.

She glanced at him. "Do you want something to eat?"

"Sure, thanks. Whatever you're having is fine."

What she wanted was a whole box of Pop Tarts, preferably Chocolate Fudge. The tension was think enough between them to cut. However, he didn't strike her as the Pop Tart kind.

"Eggs and toast okay?"

"Great. Let me get dressed." His tone did not encourage conversation.

Paige turned and left the room, nearly running down the stairs. She was greeted by a happy Finn. At least she an uncomplicated relationship with one male in her life.

After letting her puppy out into the backyard, she raided the refrigerator. She tried to shrug off her bad mood. He was still here. That had to count for something. She would enjoy the time they had before he left.

Quinn walked into the kitchen, dressed in his clothes from last night.

She stood at the stove, singing with the radio as she made eggs. "I went with scrambled since it's all I know to do with eggs. Despite years of Susan trying to teach me, I'm a terrible cook. Could you put some bread in the toaster please?"

"I'm assuming Susan is Amy's mother." He put four slices of wheat bread in the toaster and then turned back to face her.

"Yes. She's an amazing cook, and Amy never had any interest in learning. I had all the interest in the world but no actual talent. It's not unlike my singing. More enthusiasm than ability. Breakfast is ready."

She busied herself with putting food on the table. When they were seated, she looked at him. "I'm sorry for my behavior earlier. You threw me a bit."

"There's nothing to apologize for. I shouldn't have said that to you."

"Here's the thing. You have to be honest with me. I already accepted your ground rules for this." She waved her hands between them. "This thing we're doing. I need you to stick to it. Otherwise, the lines blur. Am I making any sense?"

"Of course, you are. And you're right. I should be more consistent. I will be in the future."

"Okay then, I'm glad you understand." There were so many other things Paige wanted to say. Like she was afraid she was falling for him. But she remained silent. He wouldn't want to hear that.

"So, what are your plans for today? More painting?"

"Maybe later. I'm going to take Finn for a drive to my favorite place." She didn't add her favorite place offered her comfort and a chance to think clearly. She needed to figure out what she was doing with him.

"It's good to take a break. Get some fresh air."

They finished their meal, talking only about safe, neutral topics. He got up when she finished and took her plate.

She protested. "I've got this."

"No worries. I'm used to much worse at the station."

The past half hour had nearly killed her. They had been reduced to senseless small talk, while the tension pulsated between them. As much as she hated to see him go, she couldn't stand this anymore.

He must have felt the same, for he picked up his keys after finishing their few dishes.

"I'm going to go now. Lots of work to do on my house. Have a nice time on your ride." He leaned down and kissed her cheek before leaving.

Paige stood there, watching him go. She wanted so badly to invite him along with her and Finn. But she needed some time alone to think. She put a couple bottles of water and Finn's travel bowl into a tote bag and grabbed her purse. Finn's ears perked up at the sound of her keys. He wagged his tail and looked longingly at her.

"Yes, Finn my dear, you get to go bye byes."

Hearing the phrase, the small puppy raced around her feet, almost tripping Paige. He yipped and wagged his tail.

"Okay, settle down before you kill me."

She clipped on his leash and headed out, locking the door behind her. The day was gorgeous, even if it didn't match her mood. Maybe the brilliant sunshine would make her feel better. She tried to feel optimistic about her situation as she backed out of her driveway.

Chapter Sixteen

Quinn drove home thinking about his night with Paige. Everything had been great until he had to open his big mouth. Hurting her was the last thing he wanted to do. But waking up with her had felt so right. And that feeling blindsided him. He'd never spent the night with anyone before. When he had made the comment, it was more like he was saying it to himself than her.

He understood where she was coming from, even if he didn't like it. He was the one who had set the ground rules. He was the one who insisted this could never be permanent. He was the one throwing her off balance with his mixed messages. Yet she went along with it, and he felt even worse about things.

Not once had she placed any pressure on him. She wasn't trying to change him. She was true to her word. She certainly had the right to insist he stick to his side of the bargain. So, why did it feel wrong?

He shook his head. If A.J., or worse yet Jack, could see him now, they would think he had lost his mind. Paige offered him the perfect deal; mind blowing sex without any strings. What man wouldn't jump at the opportunity? *Why did it leave him feeling a bit sick to his stomach?*

Disgusted with himself, he turned on the radio and tried not to think. He had a long day of work ahead of him. His current project was almost done and ready to be put on the market. He wanted to finish up some things today. Gabriella

Rivera, the realtor he had listed with in the past, was scheduled to come by next week for a preliminary tour of the property. He hoped to list it soon.

Several hours later, he was sweating profusely, and swearing as much. Laying the hardwood flooring in the living room was tough work. He hated to put in flooring. It was never as easy as you thought it was going to be. But it had been therapeutic. He kept thoughts of Paige, and their situation, at bay. For the most part.

Quinn looked up at banging on the front door. Throwing down his work gloves and wiping the sweat from his face, he opened the door to a grinning A.J. He wasn't sure he was in the mood to hear how wonderful things were, but that was life.

"Hey, man!" He forced a smile. A.J. didn't deserve to be the target of his bad mood.

A.J. stepped into the house and looked around, giving a long low whistle as he did. "Wow. You've gotten a lot done since I was here last. This looks great!"

"Thanks. I'm a little behind, but I plan on putting in a lot of hours in the next week or so. I should be ready to list it soon."

A.J. shook his head. "Are you ever going to have an actual home?"

He tried not to grind his teeth. "Haven't we already had this conversation? A million times?"

"I know, I know. I still don't get it."

"There's nothing to *get*. I buy homes. I fix them. I move on to the next. I make good money doing it. You know this."

"I understand that part of it. I don't get why you don't want a place of your own to live."

"I live here, A.J. And I'll live in the next house."

"But it's not the same as having something more permanent."

Quinn shook his head. "There's no point to this conversation. You and I have a different idea of what home is."

A.J. grinned at his friend. "Enough said. So, what are you doing October 15th?"

He laughed out loud. "I have no idea. What are you doing October 15th?"

"Marrying the love of my life. I was hoping you'd be my best man."

Pain sliced through his chest. Pushing it aside, he grabbed A.J. in a bear hug. "Of course I'll be your best man! I'm honored."

Relief showed on the other man's face. "Great! I wasn't sure what you'd say."

"Why wouldn't I want to be there with you?"

"Well, we all know how you feel about marriage."

"Exactly. How *I* feel about it. I don't expect to share my point of view." He still thought his friend was making a mistake, but he'd keep it to himself. "So, things went well with her family?"

"They did. I'll admit, I was nervous about going. But they couldn't have been nicer. Well, most of them anyway."

"Let me guess. Alex wasn't warm and fuzzy."

A.J. arched a brow. "You know Alex Windsor?"

"I wouldn't go so far as to say I *know* him, but I've met him a few times." He shrugged his broad shoulders. "I wasn't impressed. The feeling was mutual."

"Sounds interesting. Is there a story?"

"I met him through Paige. I came away with the feeling he looked down on me. As if I care."

"Paige, huh? I haven't heard you mention her name lately."

He hesitated, not sure what to say. "We're sort of hanging out. Occasionally."

"'Hanging out'? What are you? Fourteen? What does that even mean at our age?"

Heat crept up his neck. "It means it's none of your business."

"Ah, so there is something going on there. I knew it. Amy told me she wasn't the casual type. I guess she was wrong."

A knot formed in his gut. "She's a big girl. She knows what she's doing."

"Does she? Let's hope so. My fiancée happens to be her best friend. If something goes wrong, we are both in the dog house. Amy is not to be reckoned with."

"Don't get your panties in a twist, A.J. Nothing's going to go wrong. Paige and I are both adults."

"Well, anyway, you need to get measured for your tuxedo in the next few weeks."

"You're kidding, right? I have to wear a monkey suit?"

"Were you planning to wear your turn out gear?"

"What a great idea! Way more comfortable."

"Very funny. It's one day. More like a few hours. I think you'll manage. Anyway, I have to go. I'm meeting Amy for dinner, and I have to go home to shower and change."

"She's got you whipped already, doesn't she?" he asked with a smirk.

"Yep, and I'm okay with that. See you."

He watched his friend leave. There was a bounce to his step. Being engaged was good for his friend. Quinn knew what was good for him, and marriage wasn't it. He went back to the flooring.

*****

Miles away, Paige sat behind the wheel of her new car and turned the key in vain. Again. For the millionth time. But for the millionth time it wouldn't start. How could this be happening to her? She looked around the deserted parking lot of the Blue Ridge Parkway overlook. Although it was only late afternoon, dark storm clouds were rolling in. She had called a tow service when she realized her problem. They would give her a ride but not Finn. What was she supposed to do with him? Leave him there? No amount of begging or bribery worked. He was sorry, but it was company policy. She didn't think he sounded all that sorry.

She had called almost an hour ago, and the truck should be here any minute. In the meantime, she tried to call Amy to ask for a ride. But with her bad luck streak continuing, she hadn't gotten her nor Susan. Mike was on a golf course somewhere.

She'd thought of calling Quinn but didn't. There's wasn't that kind of relationship. And things had ended oddly with him this morning. With no other choice, she had reluctantly called Alex. Of course, he answered. Of course, he would come get her immediately. Of course, he would probably read more into it than there was. She'd deal with it when the time came. A few months ago, she wouldn't have given it a second thought. But things had been awkward between them.

The sky opened. Rain pummeled the windshield, and loud thunder shook her small car. She got out and closed all the other doors before jumping back in. Finn leaped into her lap, shivering at the noise outside. She cuddled him close and murmured reassurances to him.

She hoped Alex would be here soon. Paige had spent several hours driving up and down the parkway and was on her way back home when the car died. The majestic mountains and breath-taking vistas normally helped to soothe her. But not today. Today, her addled brain wrestled with thoughts of him. She had pulled into one last overlook when her car had failed to start again.

What to do about Quinn was the theme for the day. She knew she was falling for the hunky firefighter. Who wouldn't? He was handsome, and the sex rocked her world. But he was also so much more. She like him. He was kind and funny, loyal to his friends and family, and dedicated to his job saving others. What's not to love?

She grimaced at the thought of loving him. Where was a Pop Tart when she needed one? And when had love entered into this? It certainly wasn't in the *plan*. But she loved him. She couldn't pinpoint a specific time when she'd fallen, but there she was.

She weighed the pros and cons of remaining involved with him, which was an exercise in futility. The pros far outnumbered the cons. The only con being he would never consider a permanent relationship. That was kind of a big con.

She sighed. Who was she kidding? She was going to get smushed. She had always known this. There wasn't any debate. The only thing she needed to decide was when to stop. How much of her heart was she willing to risk?

Paige jumped at the knock on her window. She turned her head to see Alex, rain dripping down his face. She hadn't heard him arrive over the noise of the storm. She shoved her phone in her purse and grabbed it and a trembling Finn. Alex opened her door, and they both made a dash back to the safety of his car.

They were both soaked, and for once she was grateful for the heated seats in his car. Her teeth chattered. She grabbed an old sweatshirt from his back seat to wrap a frightened Finn.

She pushed the wet hair out of her eyes and turned to Alex. "Thank you so much for coming to get me."

"Don't you mean 'us'?" he replied in a rare burst of humor.

She looked down at Finn. "Did I not mention Finn was with me?"

"No, you didn't."

Alex didn't like animals, dogs in particular. Probably too messy for him. "Sorry. Would you not have come if you knew?" *What was it with not wanting to give poor Finn a ride?*

Alex blew out a long breath and pushed his wet hair off his forehead. "Of course, I would have still come."

Before she could thank him, a tow truck rumbled up beside them.

"Give me your key, and I'll deal with this."

Paige slid her house keys off the ring and handed it to Alex. She decided to let go of the fact he was telling her what to do. She would stay in the warm, dry car. Finn had stopped trembling and was now asleep in her arms. She leaned down and kissed his soft head. What a day this had been. First, she had to deal with his mixed signals. Then Zoey conked out on her. What next? She bit her lip. Although she wasn't a superstitious person, it might be better to not put *that* out into the universe. Hadn't she learned her lesson?

The door opened on a gust of wind and rain as Alex jumped back into his car. Almost at the same time, a brilliant streak of lightning split the sky. Finn awoke and growled in her arms.

"Not much of a guard dog, is he?"

She felt the need to defend Finn. "He's still a baby. Give him time."

"Huh." Alex put the car in drive and started towards town. "So, where's your boyfriend today? Off saving other people?"

"I'm not sure where Quinn is today. I didn't call him. And he's not my boyfriend. We're, uh, friends."

"Are you trying to convince me or yourself?"

She resisted sticking out her tongue at him. Barely. "It's complicated."

"Want to talk about it?"

Did she want to talk about Quinn with Alex? No way! She wasn't a masochist. "No thanks. There's nothing to say. Besides, I'd rather talk about A.J. and what you thought of him."

Alex grumbled something under his breath.

"Now, Alex, I know you're going to be more civil. Amy loves him, and he treats her well."

"Those are the only reasons I'm tolerating him."

"Those and the fact that Amy would kick your butt."

He shot her a look of derision before returning his gaze to the rain filled road. "I won't deign to answer."

"Yet you know it's true." Her laughter filled the car. Everyone knew Amy was very head strong. She wouldn't tolerate Alex being unpleasant to A.J. for even a second.

"Whatever."

They drove in silence for a while. The storm had picked up quite a bit, and Paige was glad she wasn't the one driving. The rain slashed at the windshield so hard, even on the highest setting the wipers couldn't keep up. Every few minutes lightning flashed, followed almost immediately by a tremendous boom of thunder. She continued to murmur soft words of encouragement to the frightened Finn.

After what seemed an eternity, Alex turned off the Blue Ridge Parkway and onto a road leading into Windsor Falls. She sighed in relief, and although Alex didn't say anything, his grip on the wheel lessened. From there it was only a few minutes further to her home.

The rain had all but stopped when Alex pulled into the driveway. "Well, that was fun."

"Sarcasm, Alex? I'm shocked!" She leaned over and kissed him on the cheek. "Thank you so much for rescuing us." Good manners dictated that she invite him in and offer him at least a towel, but she couldn't deal with him today. She wasn't in the mood for another stilted discussion of their future.

"You're welcome." He looked like he was going to say something else, but Paige scooted out of his car. She waved and made a dash for the porch, turning to watch him leave. She made it in the door when her phone rang. She put Finn in the kitchen before grabbing it. Thinking it was Susan or Amy calling her back, she answered without looking at the screen.

"No need for rescue now. Alex came to get me," she said by way of hello.

"Good to know you've been rescued. I wasn't aware you needed to be," answered a deep voice.

She forgot to breathe. "Oh. You're not Susan."

"What was your first clue?"

"Probably the deep voice."

"Ah, that makes sense. So, tell me why you needed rescuing."

"It's not nearly as dramatic as it sounds. My car wouldn't start, and I was on the Blue Ridge Parkway. The storm didn't help."

"What's wrong with Zoey? She's brand new."

"You remember the name of my car?"

"I remember everything you tell me."

A warm feeling surged through her belly at his words. This was exactly why she needed to guard her heart around him. "It wasn't a big deal except I couldn't get ahold of Amy or Susan. Mike's golfing, so I called Alex."

"Why didn't you call me? You knew I was off today."

She flinched at the hurt in his voice. "I thought about it. I didn't know if it was a good idea."

"Why not?"

"I don't know. I don't know what we are to each other. I didn't know if I had the right to call you for help."

There were a few, tense moments of silence. She wondered what he would say. What could he say? They were being deliberately casual about this thing they were doing.

His voice was low and rough when he answered her. "No matter what happens between us, I want you to know you can always call me. Especially if you need me."

Her heart clenched at his words. She had hurt his feelings. And even though she hadn't meant to, there it was. "I'm sorry. Next time I will."

"I called to see if you're free for the 4th of July. My mom always has a big cookout and invites the crews from the stations and their families. It's a long day and a crazy amount of people, but it's a lot of fun."

"Are you asking me on a date?"

"I guess I am. Will you come?"

"Of course I will. But right now, I have to go. I'm soaked."

"Okay. Go clean up. I'll call you later."

Paige held the phone to her ear until she was sure he was gone. Then she did a little happy dance that sent Finn into an excited whirl. She had no idea what this meant, if anything. But Quinn was taking her to meet his family didn't sound very casual to her. Against her better judgment, she couldn't help the grin spreading across her face.

Chapter Seventeen

Quinn put the phone down as soon as he hit end, to keep him from doing something else stupid. He had invited Paige to his family's party? What could he have been thinking? Alex Windsor, or any other man for that matter, was what he'd been thinking. She wouldn't sit around forever taking his bullshit. She was a beautiful woman with a heart of gold. Someone would offer her what he wouldn't.

He dragged his hands through his short hair and took a deep breath. The conversation, though brief, unsettled him. Just hearing her voice did things to him. The fact she didn't think she could call him when she was stranded left a bad taste in his mouth. But worst of all, she called Alex Windsor to help her. Alex wasn't a stupid man. He probably used the opportunity to plead his case. He would have done the same.

He looked down at the unfinished floor. Instead of starting, he walked into the kitchen and grabbed a beer and a kitchen chair. Going out through the back door, he sat on the deck. He leaned back, propped his feet on the railing, and drained half the can.

This situation with Paige was out of control. Despite his intentions, he was falling for her. He liked her in his life and didn't want to lose her. And even though he would never marry, he didn't want her to marry Alex Windsor. *How screwed up was that?* His chest ached at the thought. He could tell himself Alex was too reserved or too snooty for her, but the truth was far more disturbing. He didn't want her to marry anyone else.

The thought hit him like a line drive to the head. He felt dizzy for a moment. This wasn't his plan. This *never* happened to him. Quinn had been involved with other nice women, all of whom he walked away from in the end. Why was she different? Why was he feeling sick at the thought of ending things with her? Because she was Paige. Because she made his life better. Because she made him want to be a better man. He pulled his feet from the railing and the chair crashed to the floor when he jumped to his feet. What was he saying then? Was he ready to commit to her? *Was he even capable of it?*

He paced the deck, trying to slow his breathing as he walked. He had to think this through. There wasn't any reason to panic or rush into anything. They had a casual relationship going. Both were happy with the status quo. But if he was so happy, why was he pacing?

He knew she wasn't interested in marrying Alex. She had said so herself. And if nothing else, Paige was brutally honest. She thought of the other guy as a brother. So, there was no reason to worry about Alex. But there were so many other men out there. Men who would see how wonderful she is and not be afraid to commit. The image of a life without her in it sickened him.

Quinn drained the rest of his beer and went back inside. He had work left on the house. He'd stay busy. He'd see how things went over the next few days. Bringing her to the party should prove interesting.

*****

The next afternoon, Paige sat at her kitchen table and stared at her cell phone. Zoey was good as new, and she needed to go pick up her car. The problem was how would she get there? She thought about calling Quinn.

He had called last night, as he said he would. It had been later than she expected, and she had pretty much given up on hearing from him. But he was a man of his word. He called as she crawled into bed, and there was a lot to be said for hearing his deep voice as she slid between her cool sheets. They talked for about twenty minutes, about everything and nothing. All in all, it was a lovely way to end the night.

Before she could talk herself out of it, she hit his number on speed dial. It only rang twice before he answered.

"Hey, Paige."

"Hey. Are you busy?"

"No more than usual. Trying to finish up things in the house. What's up?"

"Oh well, if this is a bad time..."

"It's never a bad time for you."

Her chest warmed a little. "Well, I need a ride to get Zoey from the dealership, and I was wondering if you could..."

"I told you could call anytime for anything. I can be there in fifteen minutes. Give me a chance to clean up a bit. I'll see you soon."

She sat staring at the phone again, but for a different reason this time. A huge smile spread across her face, and her heart swelled a little bit. He was coming to get her, and he sounded pleased about it.

He was coming to get her! She jumped up and ran into the first-floor powder room. She gasped at her reflection. Why must she always look like death when Quinn was around? She might not be as concerned about her appearance as Amy was, but she did care.

She ran up to her bedroom. She ripped off her painting clothes and randomly picked out some clean ones. She then ran into the bathroom. She pulled out her ponytail holder and ran a brush through her unruly curls. She decided to leave it down for once. There wasn't any time for much else. So, she settled for dabbing on some lip gloss and spraying some vanilla scented body spray on herself.

Running back downstairs, she let Finn outside to do his business before shutting him into his area of the kitchen. She finished getting him fresh water when she heard his pickup in the driveway.

Quinn's hand was raised to knock when she opened the door. Her eyes drank in the sight of him. It had only been a day, but she had missed him, even though it was a bad idea. "Hey, that was quick! Thanks for coming." She grabbed her purse and phone before stepping out onto the porch and pulling closed the door behind her. He hadn't moved, and this brought her right up against his deliciously hard body.

"Don't mention it. It's nice to take a break from the house repairs. Besides, I get to do this." He backed her against the wall and covered her mouth with his.

She might have fallen if he wasn't still holding her in his arms. And with one kiss, her bones melted. Her head spun, and she had to fight the impulse to drag him inside to have her way with him. She was sure he wouldn't mind, but she needed to get Zoey.

"Wow!"

"Wow is right. Let's go. While we can…"

She tried not to laugh at his thoughts mirroring her own and followed him to his truck. Ever the Southern gentleman, he opened her door and helped her up into it. He closed it when she was safely inside before walking around to his side.

She waited until he had driven a few blocks before speaking. "I was half tempted to pull you inside and have my wicked way with you. Thought you should know."

The truck lurched. He spared her a brief look. "Jesus, Paige, are you trying to get us killed?" He turned his head back to the traffic. "By the way, why only half tempted?"

"Well, I don't want you to think badly of me. After all, I am a lady." She ruined any chance of him taking her seriously by laughing out loud.

"I could never think badly of you."

She wasn't prepared for the seriousness of his tone. The only way she was going to survive with her heart intact was by keeping it light.

"So, tell me about this party your mom throws. What can I bring?"

"She cooks for a week beforehand. You don't need to bring anything. There will be more food than you can imagine."

"Sounds great! I still want to bring something though. However, I'm a terrible cook, so maybe not. I can always buy something."

"Are you always so honest?"

"Being a terrible cook is hard to hide. All you'd have to do is taste something I made."

They arrived at the dealership. Her beloved Zoey sat near the service bays. The car was hard to miss, being the color of a snow cone.

"What do you call this color again?"

"It's blue raspberry if you must know. Zoey is an individual."

"Like her owner."

She leaned over and kissed his cheek. "Thanks again." She grabbed her purse and left his car.

*****

Quinn sat in his truck and watched her walk into the dealership. She came out a few minutes later, waved, and got into her car. He still watched as she drove away. Shaking his head at his own foolishness, he backed out of the parking space and headed home. *She'd done it again.*

He had been thrilled when she called him for a ride, stopping what he was doing to go get her. And then she was gone again. She was taking him at his word. Maybe a bit too much. And once again, he had only himself to blame.

A few hours later, he was exhausted but pleased with the progress. He could list the house for sale soon, with only a few finishing touches left. He gathered up the small brushes he had used to touch up paint and took them into the mudroom to rinse. A knock sounded at the front door. Glancing at his phone, he wondered who would be on his porch this late.

He placed the brushes in the sink and went to open the door. Paige stood on his porch, wearing a long raincoat. In late June.

"Hey! Come on in." He stepped back to let her pass.

"I hope I didn't wake you" she murmured to him.

"Not at all. I just finished some touch up painting. Can I get you something to drink?"

"No thanks. You're all I need." She smiled and pulled on the belt holding her coat closed. She wore only the briefest of matching panties and bra. The garments, more missing than there, were silky and sky blue.

Words left his brain. This was straight out of every man's fantasy.

Paige looked around. "Not much in the way of furniture."

"I have a bed. That's all we need."

"Then what are we waiting for?"

He had the presence of mind to shut his door before scooping her up in his arms. She squealed as he strode into the first-floor master bedroom. He lowered her to the floor, enjoying the feeling of her sliding down his body. Certain parts of him more than others.

She fiddled with her coat, giving away her nervousness. "I've never done anything like this before."

"You're doing a great job." Her confession pleased him. He didn't want to think of her doing this number for any other man.

She placed both hands on his chest and pushed him onto the bed. She lowered the coat off both shoulders slowly, exposing more honey toned skin as she went.

"Wow. That's all I can come up with."

"Words aren't necessary." She let the coat drop to the floor and closed the gap between them. Reaching down, she lifted the edge of his shirt to reveal taut abdominal muscles. She raked her nails across them before pulling the shirt up and over his head.

She slid her hands up his thighs, moving them further apart and stepping in between. This brought his head even with her breasts. He leaned forward and licked one nipple through the soft material. She moaned deep in her throat, reaching in between her breasts to undo the clasp. As soon as her breasts were free of the material, he placed his hot mouth on one and sucked at the nipple.

She pushed him down onto his back and licked her way up his body. Stopping at his chest, she took one nipple in her mouth and nipped lightly.

He sucked in a breath, fighting for control. "Christ! You *are* trying to kill me."

"No, I need you alive for what I have planned." Her hand slid back down his body and under the band of his basketball shorts. She stroked her fingers up and down his shaft before squeezing.

He panted and flipped Paige on her back. Running a hand down her side, he crossed it over her rounded curves until he met little resistance at her panties. The material covering her mound was wet. He slid it aside and pushed two fingers into her.

She writhed on the bed. "Please. I need more."

But he had other ideas. He moved his fingers in and out, driving her higher and higher. When he could see she was close to coming, he pulled his fingers out. Leaning down he kissed her through the now soaked material of her panties.

"Who's killing whom now?"

He stood up and removed the rest of his clothing. "Just a moment." He reached into the drawer next to his bed and pulled out a condom. As he rolled it over his penis, he glanced down at her. She was lying on her back with her eyes closed and a smile on her face. Her skin was flushed.

Rejoining her, Quinn stalked up the bed from the bottom. He hooked his fingers under the straps of her panties and drew them down and off her legs, inch by inch, teasing her flesh along the way with his tongue. Lifting her legs up and over his shoulders brought her center to eye level. She was ready for him. Her scent, all woman, drove him higher. Paige's eyes flew open. In the next moment, she grabbed handfuls of the sheet on either side of her as he lowered his mouth to her. His tongue swirled around her swollen clit, dragging moans of pleasure from her. He smiled at the strangled noises coming from her. She might pretend to be casual about them, but she couldn't hide her responses.

"Please, I need you inside me."

He raised his head. "There's plenty of time." He lowered his head again and pushed his tongue back into her. Her muscles tightened around him, letting him know the peak was close. He moved up her body and entered her with one swift thrust. She dragged her nails across his back, scoring him. He didn't care, just pulled back and entered her time and again, deeper and harder with each thrust. She clung to him. It was her turn to pant.

When he thought he couldn't hold off for another second, he felt her clench around him and then moan her release. It was enough to send him toppling over the edge. Neither spoke for a few moments. The sex only got better. He got up to dispose of the condom and then flopped back down on the bed. She had rolled over onto her stomach with her limbs strewn. He propped up on one elbow and used his free hand to trace a light pattern on her skin.

Paige mumbled something into the mattress. Something sounding like a purr.

"You sounded like a very large cat."

She turned her head to look at him. "Yep, pretty much." There was a distinct feline smile of satisfaction on her face.

"I might purr as well if it wouldn't lessen my masculinity. I have a reputation to protect."

She rolled to her side facing him and flipped her hair out of her face. "Believe me, you have nothing to worry about. If anyone questions you, send them to me."

Laughter rumbled up out of his chest. Being with her, like this, felt right. He could get used to it. He probably already was. And his heart didn't race in fear at the thought. He pulled her closer until her head lay on his chest.

"By the way, how did you know where I live? I'm not complaining, mind you. Just curious."

"I called A.J. and asked him. Which reminds me, he told me to 'not keep you up late on a school night'. That's Amy's influence. She likes to bust on me. I need to get going."

He pounced on her as she started to get up. "Not so fast. It's not too late." It actually was, and Quinn knew he would be hating life in the morning, but a warm Paige in his bed now would be worth it then.

"Are you sure? Don't you need your rest?"

A wicked gleam appeared in his eye. "Oh, I'm sure!"

There weren't any more words for quite some time.

Chapter Eighteen

Paige eased her way out of bed and went into the bathroom. When she was finished, she picked up her coat and grabbed her phone from the pocket. 3:15a.m. Time to go. Not wanting to wake Quinn, she tiptoed out of his room, stopping only long enough to grab the shirt he had been wearing earlier. Coming over here almost naked had been nerve wracking enough. She wasn't going home so scantily clad.

On the short ride home, she marveled at their chemistry. Every time was better than the last and way better than anything she had experienced in the past. She grinned at herself in the rear-view mirror. Being with him made her happy. Although she knew it was a foolish, she loved the feeling. She would enjoy it while it lasted and deal with the fall out later.

She arrived home and let herself into the house. Finn was as happy as always to see her. That was the great think about dogs. You could be gone for five hours or five minutes, and they'd be thrilled to see you. They weren't like humans. They didn't hide their emotions.

She let the puppy out and then spent a few minutes with him before heading to bed. It was a good thing she was off for the summer, or she would be exhausted at school in the morning.

She lay in the dark for a while, watching the ceiling fan blades whirl. There was no way to fool herself anymore. She loved him. And even though she knew this wouldn't end well, she didn't care. The pain would come later. For now, she would continue as they were, getting together when they could. No strings. No promises. And if doubts whispered through her brain, she chose to ignore them.

*****

Quinn lay in the dark, also not sleeping. He knew the exact moment Paige had left his bed. Even if he wasn't used to waking from a dead sleep in an instant, he would have known. His bed felt different without her in it. A little colder. A little lonelier. How had this one woman slipped through his defenses? Years of hiding from love were over. Now that he knew what having her in his life meant, his old life held zero appeal.

He didn't revel in this thought. He had reasons for not getting involved. Good, valid reasons. And yet, for the first time, those reasons didn't hold as much weight anymore. He had always focused on protecting other people, the mythical wife and children. But he had never thought about what it would mean for him. He had a good life, with a job he loved and great friends and family. But meeting Paige changed everything, made him realize how empty his life was. Now he had someone to care about. Someone warm beside him in bed at night. Now he had Paige.

Rolling on to his side, Quinn punched the pillow to get the shape he wanted and felt himself drift. He hadn't made any decisions, but he had begun to make peace with himself. He smiled as he settled back into sleep.

*****

"Tell me again how easy this recipe is, Susan." Paige tried to not grind her teeth. All she wanted to do was make a nice pie. What was more American? Yet every attempt had turned out poorly. July fourth was only a few days away, and Paige had enlisted Susan's help. She swiped at flour clinging to her face.

"I think you missed a spot."

She turned to see Amy lounging in the doorway.

"Very funny. It's not fair. Your mom always makes this look so easy."

"You're getting there. You need some practice. This last one was the best by far." Susan patted her cheek.

"That's not saying much."

Amy entered the room and stared at the piles of cooking gadgets. "I'm not even sure what half of these do. Are you sure I'm your daughter?"

Susan laughed and hugged her. "Oh, I'm sure. I was there at your birth. You just didn't get the cooking gene."

Paige wailed after tasting the latest round. The crust wasn't right yet. She wanted everything to be perfect.

"Please explain to me why you are killing yourself over a pie."

"We have been over this. I'm meeting Quinn's mother and sister for the first time. I want to make a good impression. Store bought dessert does not make a good first impression."

Amy took a forkful of the apple pie. A look of distaste crossed her features. "Honey, neither does this."

She ran a hand through her hair, depositing more flour in its wake. "That's not helpful, Amy!"

"Might I make a suggestion, dear?" Susan patted Paige's arm. "Why don't I handle the pie crust? You can help me and then put together the rest of it. Then it will turn out as you want it and still be homemade."

Relief coursed through her. "Yes! Otherwise, I'll be here all day every day until the 4th."

"You should have ordered from De Luca's like I did. It's not too late."

Her mouth watered at the mention of the family run bakery in town. Three generations of De Luca's had run the small shop. Kat, a member of their book club, was the latest.

"Next time I will. But I wanted this to be special."

The corners of Amy's mouth turned down.

"What?"

"I'm worried about you. This thing with Quinn is going to blow up in your face."

"Don't you think I know? I'm not stupid. But I love him. So, I'll take the time I have with him and worry about the future when it gets here. It's all I can do."

Amy crossed the floor and hugged Paige. "I don't want to see you get your heart broken."

"Neither do I, but I love him." She backed away. "Now Susan, shall we take one more crack at the crust?"

Susan nodded, and she turned to the pantry for more ingredients.

*****

Quinn and AJ came in from the heat, dripping sweat. They bypassed the kitchen and went upstairs to shower and change for the party. A.J. paused at the door to a guest bathroom. "Every year seems to get hotter, doesn't it?"

"It sure does. It felt like a hundred out there already. Maybe one year we'll get smart and clean off the tables and chairs the night before instead of in the blazing sun."

"I doubt it. We never seem to remember from one year to the next. But it's worth it for all of your mom's cooking."

"You got that right."

A.J. hesitated at the bathroom door. He turned back towards his best friend. "Amy told me Paige is here."

The muscles in his shoulders tightened, knowing what was coming next. "She is. What about it?"

"Nothing. She's good for you man. You've been happier lately. I'm glad." A.J. closed the bathroom door.

Quinn pondered his friend's words. Did people notice a difference in him? He was happy with Paige in his life, but the thought worried him. He wanted to have a good time today, not fend off a bunch of questions.

*****

Paige smiled at a freshly showered Quinn. "Feel better?"

"I do. It's brutal out there already." He grabbed a carrot and dipped it in ranch dressing. "You ladies have sure been busy."

"Thank you for noticing before you scarf it all down, big brother," replied Lauren, smacking his hand.

He ruffled her hair. "Always. I see you've met my baby sister."

"Argh! How many times do I have to tell you? I. Am. A. Grown. Woman." Lauren waved the knife she was holding to underscore her words.

Marie stepped into the fray. "Okay. Enough out of you both. Do I need to separate you?" The siblings shook their heads. "No? Good." She turned to him. "We've had a lovely time getting to know Paige and Amy. But now we need to move. Those tables aren't going to set themselves."

Paige, Quinn and Lauren trooped outside and got to work covering the tables with red, white, and blue plastic clothes for the holiday. Amy and A.J. filled various coolers with ice. Maria supervised everyone.

Several hours later, her head spun. She had met a dizzying array of people and had no hope of remembering all their names. Many of the guests glanced at her curiously. Despite a ton of good natured ribbing from his fellow firefighters, he seemed to be taking it all in stride.

She ducked inside in search of more sodas. Maria directed her to the garage. There she ran into Jack, who was carrying a volleyball. She had not seen him since the night at Smitty's.

"Hey! Jack, right?"

Jack turned to her and smiled. "That's right, pretty lady. I'm flattered you remembered my name."

"Don't be. Quinn told me all about you. Besides, you make an impression." She smiled to soften her words.

"So, you two are still an item? That might be a record for him." He headed out of the garage, but not before giving her a suggestive smile. "Call me when you get bored with him."

She heard a gasp behind her and turned to see Lauren standing in the doorway to the house, her face red and tears threatening. "Lauren, it wasn't what it looked like."

Lauren stepped down into the garage, pulling the door shut behind her. She stopped in front of Paige. "Oh, it was *exactly* what it looked like. But it had nothing to do with you. Jack flirts with every beautiful woman. Anyone but me." The last word came out on a sob.

She put her arms around Lauren as she cried. After several minutes, Quinn's sister gathered herself. She sniffed a few more times before speaking.

"I'm not a stupid person, despite loving a man who doesn't know I exist." She hiccupped. "One day, I'll get over him."

Paige rubbed her shoulder. "Oh Lauren, loving someone is never stupid, even when it seems impossible. Trust me. I know. We don't get to dictate whom we love." She sighed, sharing the other woman's concerns.

"Yes, Quinn has commitment issues, but he's different with you. I've been watching him all day. And he's *never* brought anyone to meet us before. That has to count for something."

"I like to think so. But he was honest from the beginning, and I knew what I was getting myself into. Understanding it intellectually is one thing but emotionally is a different thing altogether."

"All I'm saying is this is new for him. So, it might mean something. Have you told him how you feel? Maybe it would help."

"No. The last thing I want to do is pressure him, Lauren. He sends a lot of mixed signals. And we haven't been together long. There's no rush." *Brave words.* Despite everything, she would be crushed if he ended things.

"Tell me about Jack," she said to get the focus off her.

"There's nothing to tell. I've been mooning over him forever. Or so it feels. He joined Quinn's station as a rookie the summer before I left for college. He was twenty-two, and I was eighteen. He's never seen me as anything other than Quinn's 'baby sister'."

"Have you ever tried to show him you're grown up?"

"You don't get it. Dating his partner's sister is taboo. Jack loves his job and the station. He would never cross that line."

"You're right, I'm sorry. I don't understand the firefighter culture. I was trying to help."

Her pretty face fell. "No, I'm sorry. You were being nice. It's so frustrating." She blew out a breath. "I need to move on with my life. It's not like I've been sitting around pining for him. I have a job I love and great friends. I date. I've even had a few almost serious relationships."

"But they weren't Jack."

"They weren't Jack; only pale comparisons of him. Maybe I haven't met the right guy yet. Someday, someone will come along, and he won't be Jack, but he'll be the right guy. Enough about me and my messed-up love life. I came in here to help you with drinks."

"Well, good. I was looking for them when I ran into Jack. How about grabbing some water, and I'll grab some sodas?"

Lauren picked up a case of water and walked out of the garage. At the door she turned and looked back at Paige. "Thanks. I never talk about Jack, to anyone, so thanks for listening." She smiled and walked out into the bright sunshine.

She was glad Lauren felt comfortable enough with her to talk about her feelings for Jack. But the conversation scared her. Was she doing the same with Quinn?

Was she putting her life on hold, knowing he was never going to commit to a permanent relationship?

Dread pooled in her stomach. She had told herself she understood the rules and that she was only looking for a little fun this summer. But she was lying to herself. There had been a connection, a pull, with him from the very beginning. This was never just 'fun' for her. Getting her heart broken certainly wasn't going to be either.

Chapter Nineteen

Quinn was playing horseshoes, and beating A.J. soundly, when Jack found him. Although they were friends and co-workers, he had always found the other guy a bit too much. Too loud. Too cocky. Too much of a ladies' man.

"Hey. I ran into Paige in the garage. You two are still an item, huh? Isn't this a record for you?"

He gritted his teeth. Jack was probably the twentieth person to ask him. Everyone seemed surprised to see him with a date. It was his own fault. He never brought anyone to this party. Ever. It was understandable they were surprised. But that didn't make it any easier for him to keep hearing it. And for some reason the look on Jack's smug face sent him over the edge.

"It's not a big deal, Jack. Paige and I are hanging out for the summer. She was looking for some fun." He tried to not cringe. They may be her words exactly, but they didn't reflect how he felt about her.

"So, you wouldn't mind if I ask her out when you two are done having fun, huh?'

Friend or not, he couldn't help feeling like he wanted to punch the other man at this moment. "That's not what I said."

"Which is it? You're either involved with her or you're not." As usual, Jack never knew when to quit.

"It's none of your business, Jack." Quinn's game was off now since he was throwing the metal horseshoes with far more power than skill. *Being pissed off will do that to you.*

A.J. smirked at the final score. "Might be the only time I'll ever beat you by such a gap."

"Yeah, yeah, A.J. you crushed me. Let's start again and see how you do this time."

He clenched his hands into fists at his sides. He didn't want to discuss his relationship with anyone, especially Jack. They were friends, and he trusted Jack to have his back at work. But women were another thing altogether. Jack would be more than happy to call Paige. And even though he also knew she would see right through his bullshit, it still rankled him.

A.J. set up for another round, seemingly oblivious to his friend's unhappiness. He tried to shake off the bad feeling and get his head into the game. But somehow, even in the heat of the day, he felt like a black cloud had moved across the sun.

*****

Paige moved away from her place behind the tree. She had not meant to overhear their conversation. But in a way, she was glad she had. It was a big, fat reality check. Quinn wasn't in this for the long haul. And even though he had used her words, the truth still hurt. There was a heaviness in her chest making it hard to breathe. It was time to go. She walked into the house to grab her keys and purse. She almost knocked over Amy as her friend came out of the first-floor powder room.

Amy's mouth turned down. "Hey, what's wrong?"

"Oh, nothing new. Quinn will never change his mind, and I'm an idiot for thinking he would this whole time." She laughed, but it wasn't a pretty sound. "I have to go, Amy. I can't stay here. Can you please tell him I wasn't feeling well? Make something up."

"Sure, honey. Do you want me to go with you?"

"Thanks, but no. Stay with A.J and enjoy the day." She bolted from the house.

Tears streamed from her eyes as she drove away from the party. So much so that she pulled over a few blocks away. When she parked, the tears poured freely down her face. She was an idiot for believing he would change his mind.

But she couldn't even be angry with him. Disappointed? Yes. But not angry. He had been honest from the beginning. She was the one who was stupid enough to fall in love with him anyway.

She swiped her hands across her face. At least she knew for sure now. It was up to her to decide what she to do about it. The best choice would be to move on with her life. But even though she had only known him a few months, the choice seemed bleak. She could continue how they were, knowing she was risking more pain.

She regretted rushing out of the party the way she had, leaving without saying goodbye to his family. But at the time, she couldn't think of anything but leaving. She pulled out her phone to text him. It might be cowardly, but she couldn't handle hearing his voice right now.

"Hey, sorry to leave so abruptly. The sun may have been too much for me. Bad headache. Going to get some sleep. Talk to you tomorrow."

Paige held her finger over the send button for a moment. Doing this went against everything she believed in. She was inherently honest. She hit the button and turned off the ringer on her phone. Although it hurt to lie to him, it hurt more to think about talking to him.

She gathered herself and drove the rest of the way home. The time she dreaded had arrived. Now she had to decide what to do about it. But not now. Not today. Today there was a box of Pop Tarts waiting for her. And if she wasn't mistaken, it might be red velvet. Something should go right today.

*****

Quinn looked around the yard for Paige. He realized he had been playing horse shoes longer than he thought. He hadn't seen her for a while. Maybe she was in the house.

Amy glared at him as he passed her on his way to the house. He wondered what A.J. had done to cause that look. He didn't waste more time thinking about it. He had to find her. Moving on, he walked into the kitchen, only to find it empty. Opening the door to the garage, he found his sister sitting on a lawn chair near the open door to the driveway.

"Hey Lauren! Why are you in here all alone?"

She gave him a look screaming 'back off', but it didn't scare him. It didn't stop him either. "Something wrong?"

"Air pollution, global warming, the economy, men who wear capris and think they look cool. Actually, men in general."

From experience, he figured it was probably the latter. His sister had dated quite a few men over the past couple of years. Most of them questionable and none who had stuck. He was thankful. In fact, she seemed to have a lot of first dates.

"Okay, so it's men. Is there a particular one who set you off?"

Lauren turned in her chair and fixed her brother with a steady gaze, as if she was trying to figure him out. "It's not worth mentioning."

He knew she was upset, but she had the 'do not touch' vibe going. He decided to cut her a break. "I'm sorry. Have you seen Paige anywhere?"

Lauren stood up so fast she knocked over her lawn chair. "You mean the Paige who left almost an hour ago? Men!" Lauren stormed off, leaving only questions in her wake.

Another angry female. Did they not know this was supposed to be a party? But he was more concerned about her leaving an hour ago. Without saying anything to him. He pulled out his phone to call her and saw the message.

Concerned she wasn't feeling well, he called her, but it went straight to voice-mail. Maybe she had taken some medication. Did she suffer from migraines? Probably something he should know. He went back to the party in search of Amy.

Quinn found her in the kitchen with A.J., arranging desserts on a tray. "Hey Amy! Does Paige get migraines?"

The tall blonde had been laughing at something A.J. said, but now she fixed him with a cool stare. "No, Quinn, she doesn't. Why do you ask?"

"My sister told me she left a little while ago, and then Paige texted me she had a headache and had gone home. I tried calling, but she's not answering. I thought you might know something."

"Of course, I know something. She's my sister. She was gone for over an hour before *you* realized. Shall we start there?" Her blue eyes grew frosty.

Two women were treating him like crap, and he had no idea why. "Okay. I want to make sure she's doing all right."

"She's fine. Or at least she will be." She turned on her heel and carried the dessert tray outside.

Quinn turned to A.J. "What did I do? She seems pissed."

"Seems? Oh, she's pissed. Amy is not someone you want to mess with. What *did* you do?" A.J. followed his fiancée out the door. Once again, he was left in the dark. He thought about driving over to her house to check on her but didn't want to wake her.

The rest of the party passed, and the last guest left after dark. He helped his mom and sister clean up before heading home. He was still concerned he hadn't heard from Paige and hoped she was sleeping. He left another brief message, for a total of four, before going to sleep.

*****

Bright sunlight spilled into Paige's bedroom the next morning, assaulting her eyes. She rolled over and buried her head under a pillow. She had spent a restless night, more tossing and turning than actual sleeping. And now she felt like crap. Knowing she wasn't going to get any more sleep, she sat up and grabbed her phone. Only seven and she was already exhausted.

She was not surprised by the number of missed calls and voicemails. Four messages from Quinn did shock her. She listened to each one in its entirety once before doing so again. The sound of his deep voice, roughened by concern, set butterflies afloat in her stomach. The last one got to her.

"Hey it's me again. I wanted to reach you to make sure you were okay. Do you need anything? Is your headache a migraine? Lauren gets them, and they look painful. I don't want you to be in any pain. Please call me when you get this. I miss you."

She listened to it again. And then one more time. In an attempt at self-preservation, Paige considered deleting it. All the way. Not just put it in the deleted folder. But she couldn't. She didn't know what she was going to do about him, but she wasn't ready to do anything so permanent.

She felt a little queasy as she got up and then remembered why. Red Velvet Pop Tarts! The first package had been so yummy and helped to dull the pain a bit, so she figured another would help even more. And everyone knows you can't leave one pack left in the box. But now, she wished she had.

Driven by the number of calories she had consumed during her pity fest, she decided to go running. She hated running and lacked coordination, but she hated her clothes not fitting even more. She dressed before she could talk herself out of it.

Going downstairs, she let Finn out and put down fresh water and food. He was more likely to focus on that and not the fact she was leaving without him. Even this early, the temperature was near eighty with a swampy ninety-three percent humidity. No point in punishing Finn. He hadn't eaten too many Pop Tarts.

She slipped in her ear buds and set off. Not a habitual runner, she didn't have a set course. After a few blocks she remembered why. A painful stitch in her side made each breath feel like her last. She stopped and placed her hands on her knees, trying to concentrate on getting air in and out. *Pathetic.*

Once she felt like she wasn't going to pass out, she started off again. This time, her pace was more of a brisk walk. Maybe speed walking was more her style. After another few blocks, she was down to plain walking, still holding her side. She continued on until she got to Amy's condo. Her friend lived in an old Victorian on Maple Street that had been converted to several privately-owned condos. Hers was on the first floor, thankfully. Stairs might have finished her off.

She knocked softly, in case Amy was still asleep. Her friend was not a morning person, especially in the summer. But a chipper Amy answered the door. Paige heard her before she saw her.

"I can't believe you forget your key again," she called as she swung open the door. Dressed in barely there lingerie, Amy saw Paige and burst out laughing.

"I'm assuming you thought I was someone else," drawled Paige. "Maybe six plus feet of hunky firefighter?"

"Honey, come on in." She stepped back to allow room. "Andrew ran out to get breakfast for us. As you can see it will be breakfast in bed."

"Well then the last thing you need here is me. I was out running and decided to stop by."

Amy arched one eyebrow. "You? Running? Want to pull the other one?" She stuck out one long, tanned limb and laughed.

"Okay, I started out running. I had good intentions. The point is I thought I would stop by. Give me a call later. Much later!"

Amy stopped her with a hand on Paige's arm. "Are you okay? How's your headache?"

Her face warmed at the memory of her blatant lie to Quinn. "I guess he mentioned it."

"To his credit, he did call you several times, which helps to negate the fact that it took him an hour to notice you were gone." She grimaced. "Sorry! Not sure if you knew. Are you going to tell me what happened?"

"He left four messages. And that's the crux of the problem. He says one thing but then acts another way. Never mind. It's too long to get into now. Maybe lunch tomorrow? I know the guys are working."

"Lunch it is. I'll get something and bring it over. I can ooh and ah at all of your progress on the house, and you can tell me all about the evils of Quinn."

"It's a date!" Paige hugged her friend and then turned towards the door. A.J. opened it as she put her hand on the knob.

"Hey!" A.J. greeted her.

"Don't worry, I'm leaving." She hugged him. He was a good man, and Amy deserved him. One of them should be happy. Paige left the lovebirds to their plans.

Chapter Twenty

Quinn looked around the house, pleased with how it was coming together. His realtor, Gabriella, was coming later for a walk through. If they agreed it was ready to be listed, things would move quickly. Within days it would be listed and ready for showings. The housing market in Windsor Falls was brisk. He needed to find another house, or he would be sleeping on someone's couch.

He walked into the kitchen where his phone was charging. He checked it again, flattening his lips. No response from Paige. The blank screen mocked him. If he wasn't careful, he'd be growing an ovary soon. Before he could talk himself out of it, picked up the phone and sent her a brief text.

"Feeling any better?"

He deliberately left off 'call me' for the sake of his manhood. he unplugged the phone and slid it into the back pocket of his shorts. Just in case.

*****

Paige was walking into her home when she heard the text alert on her phone. Without looking, she had a feeling it was from Quinn. She resolutely placed her phone face down on the foyer table and went to see Finn. When it alerted a second time to remind her, she took the puppy out to the back yard for a game of fetch.

The summer sun was brutal. Fetch only lasted a few minutes before a wilted Paige and Finn sat in the shade of the old oak tree. She rubbed his ears while he panted.

"So, Finn, what should I do about him?"

Finn licked her arm but remained silent on the subject.

"Okay, let me spell out my options as I see them. I could continue along like we have been and not mention what I heard yesterday. Or I could end things right now and salvage what's left of my heart. Not to mention my pride."

Finn remained silent on the topic.

"That's exactly why I can't answer his text right now. It might lead to a call or God forbid a visit. I can't talk to him until I know what I'm doing."

She sent a brief text in return.

"Feeling better, thanks. Laying low today."

She hit send before she could agonize over the wording. It was brief and to the point. It also didn't invite company. Satisfied she had done the right thing, she picked up her pooped puppy and carried him into the house. She wanted to get some more painting done in her bedroom.

The next morning, she was satisfied with the progress she had made in her bedroom. The physical labor had helped to keep thoughts of him at bay. Blasting music and dancing as she worked helped more. She glanced in the mirror and flexed her arms. Although they weren't Michelle Obama arms (and whose were?), they were more toned than when she started. They also didn't cry out in pain after five minutes of painting.

Best of all, she'd be able to move back into her room in a day or so. Most of her personal belongings were stored in boxes in the garage. She had never fully unpacked when she bought the house, knowing major renovations were needed. With some of the rooms finished, she could focus on placing her personal touches on them.

The doorbell ringing pulled her from her thoughts. That would be Amy with lunch. Her stomach growled in anticipation. She ran down the stairs to let her in.

After opening the door, the two women moved into the kitchen to have lunch before Paige gave her the tour. As always, they talked a thousand miles an hour, and often at the same time. Yet they always understood each other. They devoured the gourmet sandwiches and chips.

She led Amy around the house, concentrating on the rooms she had finished. Amy gave pointers here and there, such as possible window treatments and other accessories. They ended up flopped on the couch, Finn lying in Amy's lap with a doggy grin on his face as she rubbed his belly.

"So, tell me what happened the other day." Amy fixed her with a gaze to let her know she wouldn't be getting off the hook.

Paige sighed. She had been hoping to avoid this but should have known better. "I overheard him talking with Jack, who was ribbing Quinn about being in a relationship. He set him straight."

"What does that even mean? 'Set him straight'?"

"He told Jack we were only having a bit of 'summer fun'." She held up her hand at Amy's look of outrage. "I can't even be angry. He used my words. It's what I told Quinn I was looking for when we first met. Because he was so adamant about not getting seriously involved."

"You used those words?"

"I remember saying I had been on a dating moratorium of sorts and I was only looking to have some fun. I told you this weeks ago."

"You're right. It's coming back to me now. If I remember correctly, I did say this didn't seem like you. I'm not trying to say I told you so. You know I've been worried about you all along."

She smiled at her friend. "Well, feel free to say it, because you were right. I was ridiculous to go ahead and fall in love with him. And he still sees me as a fling."

"You know I'd never do that. At least not about something this serious," she added. "But are you sure he's only looking for a fling anymore? I know what you heard honey, but he doesn't act like it around you."

"You're right. I don't know for sure. But I'm not ready to have that conversation yet. I appreciate you listening to me, but let's talk about you. Is there a bridal magazine peeking out of your bag?"

"Are you sure?"

"Absolutely!"

"Okay, great. I've been dying to get your thoughts on what you're going to wear."

*****

Across town, Quinn and A.J. finished a late lunch. Their shift had been busy, and this was their first chance to eat. Fortunately, the day had been filled with minor calls; a car reportedly on fire but not, a small brush fire on the side of a rural road, and a fire alarm in a local shopping mall. Now they could finally catch their breath.

"So, what's the deal with you and Paige?" asked A.J. around a mouthful of sandwich.

Soda threatened to shoot out his nose. He grabbed a napkin to clean the spill he had created. "What are you talking about A.J?"

"I'm not sure. She came by yesterday morning to visit Amy. There was some discussion about an incident at the party. Amy did say she was gunning for you if you hurt her friend. That's all I know."

"So, there wasn't any headache?"

"Yeah, I was shocked too. Who thought Paige would lie?"

He thought back to the party. "I have no idea what might have upset her so much to send her home and lie to me. Unless…" He stopped as a terrible possibility dawned on him.

"Unless what? Don't leave me hanging."

"I'm going to kill Jack. He was asking about my relationship, and I had already been asked the same thing by so many others. Not to mention he made it clear he was interested in her if I wasn't."

"I have a bad feeling. What did you say?"

"He kept pushing me to define my relationship with her, like we were in middle school. So, I told him it was just some summer fun."

A.J. dropped his head into his hands. "No! Tell me you're joking. What if she heard you?"

"She couldn't have."

"Are you one hundred percent sure?"

"Yes. Well, mostly. I mean I didn't see her anywhere. I never would have said it *to* her. The ironic part is those are the words she said to me at the beginning of this. She said she was just looking for some 'fun'."

"And you believed her?"

"I did then. Or maybe I wanted to. But the worst part is that it's not even true. I just wanted him off my back."

"So, you don't think this is just fun?"

"No."

"Then you have some explaining to do. I'd suggest flowers. Maybe chocolate. Can't hurt."

Before he could reply, the alarm rang once again. They abandoned what was left of their lunches and ran for their gear. Details blared over the PA system. With each bit of news, the call sounded increasingly dire.

Jack jumped in the driver's seat, followed by Quinn in the passenger's side, A.J. and two others in the back. They listened as details continued to pore in over the radio. The fire was in an abandoned industrial complex over the township line but still in their county. This wasn't their territory, but because the fire had been elevated to three alarms, neighboring personnel were needed. They would report to the incident commander for their orders upon their arrival. Because he was the senior officer from their station, he would be responsible for giving out assignments to his men.

The ride was less than ten minutes, and Quinn was on the ground before the truck had fully stopped. He checked in with the incident commander and awaited orders. The rest of his crew rolled out hoses and gathered equipment.

He rejoined his men. "Okay, listen up. This is what we know. The building is abandoned and thought to be empty. The fire was fully involved when Station Thirty-Seven arrived on scene. As you can see, they already have men working on the roof to ventilate. There's some question as to what might be in the building. The concern is there are old chemicals left behind. What they are is anyone's guess. Their chief is looking into it. There's also some suspicion the fire may be arson."

The incident commander waved him down. They suited up and strapped on their oxygen tanks. Each man was fully covered in protective gear from their helmets and hoods to their boots, with their last names in bright letters on the backs of their jackets. He knew they had every advantage to keep them safe in the line of duty. He also knew it wasn't always enough.

Station Fifteen's crew moved towards the building to take up their positions. Other firefighters began to come out. He heard a wave of excited murmuring through the first responders. He turned back to the Incident Commander.

"Chief, what's up?"

"I got a report of some belongings found near what looks like a makeshift bed. The building might not be empty after all."

Quinn's heart raced. This changed everything. "There's always the chance of squatters in these abandoned buildings, Chief. Are we sure there's someone still in there?"

"We can't take the chance, can we?" Both men glanced at the building already fully engulfed in flames. They shared a look about their doubts of finding any survivors.

"Take a look around but don't risk anyone's life doing it. You know the drill."

"Yes, sir."

He knew the drill because he had been in this situation before. Firefighters always wanted to save a trapped victim. But if they searched recklessly, they ran the risk of putting their own lives, and those of the others who would come in after them, in danger. He returned to his crew. Each would risk their lives for a stranger. That's what being a firefighter meant.

"Okay, we're up. There's report of a possible occupant." He shared the new intel he had been given. "We search in pairs. Report in anything that might lead us to the victim. Most importantly, watch each other's back. Everyone's going home today." He said those words every time they found themselves in a dicey situation. He wasn't superstitious, but he hadn't lost anyone yet.

Normally, he would stay outside as ranking officer, but they were on loan to the Incident Commander. Each set of two firefighters had an area to cover in their search. He paired up with A.J. The other man gave two thumbs up, and they entered the building. It was walking into a totally different world. Outside had been a bright, summer day. Inside was the seventh layer of Hell.

He waited until his eyes adjusted as much as they would. The interior was filled with a thick, black smoke. Flames were licking the wooden interior of the building, seemingly dancing up the walls. The heat was oppressive. They started their search. Even using powerful flashlights, he could see only inches in front of his face. They continued to sweep the floor with their beams anyway, hoping against hope to find someone still alive.

Minutes ticked by, marked by the thudding of his heart. They failed to find any signs of life. He was conscious of the amount of air they had left in their tanks. Even though a full tank was rated to last thirty minutes, the reality was far less. It didn't take into account the effort being exerted by each man. Combined with their individual elevated respiratory rates and volume of breaths they were taking, it meant different times for each man. The reality of a situation like one they were in now meant they probably had closer to fifteen or twenty minutes of air. Many times, despite being conscientious about the time, Quinn had been surprised to hear the warning bell go off on his tank. When it happened, three fourths of his supply had been utilized.

They had been in the building for over ten minutes when he heard an ominous cracking noise. Even over the roar of the flames, the sound of the ceiling above them collapsing was frighteningly loud. He turned to alert A.J. when the first of the timbers fell. He waved his arms to warn his friend, but there wasn't time. He ran towards A.J., but he was too late. He watched in horror as a large beam knocked him to the ground. Quinn screamed for help through his radio as he rushed to A.J.'s side.

*****

Paige and Amy had spent the last hour pouring over bridal magazines, searching for the perfect maid of honor gown. They found a few possibilities but howled in laughter over many others. While she was not picky about fashion, even she wouldn't wear most of the ones they had seen. No reason to subject herself to a large bow on her butt.

"What about your dress? Any thoughts yet?"

Amy sighed. "Sort of. I know what I don't want more than what I do. I've always pictured something traditional but not old fashioned, ivory instead of white with some bling but not overdone. The problem is I don't have a lot of time. The reality is I have to find the perfect dress. Of course, I have to buy it off the rack because I'm out of time. Then I have to have it tailored."

"I know. Let's find that show on TV featuring brides looking at dresses. Maybe we can spot something for you."

"Can't hurt." Amy continued to flip through another magazine.

She turned on the TV and was about to start surfing channels when a local one broke in with a special announcement. She normally didn't watch the news, but the sight of flames grabbed her attention.

"Amy? You need to see this."

Amy lifted her head and glanced at the television. Both women stood up and walked towards it. A news anchor was describing a three-alarm fire in progress at a local, abandoned warehouse. Her voice became a buzz in Paige's head as she stared at the screen. She scanned the scene, praying she wouldn't see a familiar face.

"It's not even in Windsor Falls," Amy said in a strained voice. "The guys are fine."

She nodded in response but spotted a distinctive hunter green truck parked off to the side. While a lot of fire departments went with the traditional red, she knew Windsor Falls had not. Quinn had told her his department had chosen hunter green for the mountains bordering their town.

Amy must have spotted it at the same time. A small cry erupted from her throat. The magazine she had been perusing slipped from her fingers unnoticed. She pulled an oversized ottoman closer so both women could sit and watch.

"We have been told there's been a partial collapse of the building. Apparently, firefighters were in the building searching for a possible victim. It is not known at this time if there are any injuries. Dan, I'll be sure to update you as new information becomes available."

The camera returned to a local news anchor in the station.

"For those of you have just joined us. Our correspondent, Debra Sullivan, is on site at a three-alarm fire in Darby. All we know at this time is there has been some sort of collapse in the building. Firefighters were in the building at the time of the collapse searching for a possible victim. It is not known at this time how many firefighters are still in there nor what their condition may be. We will update you from the scene with any new information. Now we return you to your regular programming."

Paige heard a woman scream "No" in a loud voice before she realized the plea had come from her. She immediately called Quinn's cell phone, but it went straight to voicemail. Amy called A.J. at the same time.

She turned to her friend and took both hands in her own. "It doesn't mean anything, Amy. They're working, and their cells are turned off. We don't even know if they were in the building." The words sounded hollow even to her own ears. But she had to believe them. The alternative was unacceptable.

Amy startled as her phone rang. She answered it immediately. "Andrew?" The immediate slump of her shoulders told Paige it wasn't him. Amy handed the phone to her.

"Hello?"

"Dear, it's Susan. I saw the news. Do we know anything yet?" The older woman's voice trembled.

"No, we don't. I need to go. One of us will call you if we hear anything." She ended the call and handed the cell back to Amy.

"I couldn't talk to her. I needed to hear Andrew's voice."

She slipped her arm around Amy's slender shoulders. "I know, honey, I know." She sent a silent prayer out into the universe for the safety of the two men they loved.

Chapter Twenty-One

Quinn shone his light to the ground where A.J. had been standing moments ago. The sound of the flames roared in his head. The initial beam was followed by more debris and a large plume of dust. He lost sight of his partner. He continued to search as others joined him. In the back of his mind, he knew their air packs would be running low soon. They had to find A.J.

A shout to his left caught his attention. Jack was waving his flashlight to summon the others. He made his way carefully over to him, picking his way over beams and debris. He wanted to hurry, but safety was more important.

After what seemed an eternity, he spotted the tips of A.J.'s boots. Training his light on them, he traced the outline of his friend. Others from his company responded, and they pulled rubble off A.J.

He tried to slow his breathing as he worked. He knew the extra exertion would eat up valuable oxygen. They lost another few precious moments freeing an unconscious A.J. from the wreckage. A.J.'s continued stillness haunted him.

He queued his radio. "Chief, there's no way to get a stretcher in here. It's too dangerous, and we don't have time. We're bringing him out." He had made the decision to move A.J. even though he knew it could be bad for any spinal injuries he may have. With their oxygen levels running precariously low, getting A.J. out of the building had to be the priority.

A.J. was lying on his back, the oxygen mask miraculously still in place. They didn't have anything on which to carry or drag him. He motioned two firefighters to A.J.'s head and each one grabbed his turnout coat at the shoulder. The other two went to his knees.

He stood at the head and motioned to the other members of his crew. It was impossible to hear anything over the insistent roar of the fire. He gestured towards the door and walked ahead of them, making sure the path was clear. They all needed to be out of the building as quickly, and safely, as possible.

The other firefighters nodded in response. As one, they lifted A.J.'s unconscious body and started to move. Quinn shone his flashlight on their path and kicked various pieces of debris out of the way. He couldn't see the exit yet, but he hoped they were close. More than anything he prayed they hadn't gotten turned around. Disorientation in a fire had killed many firefighters.

He continued to look back over his shoulder at his men, assuring himself they were still with him. Suddenly, he heard the high-pitched bell that was every firefighter's nightmare. He cursed under his breath as others joined in the unholy choir. They were running out of time.

Up ahead, he thought he saw a weak light. He motioned towards it with his gloved hand, letting the others know they were almost home free. Suddenly, the building was filled with the loud crashing of more of the upper floor. As one, the men pushed forward to where he pointed. Flaming debris fell around them.

Relief flooded his body as he stumbled out into the bright afternoon sunshine. He ripped off his mask and screamed for the medics. Turning, he helped the others the last few feet to safety. As they carried A.J., Quinn removed his partner's mask and oxygen tank. The medics took over, laying him on a back board

The next few moments passed in a blur. He saw Mac and sighed a breath of relief. The medic was a friend of his. He would know what to do. They placed A.J. on a backboard and secured a stiff collar around his neck. Within two minutes, they loaded him into the back of the ambulance. He jumped in as the doors were shutting. He stayed out of Mac's way, watching with growing horror as the medic worked on A.J. with a pair of shears. Within minutes, A.J. had been stripped of his turnout gear. Mac started an IV, giving A.J. fluids.

Quinn listened when the medic gave report to the ER over the radio. He was not encouraged by what he heard. A.J.'s vital signs were dangerously low despite the large volume of fluids being pumped in. There were large contusions across his abdomen and chest from the falling beams.

He shook his head to clear the horror of what was happening. He knelt on the floor at A.J.'s feet and placed a hand on his bare leg, silently begging his friend to open his eyes. As if he had heard Quinn's plea, A.J. struggled to speak.

Mac motioned for him to come up to the head of the stretcher. "Just stay out of my way."

He nodded, unable to speak past the lump in his throat. He stepped around Mac, who was palpating A.J.'s abdomen. He placed a hand on his friend's shoulder.

A.J. weakly lifted a hand and batted at the oxygen mask on his face. He muttered something Quinn couldn't understand.

"I'm right here, A.J. You need to breathe. I've got you."

A.J. knocked the mask from his face. "Tell Amy for me," came his weak plea.

Unshed tears burned in his throat. "No way, man. You tell her whatever it is yourself."

A.J. grabbed at Quinn's hand. His eyes widened. "Promise me," he gasped. "Tell her…" He stopped, panting for breath. "Tell her I love her. And tell her I'm sorry."

He placed the mask back on AJ's face and tightened his grip on his friend's hand. "I won't do it, A.J. I need you to fight. You tell her yourself."

A.J. squeezed Quinn's hand. "We both know I'm not going to make it. You have to tell her I'm sorry."

He swallowed the lump in his throat. "Why are you sorry?"

A.J. took another rattled breath. "Promised her I'd always come home to her."

Quinn felt as though a beam had fallen on *him*. He couldn't get air in and out of his lungs. He clung to AJ's hand as the hot tears poured down his face.

"I'm sorry, but I need you to move now. His oxygen level is dropping. I need to intubate."

He nodded to Mac. Before he moved, he put his face in front of AJ's. He did the most difficult thing he ever had to do and nodded. "I'll tell her anything you want, A.J."

*****

An hour crept by, measured more in the frantic beating of their hearts than minutes. Paige and Amy had come to an unspoken agreement they wouldn't leave the TV until they got word on the guys.

"I get it now," murmured Amy.

"What do you get?"

"Why Quinn feels the way he does. It never made sense to me when you told me his feelings on marriage. I mean lots of firefighters get married and have children. So why was he so set against it? I understand now."

Paige thought about that. "You're right. I thought I understood. How could I? He told me how it had affected his mother all those years, first with his dad and now him." She gasped. "Oh, his mother. I wonder if she knows about this."

She debated calling her but decided against it. She had only just met Maria. She didn't have the right.

Amy dug her fingers into Paige's arm. "They're coming back on!" She grabbed the remote and turned up the volume.

"*We interrupt this program to bring you an update from the Tanner Avenue fire. If you're just joining us, we have been covering a fire in an abandoned warehouse in Darby. The three-alarm fire has been burning out of control for several hours. Our Debra Sullivan is on the scene. Debra, what can you tell us?*"

The camera panned the scene before settling on the petite reporter. If anything, the background looked worse to Paige.

"*Thank you, Dan. As you can see, the fire continues to burn out of control. I spoke with the Incident Commander who would only say there may be flammable materials inside this abandoned warehouse. As for the earlier partial collapse, I can tell you one firefighter has been taken out by ambulance about fifteen minutes ago. We do not have any word on their identity or condition.*"

The scene shifted to earlier footage. She gasped as it showed someone in turn out gear being loaded into a waiting ambulance. Several other firefighters could be seen standing near it, but they were too far away for Paige to identify. As she continued to watch, the channel once again switched back to regular programming. "This is torture," she said to no one in particular.

*****

Quinn opened the back doors of the ambulance as soon as the truck came to a halt at the emergency department. The hospital had been alerted to their arrival, and a trauma team was waiting for them. He caught a brief glance of Dr. Charlie Avery in navy scrubs barking out orders before A.J. was taken into one of the rooms. The doors closed firmly behind him. A. J. was in good hands. There was nothing he could do for his friend now.

He stood staring at the doors until a staff person came and showed him to a waiting area. He was grateful for her kindness. He couldn't handle being out in the hallway right now with all the people and noise.

He wasn't a particularly religious man; hadn't been since his dad was killed. But he struggled to remember some prayers he had learned as a child. He didn't know if they would help A.J., but he figured they couldn't hurt.

He sat in silence for what seemed like an eternity. He knew no one would be coming to wait with him. The fire still burned out of control. He should be with his crew, but he couldn't leave A.J. He picked up a well-worn magazine, just to have something to do with his hands.

The door opened, and Charlie slipped into the room. Her bleak eyes told him what he didn't want to know.

*****

She was going to lose it. The news station kept repeated what they already knew. One firefighter had been sent to the hospital in 'serious condition'. *What did that even mean?*

There was a knock at the door, and both women startled. Paige rose to answer it, dread weighing her steps. She opened the door to Quinn, still wearing his turnout gear pants and boots. Grateful tears slid down her face.

"Oh, thank God," she whispered and hurled herself at him. All her doubts and fears melted away. He was safe. She covered his dirty face with kisses before backing up to drink in the sight of him. Then she noticed the grim expression on his face. A chill wrapped around her heart.

He looked over Paige's shoulder. He moved around her and took a step towards Amy.

"Stop right there! Don't you dare tell me something has happened to Andrew." Amy stood with her arms wrapped around her middle.

He stepped further into the room until he was within arm's reach of her. "I'm so sorry, Amy. There wasn't any warning. The ceiling gave way and A.J. was in the wrong place at the wrong time." A breath shuddered out of him. "He wanted me to tell you he loved you. And that he was sorry."

Paige watched in horror as the color bled from Amy's face. "Are you telling me he's dead? Andrew is dead? He can't be. He promised." She beat her fists against Quinn's chest, sobbing as she did. He took the blows, arms hanging at his sides, tears running down his face.

Paige took Amy by the arms and led her to the couch. She sat next to her and folded her friend into her arms, stroking her hair as Amy sobbed. Her own heart ached for her friend.

She motioned to Quinn. She held up her phone and pointed to Susan's contact information. "Can you call her and ask her to come please?" He took the phone and stepped into the kitchen to make the call. She could hear his soft murmur.

Paige continued to hold Amy as she cried. "I'm right here with you. We will get through this together, Amy. I'm so, so sorry." If Amy heard her, she didn't know. The words were nothing against the tide of grief washing over Amy, but they were all she had.

Less than fifteen minutes later, a car pulled into the driveway. Susan ran into the house. She sat on the other side of her daughter and held tightly to her without saying a word. Paige heard the door close and realized he had left. Although she knew he was hurting too, her place was with Amy right now.

*****

Quinn got into his truck, grateful a hospital volunteer had been able to drive him from the emergency department back to the station to pick it up. He checked in with his chief and learned the fire was now under control. His crew had been released and were en route back to the station. He drove there on auto pilot.

The memory of Amy's grief tortured him as he drove. Her sobs mingled with the memory of the long-ago ones of his mother. This was exactly why he told Paige he would never get married.

Her relief at finding him alive on her doorstep had been a palpable thing. It meant she had been worried for some time, maybe even seen the fire on the news. He refused to put her through this again.

He pulled into the station remaining in his car and watching as the engine pulled into the bay. He could make out the somber expressions of his friends. He got of his truck and walked towards the station. The thought of A.J. lying in the morgue instead of riding on the truck almost brought him to his knees.

Jack approached him. He knew the stark expression on his friend's face mirrored his own. "What do we do now?" His eyes were red from more than smoke.

He shook his head. "I don't know, Jack. I just don't know." He put his arm around Jack's shoulder and walked him into the station. Everyone was gathered in the dining area. It was eerily quiet. He looked around and noticed many of the off-duty crews had shown up. Bad news travelled fast.

Chief Wells entered the room. All eyes were on him. None were dry. The Chief cleared his throat. "This is the day every firefighter dreads. When one of our own doesn't make it home. A.J. was like a son to me, as you all are. He was a good man and a good firefighter. I won't lie to you. The next few days are going to be hard. We're going to have to say goodbye to A.J. I've taken us out of service until the funeral is over. Stations Twenty-Two and Thirty-Five will be covering for us. In the meantime, we need to be here for each other." A few men nodded in response.

Quinn left the room. Tears coursed through the grime on his face. He didn't bother to wipe them away. He stopped at the plaque for fallen firefighters. He traced his father's name with a finger. Soon, another name of someone close to him would grace it. A heavy hand dropped onto his shoulder.

"I won't ask you how you're doing. Just wanted to let you know I'm here for you." He glanced at the metal plate that bore the name Joseph Adams. "Your father was my best friend. Losing him almost killed me."

"How did you keep going? How did you go to the next fire? And the next? I don't think I can, Chief."

"Those are questions for another day. Right now, all you need to grieve for your friend. Don't think about the job. Go home. Be with family. Be with Paige. Get through this first before making other decisions." He squeezed Quinn's shoulder before leaving him to his grief.

He turned and watched his chief walk away. His steps were heavier and slower, as if losing A.J. had aged him. Fatigue washed over him. He went into the TV room and collapsed in a recliner. Leaning back, he stretched out fully and closed his eyes. But rest wasn't coming. All he could see were images of A.J covered in rubble.

He was too restless to stay here. Knowing what he had to do, but dreading it, he left the building. A.J. had been an only child, born to older parents who had given up the dream of having a family. This would crush them.

Chapter Twenty-Two

Paige drove to Amy's condo to gather some of her belongings. Susan had taken her daughter home with her. After her initial bout of sobbing, she had retreated into a world of silence. The light vanished from her eyes. She shuddered at the memory of that kind of grief. She knew it all too well.

She randomly threw clothing into a small suitcase. Turning to leave the condo, Paige halted by a framed photograph on the entry table. It was of Amy and A.J. and had been taken the night of the dinner at her parents' home. Both were relaxed and smiling. A.J. had his arm thrown around Amy's shoulders. He looked happy. And alive. She had taken the picture with her phone and sent it to Amy the next morning. She had no way of knowing tragedy was right around the corner when she snapped the photo.

She arrived back at the Windsor home. Her heart ached as she carried Amy's suitcase inside. As hard as it had been to hear her friend sobbing, the eerie silence was more difficult to take. She found Susan in the kitchen. She set the suitcase down in the doorway and hugged the older woman, who sobbed into Paige's shoulder.

"What are we going to do? How do we help her? I can't stand to see her in so much pain. I want to take it from her."

She held onto her and thought about that day so long ago when Susan had been there for her. Their roles had come full circle. "I know you do. It's what makes you such a good mother. But you can't. This is a journey she has to take. We can only be here for her."

Susan straightened up and grabbed a handful of tissues. "I'm so thankful she has you. She's going to need every person who loves her to get through this awful time." She turned to the counter and resumed peeling potatoes.

"What are you doing?"

"I'm making potato salad. Then I'm going to move on to pasta salad and maybe some desserts." She smiled through her tears. "You know me, when in doubt, cook."

She smiled back at her. She doubted she could swallow past the painful lump in her throat. But they would have to eat at some point. And Susan Windsor would be ready.

She looked out to the patio. Mike and Alex sat in the shade of the awning with glasses of sweet tea at their elbows. Theirs heads were bent close in conversation, so she decided to not interrupt.

"I'm going to go check in on Amy."

She mounted the staircase, her heart pounding with dread. Amy's grief was palpable. Like Susan, she wished she had a way to take it away. She knocked before entering.

Amy lay curled up on top of her bed, legs drawn up to her stomach and arms wrapped around them. She looked as though she was trying to fend off some invisible blow. He eyes were open but unfocused.

She entered the room and sat on the bed. "I'm here with you. Is there anything you need?" She hadn't expected an answer. "It's okay. I wanted you to know I'm here. I brought some of your things. I thought you might be more comfortable staying here for a few days." She glanced at her friend. The blank expression on her face shook Paige. It was as if there was nothing left to her.

She stayed there until Susan came in. She got up and walked out into the hallway with her. "She hasn't moved. Hasn't spoken. Hasn't cried. She's barely even blinked. I feel so helpless."

"I know dear. I'm going to call Dr. Farnsworth. He'll know what to do." She moved off down the hall.

She went down to the kitchen to see what she could do. She got out a large pot to boil the pasta Susan had set on the counter. She was lost in thought and didn't hear Alex come in.

"Hey, Paige. How are you holding up?"

She turned towards him, fresh tears threatening at his subdued tone. "Not great. It's so hard to watch her grieve."

"I know." He closed the distance between them and folded her into his arms.

The tears that had been threatening now slid freely down her cheeks. She pressed her face into his chest and sobbed. He stood holding her and murmuring softly.

After a few minutes, she stepped out of his embrace and smiled through her tears. "Luckily for you, I'm not a big believer in mascara."

Alex glanced at his soaked shirt. "It wouldn't have mattered if you were. I'm here for you. I always have been."

She felt a quick stab of remorse at his kindness. Alex was a great man. If only she could have fallen for *him*. "I know you are, Alex. And I appreciate that. This is so awful."

She turned back to the stove and turned on the burner. "And now I am going to keep busy. It's all I can do." Reaching around him, she ran water into the pot before setting it on the burner.

Late in the evening, Paige drove to Quinn's house. She had finally left to go home to shower and change but decided on the way she would rather see him. She wondered how he was holding up. She had thought about him throughout the day but had not wanted to leave Amy's side.

She wasn't sure if he even wanted to see her. But she needed to know he was okay. She parked next to his truck and walked to the front door. She knocked softly and waited.

He appeared in the doorway. If he was surprised to see her, he didn't say. He merely held open the door for her.

She walked in and waited while he shut it again. She stood uncertainly, not knowing if being here was the right thing.

"How's Amy?"

"She hasn't eaten or spoken all day, but she's asleep now, which is probably the best thing for her. Earlier, Dr. Farnsworth stopped by to check on her. He's an old friend of Amy's dad. He gave her a shot of tranquilizer and left a prescription with Amy's mother."

"I went to see A.J.'s parents." The lines on his face told the story of how that had gone.

"I wanted to see how you were. You must be hurting."

"I have no idea how I am. Numb maybe. I thought about having a drink, or maybe ten. But there isn't enough alcohol in the world to help. A.J. will still be dead."

She reached out and took him by the hand. She led him into his darkened bedroom. She removed her shirt and shorts before turning to him. Without a single sexual thought, she removed his clothing as well and pulled him down to the mattress. When they were both lying down, she reached for the sheet to cover them and put her arms around him.

He laid his head on her shoulder and cried. She remained silent as his hot tears ran down her chest. She stroked his arm and tried to give him strength. Her own tears flowed freely as she listened to this big, tough firefighter sob like a small child.

After a while, his tears slowed. Without moving or looking at her, Quinn began to speak. "He was a good man. A.J. would do anything for anyone. And he was so happy since he met Amy. I can't believe he's gone."

"I know. It doesn't seem real to me. We were sitting there talking about her wedding dress when the news broke. I always knew there was an element of danger to your job, but I never thought this would happen. Amy is devastated. It's so hard to watch her be in so much pain."

"I can't get the scene out of my head. We were looking for a victim thought to be in the building. One minute A.J. was fine, and then he wasn't. There was this horrible sound as the ceiling gave way." He drew in a ragged breath.

She traced her fingers up and down his arm to remind him she was there.

"I tried so hard to get to him on time, but it all happened in the blink of an eye. All I could do was yell. But it was too late. I couldn't reach him. I couldn't save him."

His powerful body shuddered as waves of grief rolled through him. All she could do was hold on to him. Paige's own tears continued to fall. She grieved for all of them. For Quinn losing his best friend; the second time had lost someone he loved to fire. For Amy who had been so in love with A.J. and eagerly planning their future. And for herself. For having to stand by and watch as two people she loved had their lives changed irrevocably.

She tentatively kissed his face where she could reach him. She meant only to offer comfort, but he responded with a white-hot desire. He groaned and flipped her underneath him, hands wild and lips devouring her. She went up in flames as he covered her body with his own. His lips seared her breasts as his fingers found her wet and waiting for him. He looked into her eyes and hesitated, but she made the decision for him, wrapping her arms around him to pull him close. With a groan, he slid into her warm depths.

Paige gasped at the sensation of him inside her. He hadn't stopped to put on a condom, and she hadn't thought of one. But it was a safe of the month, and she couldn't have stopped now even if she wanted. She raked her nails up and down his back, encouraging him to move faster, harder.

In a moment of blinding sensation, she was tumbling into her release. She felt Quinn contract within her before she was filled with his warmth. He pulled out and flopped on his back next to her. They both panted hard, trying to catch their breath.

"I'm so sorry. I wasn't thinking."

"Shhh," she soothed him. "It's okay. I wasn't thinking either. We should be fine. Between the timing and the birth control pills I take, we're okay."

He dragged a hand though his hair. "Still, I should have been more careful."

"We're fine. Go to sleep."

"I can't sleep. I can't close my eyes without seeing A.J." But his eyelids drooped.

Amy drew the sheets back up to cover them. She had only intended to offer him comfort. Sex had not been on her agenda. But the closeness of their bodies was exactly what both of them needed. She lay in the dark and held him, listening as his breathing slowed and evened out. His body relaxed as he slid into sleep. Paige was emotionally exhausted from the day and followed shortly afterwards.

*****

Quinn awoke to the sound of his text alert. He grabbed the phone and saw Chief Wells had sent him information for A.J.'s funeral, which would be held in two days. He placed the phone back on the table. The other side of the bed was empty, with only the scent unique to her remaining as proof she had ever been there.

He had no idea when she left. For once, he had slept through it. He got up and relieved himself in the bathroom before throwing on running shorts and a tank shirt. The grief so blissfully absent for a few short hours was back with a vengeance. His lungs burned with the effort of breathing. He grabbed his phone and headed out.

Setting a punishing pace, he ran through the quiet streets of Windsor Falls. It was still early; barely past dawn. Most people would still be asleep. He loved this time of the morning for a run. Although warm, he avoided the brutal heat that would come later. Usually, this was a peaceful time, with only the sound of his shoes on the pavement and his own breathing. But not today.

He couldn't believe his actions last night. He had been hurting so badly when Paige had appeared, a temporary relief from the pain of losing A.J. And while she had freely given him the comfort he needed, he had responded by taking her roughly and without any thought to consequences. He had wanted to feel something other than crushing grief or guilt.

He cringed as he remembered entering her without so much as a thought of using a condom. All he wanted, needed, was to feel her wrapped around him. He needed to blot out the memory of A.J.'s final moments, even for a few minutes.

And then he had fallen asleep. He was thankful to her for this. He had been dreading nightmares. Those would come, but for one night he had been able to sleep.

Sweat dripped off him by the time he returned home. He went straight to the kitchen to grab a bottle of water. That's when he saw the sticky note posted there.

"Sorry about leaving like this. I need to get back to Amy. Hope you're doing okay. Call me later. Paige"

He traced his finger over her signature. It explained why she was gone when he awoke. It made sense, and he knew she needed to be with Amy today. But he couldn't help feeling a bit lost. She never put any demands on him. She still did exactly what he had asked of her.

*****

The day of A.J.'s funeral dawned too beautiful for burying her best friend's fiancé. This thought greeted her when she awoke. It had been three days since A.J. died, and Paige was dreading it. She couldn't even imagine how Amy was feeling.

Amy still hadn't spoken much, a few words here and there. She had eaten a couple times, but usually only enough to keep a bird alive. Still, she hadn't taken any more of the medicine Dr. Farnsworth had left for her. Whether or not she was sleeping was anyone's guess.

She had moved back into her old room at the Windsor home. Long gone were the pink walls and boy band posters. Susan had turned it into a beautifully appointed guest room in calming shades of green.

She sat there now, on a chintz covered chair, staring out at the beautiful morning. She had showered and was putting on a bare minimum of makeup. Her plain, black sleeveless dress hung in the closet. The weather forecaster had promised scorching temperatures near one hundred. The sky was an almost painfully brilliant blue without the trace of a cloud.

She shook her head. The weather didn't matter. This would be a long, brutally difficult day. There was a viewing this morning which led right into the funeral service. Afterwards, A.J.'s fellow firefighters were hosting a wake in his honor at the station. This she had learned from Susan, who had spoken to A.J.'s brokenhearted parents. She hadn't heard a single word from Quinn.

She sighed and stepped into her dress, reaching behind to zip it up as far as she could. She wasn't surprised she hadn't heard from him. She had crept out of his house in the wee hours two days ago. And even though she had left a note, she hadn't liked leaving without so much as a goodbye.

Looking in the mirror, Paige squared her shoulders and her resolve. She would get through this day. More importantly, she would help Amy get through it. Later, when it was all over, she would find Quinn. Only Amy mattered today.

She turned at the soft knock on the guest room door. She opened it to find Amy standing there in a black dress. She looked better than Paige had expected, until she saw her eyes. They were empty. Amy was barely hanging on.

"Are you ready?" she asked in a dull voice. "I need this day to end."

She nodded and grabbed her small black purse in which she had stuffed a mountain of tissues and her phone. She reached forward to hug her friend.

"Don't." Amy stepped back into the hallway. "I'm sorry, but if you hug me I may break into a thousand pieces."

"Okay." She followed Amy down the stairs. Susan and Mike were standing near the front door. Alex walked in from the kitchen.

"I'm going to say this once." Everyone looked at Amy as she spoke. "I have to get through this day. I have to say goodbye to Andrew one more time. I will do so in my own way. Please don't try to make this easier for me. There isn't anything you can do or say."

Susan clasp her hands tightly together as if stopping herself from touching Amy. Mike took his keys from his pocket. "Are we ready to go?" Everyone nodded solemnly. They walked out the front door.

Alex came up beside Paige and touched her on the arm. "I was thinking I would drive as well. Do you want to come with me?"

Amy and her parents were already in their car. "Sure, Alex. Thanks."

The short drive was completed in relative silence. There wasn't anything to say. When they arrived at the funeral home, Paige gaped at the number of emergency apparatus lining the street. Quinn had mentioned fellow firefighters would come from near and far to say goodbye to one of their own. But she had no idea how many would come.

Alex parked the car and turned to her. "I did like him you know. He may not have been my first choice, but he made my sister happy."

"Yes, he did. I was there when they met. A.J. took one look at your sister, and he was gone. And it wasn't the usual reaction men have; drooling over her stop-you-in-your-tracks beauty. He just wanted to be with her. And she felt the same way. I don't know if I ever believed in love at first sight. I do now."

Alex was silent for a moment. "Is that what happened with Quinn?" He asked so softly she barely heard him.

She didn't want to discuss her relationship with anyone, especially Alex. "It's complicated." She knew it sounded lame and raised more questions than it answered, but she didn't care.

"You love him."

"I do." She had never admitted it to anyone. Not even herself really. Funny Alex would be the first.

"Is he good to you? I can handle your loving someone else as long as I know he's good to you." He pulled into a parking spot.

Paige smiled for the first time in days. "He is, Alex. You never have to worry." She picked up her purse and opened the car door, dreading going into the building.

Schumacher & Sons Funeral Home was where they had buried her parents so many years ago. She had not been back since.

Alex came behind her and placed a hand in the small of her back. "That's the problem with small towns. Only one funeral home. I've got you."

Although Paige liked to think she was tough, she was grateful for his support. They walked across the parking lot, the ferocious heat coming off the black top in waves. If nothing else, she was thankful for the blast of cold air greeting them when they entered the building.

She signed the guest book, noting Quinn's name was already there. Knowing he was somewhere near gave her comfort. She turned as Amy stepped behind her. She looked as though a strong wind might blow her over.

"I know you're worried about me. I'm going to be fine. I'm going to be fine." She wasn't sure if Amy was assuring her or herself.

"Of course, you're going to be. I'm just here for whatever you need." Paige gripped Amy's icy hand and led them into the viewing room.

*****

Quinn watched from the corner of the room as Paige entered with members of the Windsor family. He had been standing in the parking lot with Jack when Alex's shiny black Mercedes pulled in. He believed she didn't have any romantic feelings for Alex, but the sight of the other man's hands on her was tough to swallow.

He had followed them inside, keeping his distance. He wanted to be with Paige, but he also had a duty to perform. He and Jack, along with four others, would act as pallbearers later. Just another thing to dread on an already terrible day.

He stood in the corner of the room, unwilling to look at A.J.'s body again. He had already approached the casket containing his friend when he first arrived. The essence of what had made his friend great was long gone. The shell left behind served as a cruel reminder of the loss that clawed inside him. Two members of his station stood at either end of the casket as honor guard. He watched A.J.'s parents greet each new person. Someone had brought them chairs to rest in between the seemingly endless waves of people paying their respects.

From his vantage point, Quinn watched as she entered the room with Amy. Alex and his parents were right behind them. The hollow look to Amy made his chest ache. It was the look his mother had worn so many years ago. The thought of her ever having to look like that made him ill. It also strengthened his resolve.

*****

Paige climbed into the long, black limousine with Amy for the ride to the fire station. The past few hours had passed in a blur of sorrowful faces and bitter tears. A.J.'s parents had insisted Amy stay with them throughout the viewing and funeral. She stayed with her for support. And so, she had ended up across the casket from Quinn. Even with dark sunglasses shielding his eyes, she could feel him watching her throughout the service. They still had not spoken.

"It's a comfort to know A.J was so well thought of," said his mother, Linda, from the seat opposite from Paige. "I had no idea so many people would come." She turned her head to the window as fresh tears ran down her cheeks. She seemed to have aged ten years in the past few hours.

Watching others grieve this senseless loss devastated Paige. "I didn't know him as well as I would have liked, Mrs. Jefferson, but I was looking forward to getting to know him better. Amy and I…" She broke off, not wanting to continue the sentence. There wasn't any point now. A.J. was dead.

Amy stiffened next to her. "She would have gotten to know him a lot better as her best friend was going to marry him. That's what she was trying to not say." She turned to Paige before continuing. "It's okay to talk about it. I loved Andrew. I will always love him. The fact that he died before we could marry doesn't change it."

A.J.'s father spoke for the first time. "You were a gift to him, Amy. I've never seen him as happy as he was the past few weeks."

Amy nodded, tears sliding down her face. She clutched Paige's hand.

Several hours later, Paige got up from the table and stretched. People milled around in small groups, standing together or eating. Food equaled love, and this tight-knit community had poured all of its love into today. Good-intentioned women tempted her with yet another dish she 'just had to try'. So, she ate, but even good old Southern comfort food couldn't pierce the veil of grief.

She walked over to Amy, who was speaking with Jack. "Are you ready to go home?"

Amy nodded. "Jack, it was lovely to catch up with you."

An unusually subdued Jack leaned in and hugged her awkwardly. For all his reputation as a ladies' man, Jack was sweet. She smiled at him and then guided Amy to where her parents waited.

Susan took Amy by the hand and led her out into the bright sunshine of late afternoon. Mike followed behind. "Are you coming with us or Alex?"

"I guess I'll go with Alex so he's not alone in the car. Have you seen him anywhere?"

"I think he went in search of a restroom. He should be right out."

"It's fine. I want to say goodbye to some people. You guys go on ahead." She watched as Amy's father left the building.

She looked for him but didn't spot him right away. She walked into a hallway and found him staring at a plaque on the wall. Approaching, she realized it was for fallen firefighters. His father's name was the last one listed.

He turned his head and looked at her with no expression on his face. A chill ran down her spine. She hadn't spoken with him all day, and now he didn't seem pleased to see her.

She closed the gap and placed a tentative hand on his arm. "I just wanted to say goodbye. I'm going home with Amy's family. It's been a long day, and I'm worried about her."

For a long moment, he didn't reply, and she was afraid he wasn't going to say anything. Just as she turned to leave, he reached out and grabbed her arm.

"Do you get it now?" There was only despair in his voice.

All of the comfort food threatened to come back up. She knew what he was asking but couldn't get the words out. She stared at him mutely.

"Today is exactly why I have avoided any type of serious relationship. I watched Amy all day. It would have been easier if she had broken down and cried, but she just moved through the day, trapped in her grief. I don't ever want to be the reason for someone feeling that. For you feeling that."

The dread in her stomach turned to ice. Paige knew what was coming. And there was no way to protect herself from it. "You're right about today. Watching my best friend in the world bury her fiancé was awful. But you take that chance when you open your heart to someone."

He dragged a hand through his hair and turned partially away from her. She laid her hand on his back to comfort him, but he shrugged it off.

"At least have the decency to look at me when you break up with me." She hated the desperation she heard in her own voice but couldn't help it.

He turned to face her, his eyes bleak. "I told you from the beginning. I told you I don't do long term. You promised me you understood."

She felt the ice in her stomach swell to encase her heart. She knew this day was coming, but the reality was so much worse than she ever imagined.

"You're right. This is on me. You have been nothing but honest. But I was stupid enough to fall in love with you anyway." She wiped at the lone tear that escaped.

He stared at her for a moment. She thought she saw the tiniest expression flare in his dark brown eyes, but it was gone as quickly as it had appeared. "I won't risk doing to you what A.J. just did to Amy. I won't break your heart."

"Too late, Quinn. You already did." Paige turned on her heel and headed blindly towards the exit. She plowed straight into Alex.

He steadied her and looked into her eyes. "Hey! Are you okay?"

She raised her head and shook it, not trusting herself to speak.

Alex took her by the arm and escorted her out to his car. After handing her into the passenger side, he walked around and climbed in next to her. He drove for several miles before pulling over and placing the car in park.

"This is not about A.J., is it?"

That was all it took to set her off. Paige covered her face with her hands and sobbed. "I'm such an idiot! He told me from the very beginning he didn't do relationships. I promised I understood, and I thought I did." She covered her face with shaking hands.

Alex leaned over the console and wrapped his arms around her. "You're not an idiot. He was lucky to have you. Don't cry. Please don't cry."

Paige straightened up and dashed the tears from her face. "You're right, Alex. I shouldn't be crying about Quinn, today of all days. I can't let Amy see me like this." She straightened her shoulders. "I love him, Alex."

"I know you do, sweetheart. I'm so sorry."

She sniffed again. "Today and the next few days are about Amy. Then I'll give in to my broken heart. How's that for a plan?"

"It's brilliant," replied Alex. He put the car back into drive and continued on to his parents' home.

Chapter Twenty-Three

Quinn sat in the station parking lot and stared at the building. This had been his true home for so many years. Now his stomach rolled at the thought of entering. He had not been back in the two weeks since his friend's death. Technically, he was still on leave. But he couldn't put this off any longer.

He went inside and slipped into the hallway containing his chief's office. He needed to have a conversation with him that was long overdue and didn't want an audience. He raised his hand and knocked on the open door.

"Come in," came the gruff reply. Chief Wells swiveled in his chair to glance towards the doorway. The two men exchanged a look before he entered the room.

Acid swirled in the pit of his stomach. The chief had always been a part of his life, first as his father's friend and then as a sort of surrogate father after Joe died. He had been Quinn's boss for the past fourteen years. Henry was tough but fair. There was no reason for him to be nervous. But he was afraid he was about to disappoint the one man he never wished to.

"So, you've decided to not come back. Isn't this what you're trying so hard to not tell me?"

His mouth dropped open. He stared in silence for a long moment before answering. "Yes, sir. I'm sorry."

"Why are you sorry?"

He could barely look at the older man since entering his office but deliberately raised his eyes to do so now. "I'm sorry for disappointing you, sir."

Henry got up and came around the desk, taking the chair next to him. He placed one big hand on the younger man's shoulder. "What makes you think you've disappointed me?"

Quinn tried to swallow the bitter emotion lodged in his throat. "I just can't come back, sir. Not after A.J. My heart's just not in it anymore."

"Then you're making the right decision. This is not a job you can give less than one hundred percent to, as you know. So, you're doing the only thing you can do. Why would I be disappointed?"

"Well, I'm quitting, sir."

"Yes, you are. But for the right reason. It takes a brave man, a smart man, to know when he's done. Staying would be easier in the short run. But you're a better man."

"Thank you, sir."

"You're welcome. So, what's next?"

Quinn barked out a short, humorless laugh. "I have no idea. I have a ton of leave stored up. And I'm looking for my next house project, so maybe I'll do that full time for a while. See how it goes." But even as he said the words, he knew they weren't true. While he enjoyed the house flipping, he knew in his heart it wasn't what he wanted to do for the rest of his life.

"I have a better idea. There's about to be an opening on the county arson squad. Smith is retiring, and his second in command is taking over his position. So, the full-time arson investigator spot will be open. I already told them about you. You'd be perfect for it."

For the first time since the fire, he felt a smile tug at the corners of his mouth. "I could stay involved in the fire service without having to be in the thick of it, so to speak. You've known this whole time, haven't you?"

"I saw your expression the day we buried A.J. It wasn't just grief or sorrow. I knew you were done. I thought about quitting after your father died. But the fire service was all I had."

"How am I any different? This is all I have."

"That's not true. You have a young woman who's crazy about you. And if you were honest, you're just as crazy about her too." He grinned as Quinn squirmed in his seat. "You've been playing it safe all these years, never getting involved. I get it. I do. But it's a sacrifice you made to be a firefighter. If you take the other position, you can have both. You don't have to choose anymore."

The first bit of hope since A.J died stirred in his chest. *Maybe it wasn't too late.* Maybe Paige would understand and forgive him. "So, what do I have to do, Chief?"

"Well, first you have to stop calling me Chief. It's Henry. I'm not your chief anymore. I'll start the paperwork on this end. You need to contact the county and let them know you're interested. They're waiting to hear from you."

"Just like that?"

"Oh, you'll have to get up to speed with the science behind arson investigation. I imagine you'll have to take some classes. But you'll be fine."

He rubbed a hand over his face. "I miss him, Henry. Everyday."

"I know you do. I still miss your father every day. A.J. was a good man. We all miss him."

Both men stood, and Henry slapped Quinn on the back. "Go on, get out of here. You have a lot to do."

He grinned. "I certainly do." He exited the building with a much lighter step than he had entered. He got into his truck and headed back to his house. House. Not home. Paige lived in a home. He had felt the difference the first time he had stepped into hers. Even in its state of reconstruction, with drop clothes everywhere and a distinct lack of her personal belongings, it felt more like a home then where he actually lived.

But now his house was on the market, and Gabriella had just informed him of an offer this morning. It was time to look for the next project. For the first time ever, it wasn't a pleasant thought.

Without thinking, he turned down Paige's street. He slowed as he passed, noting her empty driveway. She might be at Amy's. He remembered her awful grief at the funeral. It had been painful to watch. It was exactly what had pushed him over the edge and caused him to end things with her. Also, not a good memory and not his finest moment. He needed to set things straight. He would beg if necessary. But first, he had to find her.

*****

The lawn around the gazebo filled as daylight faded. Paige sat with Amy and her family, awaiting the start of the concert. A local band that played a mix of country and rock would be starting any minute. She leaned across Susan to address Amy. "I remember seeing them play when we were in high school."

Her friend nodded. Amy had been very quiet since A.J.'s death. It had taken all of them to get her to come out tonight. Her friend was still caught in the depths of grief and she remembered how difficult that was. Still, she worried about her. Normally slender, Amy couldn't afford the ten pounds she'd dropped.

Alex shifted in his lawn chair on the other side of her. She turned to look at him. He seemed edgy, which wasn't like him. She laid a hand on his arm. "Are you okay?"

"Of course. Why wouldn't I be?"

"I don't know. You seem a bit off."

He flashed his million-dollar smile at her. "You worry too much."

She nodded, still not convinced. "If you say so."

A murmur rippled through the crowd. Paige turned towards the stage as the band took their places. Will Simms, the owner of the local pharmacy and lead singer, approached the mike.

"Good evening, Windsor Falls. Thanks for coming out to listen tonight. We've got all your favorites lined up. But first, we have a surprise for you. Alex, if you're ready."

Alex stood and joined Will on the stage. She turned to his parents. "What is he doing? Alex can't sing." Her stomach dropped when both Mike and Susan averted their gazes. *What in the world?*

"Good evening, ladies and gentlemen. For those of you who don't know me, I'm Alex Windsor." Clapping and a few whistles followed his introduction. "If you do know me, don't worry. I'm not here to sing." He paused as the crowd cheered.

Alex cleared his throat, and for the first time she could remember, looked nervous. "I wanted to ask a certain someone a special question. Paige Harrington, could you please stand up?"

Her hands turned to ice, but she did as he asked. She had a very bad feeling what the question might be. Her knees wobbled. *Please don't do this, Alex.* She stood very still and waited for the inevitable.

"Recent events have caused me to take a look at my life. And while I love my job and my family, I realize there's something missing. I've known Paige since she and my sister were babies together. We've been friends a long time. She's a wonderful person. A good person. She's the kind of person you build a life with."

The crowd gasped as one. She gasped for air. This was really happening. Alex was motioning her to join him on stage. The crowd cheered. Why couldn't the earth open up and swallow her whole? On wooden legs, she walked up the stairs to the gazebo. Alex covered her icy hand with his. And dropped to one knee.

"Paige Harrington, I have a very simple question for you. Would you do me the honor of becoming my wife?"

The few hundred people on the lawn all seemed to lean forward, waiting for her answer. Suddenly, the heat from the lights of the gazebo overwhelmed her. The edges of her vision blurred. Paige reached out to grab onto Alex. And passed out at his feet.

*****

Quinn had just arrived at the town green, hoping to find Paige. He had already looked everywhere else. On stage, with Alex Windsor proposing to her, was the last place he expected to find her. Then she fainted. He ran through the crowd, dodging blankets and jumping over coolers, to reach the gazebo. By the time he did, Alex had picked her up and carried her off to a bench behind it. He heard someone on the phone with 9-1-1.

Not caring what Alex thought, he rushed to her side. She lay cradled in the other man's arms, a sight which made him want to punch him. "Are you all right?"

"Back off, Adams. Haven't you done enough?"

He clenched his hands into fists at his sides. "I'm not the one who caused her to faint, Windsor."

"Quinn, what are you doing here?" Paige opened her eyes, but her voice was very faint.

"I've been looking for you everywhere. How are you feeling?"

"Alex, let me go." She struggled for a moment before sliding to the bench next to him.

"What happened?" Amy ran to her side, her parents on her heels.

He grew impatient with the growing crowd. He needed to speak with her. Alone. "If I could just have a moment with her, please." The wail of an ambulance drowned out his words. Sure enough, Mac jumped out of the truck and strode towards them.

Mac hunkered down in front of Paige. His face softened. "I know you."

She lifted a hand in greeting. "We have to stop meeting like this," she joked.

"I hear you fainted. Let's take a look." Quinn watched as Mac took out a blood pressure cuff and stethoscope, chatting with Paige as if they weren't in the middle of a growing crowd of onlookers. The situation was spiraling out of control.

Alex held her other hand. "I've got this, Adams. Maybe you should leave."

The urge to punch him in his perfect face bubbled to the surface again. Through gritted teeth, he responded. "I'm staying."

Mac finished his survey. "Your vital signs are fine. It could be the heat."

She nodded. "I skipped dinner. I feel better, Mac. Thanks so much for rescuing me again." She pulled her hand from Alex's and stood. Quinn and Alex both stood at her side.

She turned to Alex. "Could you take me home, please?"

Quinn's heart clenched. She hadn't even looked at him. "I'm glad you're okay." He turned and walked into the night.

*****

Paige's head spun as he walked her to his car. And it wasn't from fainting. She waited until they were seated before turning to him. "What were you thinking, Alex?"

Even in the dark car, she could spot the dull red creeping across his cheekbones. "I thought a grand gesture might convince you."

Her heart swelled with love for him, just not the kind he wanted. She laid a hand on his arm. "Oh, Alex, I'm not looking for a grand gesture. Not from you or Quinn. The fact you don't know that should tell you something."

"I know now," he mumbled.

"Alex, you know I love you. Just not in the way you think you want me to. We're friends. You're the brother I never had. You may not want to hear this, but it's the truth. I've been honest with you all along."

"What does love have to do with anything?" He smiled down into her incredulous expression. "You know I have big plans for my life. I need a partner. Someone from a good family who gets me. That's you. We've known each other our whole lives. We get along. My parents already love you. This is right."

Paige's blue eyes widened. "I would ask if you were kidding, but obviously you're not. Alex, I would never entertain such an arrangement. Your parents love each to distraction, as did mine. They were happy. I want the same. I'm not interested in marrying someone based on their pedigree."

"Love? You've been miserable for the past two weeks. I haven't seen you smile or be yourself. Loving Quinn did that to you. Is that what you want? I would never hurt you like he did."

She sighed. He wasn't getting this. "Yes, he hurt me. But it's my own fault. He was honest from the very beginning. I should have never entered into a relationship with him knowing how he felt. But I did, and I fell for him." She lifted her chin and stared him down. "And I may be 'miserable' right now, but I don't regret what I did. I won't go through my life being afraid to live. And to love."

He started the car. "I'm sorry. I thought we would be a good match." He smiled at her. "I still do."

There was nothing more to say, so she turned to look out the window on the short drive home. They arrived at her house in a few minutes. Ever the gentleman, Alex walked her to the door. He leaned down and kissed her cheek. "You know where I am, if you change your mind."

"I'm not going to. But I don't want things to change between us."

He nodded and left.

She went inside, scooping up Finn and taking him to the back yard. She sat on the patio while he ran around searching for the perfect spot. Leaning back, she stared at the stars and wondered how her life had spun so completely out of control. Alex proposed to her, in front of hundreds of people. Hundreds! She'd never hear the end of this.

And then Quinn appeared out of nowhere. She had not seen nor heard from him in two weeks, and he shows up when she's unconscious. She squeezed her eyes shut. How long had he been in the park? Had he seen the debacle of Alex proposing to her? Of course he had. That's the way her life went.

Finn pounced on her bare toes, pulling her out of her gloomy thoughts. She threw his ball and watched in amusement as he scampered after it. Paige straightened up in the chair and mentally gave herself a talking to. She was just fine, thank you very much. She'd never been the kind to need a man, and she wasn't going to start now.

Her home was coming along well, and she would be done before her summer break was up. Maybe she'd take Amy up on her idea to get away. They could both use a change of scenery.

Chapter Twenty-Four

Paige turned off the car and rested her head back against the rest. She squeezed her eyes closed, hoping to blot out thoughts of Quinn. No such luck. She sighed and opened her eyes. Finn barked from his seat in the back. She smiled and turned to him. "Okay, let's get out."

She released his travel harness and clipped on a leash. Finn burst out of the car with his usual enthusiasm, sniffing each individual blade of grass. She breathed in the mountain air. Following a small path down from the parking area, she found her favorite shade tree and sat, resting her back against it. Finn walked around her in all directions as far as the leash would allow. Satisfied when he had smelled everything, Finn returned to Paige and flopped down in the grass against her leg.

The past few weeks had been tough, more than she could have predicted. But both she and Amy were going to be okay. Just thinking about it made her angry all over again. A.J. had died, not left Amy. He didn't have a choice in the matter. But Quinn did. He had chosen to leave her. Knowing he had been honest from the beginning didn't make it any easier. But she had been so consumed with taking care of Amy, she had buried her own grief.

She allowed the pain to roll over her once again. Hot tears ran down her face. She let them flow unchecked, wondering for the hundredth time when this was going to get any easier. She was careful to only think about him when she wasn't with Amy. She had enough to deal with just putting one foot in front of the other each day.

Lost in thought, she didn't notice at first when Finn sat up and started to wag his stubby tail. Her text alert sounded.

"Please don't cry, Paige. I'm so sorry."

Finn broke out into a chorus of delighted yipping. Paige turned and looked around the tree. Quinn stood less than twenty feet away, looking more ruggedly handsome than was fair. She turned back and stared ahead blindly, not seeing the beautiful sea of green in the mountains ahead of her. For the first time ever, the scene wasn't curing what ailed her.

She texted him back.

"I'm not crying. I'm certainly not crying over you. Something got in my eye."

"I'm still sorry." Instead of a text, his words drifted down to her. She looked up to see him standing next to her. Finn did his best to crawl up Quinn's body.

"Hey little man." He reached down and picked up the squirming pup. Finn licked every inch of his face he could reach. Quinn laughed. The sound of it did Paige's heart good. There had been so little laughter lately.

"What are you doing here?" She still didn't look at him.

"You weren't at home, so I took a chance. I know how you love the mountains."

"I do. But how did you know where to find me?" She peeked out of the corner of her eye and saw a mile of firm, tanned leg. Not helping her resolve.

"I guessed."

She shot him her best teacher look.

"Okay, I actually took a lot of guesses and eventually found you." He shook his head. "There are a lot of overlooks." He sat on the ground next to her, as close as he could without touching her. Finn happily jumped in his lap.

Traitor! "Why were you looking for me? There's nothing left to say."

"I'm so sorry."

"So you've said. But here's the thing. It doesn't matter anymore. I understand. You're not willing to risk anything in a relationship, and I am. We've already covered this. So please go." She turned her head and gritted her teeth, willing herself not to cry. She was done crying over him. At least while he was still here.

He placed one hand under her chin and turned her head back to face him. He wiped a tear off her face. "That's just it. I don't want to go. I want to be with you. I need you."

She closed her eyes against the promise, and the pain, in his words. "We tried. Remember? I got my heart broken, even though you didn't mean to."

"I'm not saying this right. Please look at me." When she opened her eyes, he continued. "I want to be with you. I want a real relationship."

She thought for sure her heart had stopped. "What? Why? I thought you didn't do relationships."

"I never did, until you came along. I was fine with my life the way it was. Or at least so I thought. But I was living an empty shell of a life in an endless series of houses. It's not what I want anymore."

"What do you want now?"

He smiled down into her eyes. "You're not going to make this easy for me, are you?"

She didn't return his smile. She was too busy protecting what was left of her heart. "Why should I? *You* broke my heart. I've been grieving, but I've been doing so in private. Away from Amy and my family because she's grieving too, and she needs me to be there for her. So, guess what I do. I drive back to my own house or here, and I cry until there aren't any more tears. Because of *you.*"

His expression changed with her words. "I'm sorrier than you could ever imagine. I just didn't know what to do. A.J.'s death hit me hard, and I was lost for a bit."

"His death hit all of us hard. You didn't have to be lost or alone, but you chose to be. I was here for you. Or I would have been if you had let me in."

He placed his hands on either side of her face and spoke directly to her. "I know, but at the time, all I could feel was pain. I wasn't ready to admit I loved you or that I wanted to build a life with you."

Hope stirred, a fluttering in her chest. "Are you saying those things now? Because if you are, I'm going to need to actually hear you say them."

This time, he laughed. He kissed her and then released her face. "Paige, I love you. I have for a while. I was just too scared to admit it to myself, let alone you. I need you. Before you say anything, I need to tell you something. I'm not a firefighter anymore."

She gasped. "But you love being a firefighter! Please don't tell me you gave it up for me, because I would never ask you to." Fresh tears gathered in her blue eyes.

"I *loved* being a firefighter, but not anymore. I didn't do it because of us, Paige. I did it because I couldn't face going back into a burning building. Losing A.J., watching him die, changed everything for me. I don't have the heart to go back in there."

"Maybe you just need time." She resisted crossing her fingers, hoping against hope she was wrong.

"No, what I need is you. Please tell me you'll forgive me. I'll spend the rest of my life making it up to you if you let me."

Paige was lost in the pleading she heard in his voice. She stood up and threw herself at him. Covering him in kisses, she stopped only long enough to answer. "Of course I forgive you, Quinn. I love you too. Who would have thought we'd end up here when you saved me that day?"

He kissed her back. Raising his head, he smiled down at her. "We both know you really saved me."

Epilogue

"I'm sorry to do this to you when you walk in the door, but I need an answer now." Paige thrust several choices of paint colors in his face.

He took them from her hand and dragged her close for a bear hug, his mouth wide with a grin. "It's for your library/study. You should pick." He waited for the protest. He didn't wait long.

"We decided that room was going to double as your home office as well. Which means you should help pick the color."

"I have a better idea." He tossed the cards aside and plucked her off the ground. Taking a few steps, he landed on the couch, a squealing Paige in his lap. He lowered his mouth to hers, cutting off any conversation about paint colors.

Several weeks had passed since that day on the side of the Blue Ridge Parkway. His remodel was under contract. She had helped him to pick out the next flip. But he wasn't a nomad anymore. Last week, Quinn moved his belongings into this house. Their home. They were officially living together.

She came up for air, grinning. "Don't think this gets you out of picking a color." She used her 'I'm a teacher voice', but love shone from her eyes.

He really was a lucky man. "I wouldn't dream of it."

"Have I mentioned lately I love you coming home to me each night?"

He nodded. "Yes, but I never tire of hearing it."

"I wish Amy could be this happy," she said on a sigh.

"I do too." He missed A.J. every day. He still had nightmares about his best friend's death. On Monday, he would start with the county arson department. The fire that took A.J.'s life was already under investigation. Although it wouldn't bring his friend back, there would be justice.

"We're so lucky." She snuggled into him, resting her head against his heart.

He wondered if she could hear it beat for her. His life had been good, fulfilling, before he met her. Now it overflowed with love and joy.

The End

Acknowledgments

I wouldn't be able to do this without my family and friends. They support me in more ways than I even know. I've been travelling to signings and conferences a lot this year, trying to get my name out there. I've missed soccer games and meals around the table. But even when I'm there, I'm not always present. Thank you for your patience and love.

Jeni Burns agreed to edit another book for me. Apparently, I didn't scare her off last time. Jeni, I am so indebted to you. Thank you for not reaching through the phone to kill me when I text you with "What am I doing?". One day I will know my external conflict all on my own. I promise.

For every cover, I have turned to the magic of Rebecca Pau of The Final Wrap. She is so very talented and even more understanding. I give her a word or two, and she nails it. Every time. I love my covers. Thank you for working with me to create such beauty.

To the most patient PA in the world, Margie Greenhow. Where would I be without you??? You keep me focused, on track, and organized. That last one alone deserves a bloody medal. Your humor and kindness are lifesavers for me, more than you'll ever know.

Thank you to all of the wonderful romance writers I have met over the past year. Without exception, y'all have been gracious and generous. I am indebted to you for your words of wisdom and advice but even more so for your company and friendship.

How to Help an Indie Author

Reviews, reviews, reviews! Even if you didn't love Saving Quinn, please take the time to review it on Amazon and/or Goodreads. Reviews are so much more important than you could ever imagine.

Follow me everywhere:

Facebook: https://www.facebook.com/profile.php?id=100012114317732
Twitter: https://twitter.com/K_OMalley67
Instagram: https://www.instagram.com/kimberleyomalley67/
Amazon Author Page: www.amazon.com/author/kimberleyomalley
Good Reads Profile: https://www.goodreads.com/author/show/16545063.
Kimberley_O_Malley
Book Bub profile: https://www.bookbub.com/profile/kimberley-o-malley

***

We're coming to the end of the Windsor Falls series. Just two more books to go. Read an excerpt from the next Windsor Falls novel, *Finding Kat,* by Kimberley O'Malley. Keep in mind this is a work in progress and is therefore subject to change. *Finding Kat* will be available in the Summer of 2018.

Finding Kat

Early morning was Kat De Luca's favorite time in the bakery. The delicious scents of yeast, cinnamon and other ingredients filled the air. Darkness still reigned outside the windows. Her father was still sleeping. That was probably the best part.

Kat sighed and reached for her first sip of coffee. There was a time when she loved working with her father. In grade school, Kat would be glued to his side, soaking in both his presence and his knowledge. Her fondest memories of childhood were spent right here, pounding dough and decorating cookies.

By high school, their differences became a wedge between them. Marco De Luca was old school. He made recipes handed down to him from his father and grandfather. And that worked. For him. De Luca's Bakery was a thriving business in Windsor Falls; had been for three generations.

And that was the problem. Kat didn't just want to be the next generation of De Lucas to run the bakery. She wanted to do different things. Big things. Baking the same things her great grandfather made wasn't enough for her. And it was all her father wanted. There in lie the issue.

Sighing, Kat pushed the troubling thoughts from her mind and inhaled through her nose. The scents always calmed her. They were in her blood. She pulled racks from the oven and put in others. The constant cycle of baked goods in and out soothed her. She could do this in her sleep.

Soon, people would be outside the door, waiting to come in. She loved the people of Windsor Falls. It was a small town but had everything Kat needed. There was a lot to be said for knowing the people you passed on the street, sharing the news of the day with them. Going to pastry school in Paris had been her dream, and she had loved every second of it. Despite offers to stay and work there, Kat came home to the town she had missed so much. The fact that she rarely got to use what she had learned there was another layer of the resentments between she and her father.

She turned up her music and danced along to Justin Timberlake, shrugging off the negativity. What she would do about that problem was a thought for another day. More than an hour passed, and Kat had filled the display cases for the morning rush. She was walking back through the swinging door leading to the kitchen when she heard a knock on the front door. She turned around to tell whoever was there that they weren't open yet. And stopped dead in her tracks. The words stuck in her throat. Standing beyond the locked door was six feet of smoking hot male. One she had never seen before. Not an easy feat in Windsor Falls. She loved her hometown, but it wasn't exactly dripping in single men she hadn't gone to school with.

She walked towards the door, shaking her head. She glanced at the wall clock. Another thirty minutes before opening. "Sorry, we're still closed." More than three feet and a glass door separated them, and yet her blood bounded in her veins. *Who was this guy?*

The man in question smiled, and a dimple appeared on his face. Kat's ovaries clenched. Wow! She hadn't even heard his voice yet.

"What if I beg?" His bright blue eyes held her gaze. She noticed faint lines at the edges. He wasn't a puppy. And he smiled with his eyes. That was a good thing.

Her ovaries unclenched, stood up straight, and sang The Halleluiah Chorus. Before she realized it, Kat unlocked the door. Humid air assaulted her lungs, making breathing difficult. The calendar might say September, but it was still summer in North Carolina.

"Can't have a grown man begging." She stood back, holding the door and allowing the stranger to enter. He passed within inches of her, his clean, male scent sending her brain into a tailspin.

"No, we can't, can we?" He grinned at her, and she felt it through to her toes.

"What can I get you?" Was that her talking in a bedroom voice? It had been so long, she almost couldn't remember. *How about me, naked in your bed?*

She tripped over her own feet. He saved her from face planting with his strong hands at her waist. "First day with the new feet?"

Kat straightened and grinned at him. She loved a man with a quick wit. She walked around the counter to give herself some breathing room. "I'm not usually that clumsy. Thank you for saving me. Now, what's the baked goods emergency?"

"I have to be in early for a staff meeting, and I promised something yummy. Of course, I remembered while getting in my car this morning." He broke off and gave her what could best be described as a puppy face. "Please save me from them."

Kat couldn't help it. She burst out laughing. "Well, since you're already in the bakery, and I'm a nice person." She spread her arms wide. "Anything here will win over their good graces."

He tilted his head, a lock of blonde hair falling over his forehead. She fisted her hands in her apron to avoid brushing it back. Who was she kidding. The thick locks begged for her hands to run through it. "Confident. I like that in a woman."

Kat cleared her throat because she knew her voice would come out as a squeak if she didn't. She tried to ignore the heat she felt creeping up her face. "De Luca's is a third-generation bakery, sir. I stand behind anything here. Especially since I made everything myself." A cocky grin completed her vow.

"Well, then, what do you recommend. I need a dozen of whatever you choose. And one has to be a cranberry scone."

Kat arched a dark brow but didn't ask. She grabbed one of the bright pink boxes that De Luca's was known for and folded it into place. "How about a variety? Then people can choose." She didn't wait for his answer and set about picking a selection of scones, muffins, and donuts. She didn't miss the look of appreciation on his handsome face as he tracked her progress. A smug smile lit hers. Maybe she wasn't the only one feeling it.

She closed the box and tied it with string. "Is there anything else I can get you?" Again with the bedroom voice. What was wrong with her? *Too long since you've gotten laid.* Sad but true. And yet, there was something else at play here.

He pulled two bills from his wallet and handed them to her, a grin on his face. "I'm already late, so I think that's all. For this time, anyway." His fingers brushed hers as she took the money. It took all of her will power to not jump in surprise. Tingles shot up her arm.

Kat rang up his purchase and counted out his change. Before she could hand it to him, he swiped a finger across her cheek, burning her as he moved. He held up the finger in question, which was coated in flour. "Couldn't have you running around all day with this on your face," he murmured.

"Certainly not," she muttered in reply. So much for witty repartee. She handed him the change, which he stuck in his pocket. Once again, tiny bursts of energy raced along her skin where their hands had touched.

Wicked hot man, as she had begun to think of him, nodded at the box in his hands. "Thanks again for saving my life. I owe you one."

"I'm going to hold you to that." *Or you to me.*

"You do that."

The door closed behind him, the bell dancing with the motion. Kat stood there, hand pressed against her face where he had touched her. And grinned. Then she pulled her phone from her back pocket. Surely, Katie would know who wicked hot man was.

www.ingramcontent.com/pod-product-compliance
Lightning Source LLC
Chambersburg PA
CBHW060545180626
46817CB00002B/736